REDEMPTION

REDEMPTION

JACQUELIN THOMAS

NAL
PRAISE

NAL Praise

Published by New American Library, a division of Penguin Group (USA) Inc., 375 Hudson Street, New York, New York 10014, USA • Penguin Group (Canada), 90 Eglinton Avenue East, Suite 700, Toronto, Ontario M4P 2Y3, Canada (a division of Pearson Penguin Canada Inc.) • Penguin Books Ltd., 80 Strand, London WC2R 0RL, England • Penguin Ireland, 25 St. Stephen's Green, Dublin 2, Ireland (a division of Penguin Books Ltd.) • Penguin Group (Australia), 250 Camberwell Road, Camberwell, Victoria 3124, Australia (a division of Pearson Australia Group Pty. Ltd.) • Penguin Books India Pvt. Ltd., 11 Community Centre, Panchsheel Park, New Delhi - 110 017, India • Penguin Group (NZ), 67 Apollo Drive, Mairangi Bay, Auckland 1311, New Zealand (a division of Pearson New Zealand Ltd.) • Penguin Books (South Africa) (Pty.) Ltd., 24 Sturdee Avenue, Rosebank, Johannesburg 2196, South Africa

Penguin Books Ltd., Registered Offices:
80 Strand, London WC2R 0RL, England

First published by NAL Praise, an imprint of New American Library, a division of Penguin Group (USA) Inc.

Copyright © Jacquelin Thomas, 2007
Readers Guide copyright © Penguin Group (USA) Inc., 2007
All rights reserved

NAL Praise and logo are trademarks of Penguin Group (USA) Inc.

Scripture taken from:
The *Holy Bible, New International Version*®. Copyright © 1973, 1978, 1984 International Bible Society. Used by permission of Zondervan. All rights reserved. The "NIV" and "New International Version" trademarks are registered in the United States Patent and Trademark Office by International Bible Society. Use of either trademark requires the permission of International Bible Society.
The New King James Version. Copyright © 1982 by Thomas Nelson, Inc. Used by permission. All rights reserved.
The *New American Standard Bible*®, copyright © 1960, 1962, 1963, 1968, 1971, 1972, 1973, 1975, 1977, 1995 by The Lockman Foundation. Used by permission.

ISBN 978-0-451-21764-6

Set in Centaur
Designed by Ginger Legato
Printed in the United States of America

For my sister Carmen—

you are loved. . . .

ACKNOWLEDGMENTS

My heavenly Father, I have to thank You for trusting me with this gift. I will always strive to tell stories that will not only entertain but also glorify Your precious Name.

Pastor Rodney and Pastor Valerie Frazier, Pastor Danny Peebles and Dr. Seymour, thank you all so much for your teachings, for your willingness to reach out and help others, and for making my family and me feel welcome at Wakefield Family Church. Thank you for showing me what it means to be a Christian. You wear your faith like a badge of honor, and because of it, my own faith has grown.

My wonderful husband and best friend, where would I be without you? I can't thank God enough for placing you into my life. I'm a better person having met you.

My mother—this book would not have happened without your help when I needed to focus on my writing. You unselfishly moved in with us for two months and took care of my family so that I could make my rapidly approaching deadline. I thank you so much for the sacrifice you made on my behalf. I can't wait for the time when you decide to share your stories with the world.

Alicia Thomas, Pamela Kennedy, Shatoya Johnson and JoAnn Turner, I would be remiss if I didn't publicly acknowledge you here. You ladies read the raw manuscript and gave me some wonderful feedback and constructive criticism to help make this story better. Thanks so much for the unselfish giving of your time and your constant show of support of me and of my novels. You all hold a special place in my life.

The Lord said to me, "Go show your love to your wife again, though she is loved by another and is an adulteress. Love her as the Lord loves the Israelites, though they turn to other gods and love the sacred raisin cakes."

—HOSEA 3:1 (NIV)

REDEMPTION

PROLOGUE

PASTOR WARNER GARFIELD BRICE WEDS ACTRESS MARIN ALEXANDER

Los Angeles (AP)—Marin Alexander managed to find time for love amid her burgeoning career when she recently wed Pastor Warner Garfield Brice at the Victory Baptist Church in Los Angeles, CA. Brice is its senior pastor. The Reverend Andrew Maxwell officiated at the ceremony.

The bride's father escorted his glowing daughter down the aisle. NFL legend Adrian Reed served as best man. Bridesmaids included actresses Monique O'Neill and Carol Leon-Grady, while Dru Wilkerson served as matron of honor.

"The ceremony was not only elegant, but very spiritual and sacred," wedding coordinator Karen Jones-McBride said. The groom sang a heartfelt tune to his lovely bride. Mark Koster, of the Grammy Award–winning gospel group For His Love, performed a soulful rendition of "The Lord's Prayer."

Guests included several dignitaries and a host of celebrity guests, among them Starla Hancock, legendary singer Mamie Bryant, gospel musician Benson Taylor, Regina Hall, Lily Song and comedian Harvey Maxwell.

The groom is the son of legendary gospel songbird Millicent Brice and actor Garfield Brice. The celebrated bride is the daughter of Judge Robert E. Alexander and Shirley Miller, the assistant district attorney handling the high-profile case of Miami Dodgers' Roy Kelly, on trial for the murder of his ex-wife and her lover.

After the ceremony, the wedding party enjoyed a private reception at the Beverly Hills Hotel. This is the first marriage for both.

CHAPTER ONE

🌿 *August*

She had the type of body that could make a man forget his own thoughts. Warner Garfield Brice cleared his throat noisily as his eyes rapidly scanned the gathering to see if anyone had noticed his blunder.

The moment Marin Alexander sauntered into the room overflowing with a hundred and fifty industry types at the Four Seasons Hotel in Beverly Hills, Warner immediately forgot the words of his speech. The same one he'd rehearsed all week long and knew like the back of his own hand up until a few minutes ago.

Straightening his glasses, Warner stole a quick peek at his notes, relocated his place and regained his composure.

He began again.

"There are people in the world—even in your own family—who won't understand your decision and they might try to convince you that God would never call someone to Hollywood. They might tell you that Hollywood is evil. That it's a place filled with nothing but drugs, sex and violence." Warner paused for effect.

"Let's be truthful—this *is* the liberal mecca of the world. But let me paint you a different picture that I hope encourages you and encourages your well-meaning friends and family . . ."

Warner's eyes settled briefly on Marin, and then moved on. "I can tell you truthfully and with great conviction that God is moving in Hollywood. I have seen God bring actors, media and other industry professionals to me that are unfulfilled, searching and spiritually hungry. I've had the privilege of building deep friendships with them, earning their respect and being able to share the Gospel of Christ with them."

When Warner finished his keynote address, he was met with a round of applause and a standing ovation. He awarded them a grateful smile before taking his seat.

From his position at the head table, Warner had a clear view of Marin, who was watching him boldly, without shame.

He was the first to turn his attention away but he vowed he would not leave the room before speaking to her.

The meeting for the Entertainment Fellowship drew to a close and people swarmed to Warner, thanking him and acknowledging the truth in his words.

Every now and then his eyes traveled the room, trying to find Marin and hoping she wouldn't leave before he could talk to her.

But Marin didn't look like she was in a hurry to go anywhere. She stood a few yards away, waiting patiently to talk to him.

Warner relaxed.

After what seemed like an eternity, they were finally face-to-face.

"I really enjoyed your speech, Pastor Brice. It was very inspiring."

Her infectious grin made him smile. "Thank you, Miss Alexander. I have to tell you that I really enjoyed your last movie." Warner couldn't stop smiling.

Marin was radiant, with sparkling medium-brown eyes, a friendly smile and a tiny spray of freckles lightly brushed across her nose.

"I've visited your church a few times," she was saying. "I'm actually planning to come tomorrow, but had no idea you'd be speaking at the meeting. I enjoy your sermons, and your speech today was something I needed to hear." A tiny smile softened her lips. "I guess this is a sign that I should definitely attend."

Warner pushed the frame of his glasses up the bridge of his nose. "I look forward to seeing you then."

More people had gathered behind her, waiting to talk to him, so Marin didn't linger.

A wave of disappointment spread through Warner's body when she disappeared through the exit doors and was gone. He wasn't worried though—Warner knew he would see her again.

She was destined to be his wife.

God had spoken it into his spirit the moment Marin came through the doors. She was the answer to his prayers for a partner in life.

When Warner left the hotel a short time later, he drove straight to his parents' home in Hollywood Hills. It was his mother's birthday and his father was hosting a barbecue in her honor.

His younger sister, Chanelle, greeted him with a kiss on the cheek when he strode into the house.

"How did your meeting go?" she inquired. Chanelle waited for him to remove his jacket before taking it from him and hanging it in a nearby closet.

"Great." Warner wrapped an arm around her. "In fact, I met the woman I'm going to marry."

Chanelle's mouth dropped open in her surprise. "Really? At the meeting?"

He nodded.

Their father walked out into the foyer where they stood talking.

Garfield Brice was a prominent figure in the entertainment industry, best known for his role as Middleton Greene, a neurosurgeon on a popular television series.

"Chanelle, your husband's looking for you."

"We're on our way out to the patio," she responded. "Warner just arrived."

Warner and Chanelle followed their father to the poolside kitchen and grill.

"So, tell me about my future sister-in-law." Chanelle's smile turned to a chuckle as she sat down in the empty chair beside her husband at one of the glass-topped tables scattered around the Olympic-sized pool. "Who is she?"

"Marin Alexander."

Chanelle's smile quickly faded. "Who did you say?"

"Marin Alexander," Warner repeated. "You know who I'm talking about. We just saw her in——"

Holding up her hand, Chanelle cut him off. "I *know* who she is. Warner, she's definitely not the wife for you. Marin's not your type at all."

Garfield turned around, facing his children. "Warner, did I hear Chanelle right? Are you getting married?"

Before he could speak for himself, Chanelle replied, "He's interested in Marin Alexander, Daddy. Wasn't she in *Code Red* with you?"

He nodded. "She's a nice kid."

"Beautiful, too," Chanelle's husband, Mitch, interjected.

Elbowing him, Chanelle said, "I was just telling Warner that she's all wrong for him. He needs someone closer to his own age, I would think. Not ten years younger."

Warner sat down across from his brother-in-law. "How do you know how old she is?"

"I don't know exactly," Chanelle admitted. "But I read somewhere that she's either twenty-four or twenty-five. She could be older, I guess. Women do lie about their age all the time. Especially in Hollywood."

Shrugging, he stated, "Age doesn't matter to me. Besides, I'm thirty-five—I'm not that much older."

"I doubt Marin can handle the responsibilities that come with being your wife. How do you know if she even has a relationship with God? Can she truly stand with you in leading your church? I don't think so."

"You really don't know anything about her, honey," Mitch said.

Chanelle sent her husband a sharp glare.

Garfield asked, "Well, how much do you know about her, Chanelle?"

"I don't think she's cut out to be the wife of a pastor. I'm not sure she could even act the part in a movie. She's too . . ."

"Sexy," Mitch offered.

Rolling her eyes, Chanelle responded, "That wasn't quite the word I was looking for."

A tall, striking woman with salt-and-pepper hair walked out of the house, asking, "What are you all talking about? Warner, you look so intense. What's going on?"

"Millicent, dear, our son is interested in Marin Alexander," Garfield announced as he handed her a glass of iced tea.

She took a deep breath and adjusted her smile. "You're not serious, are you, son?"

Warner gave them all a look of astonishment. "What is the big problem? She's an actress. You all act like I've come in announcing that I plan to marry a prostitute."

"Some would ask what's the difference?" Millicent responded dryly. "I can't imagine what your congregation would think of your getting involved with an actress."

"I'm not worried about other people or what they think, Mother. When I saw her today, God spoke to me. I told you how He'd laid it on my heart that it was time for me to take a wife. Well, today He told me that Marin is that woman."

Warner looked from one person to the other, frowning in exasperation. "I can't believe any of you. Dad is an actor. What makes Marin so different?"

Chuckling, his sister responded, "I think you know the answer to that. Are you *sure* it was God talking to you?"

Warner was not amused. "Chanelle, you know I don't play about that."

"Just pray about it some more, Warner," his sister advised. "Maybe the Lord is telling you something else."

Their parents joined them at the table.

"Marin comes from a good family," Warner said. "You know who her father is, don't you? Judge Robert Alexander."

"Shirley Miller is her mother," Millicent announced. "I met her last year at the Gospel Celebration. She's a real nice lady. Very intelligent."

"Warner, I have someone I really want you to meet. We went to college together and she's a good friend of mine. Her name—"

He interrupted her. "Sis, I don't need to meet anyone. Marin Alexander is the woman for me." Warner pressed a hand to his heart. "God spoke it into my heart. Even you can't argue with that."

*   *   *

Marin pulled her brand-new BMW 525i into a circular driveway, parking in front of her parents' house in Baldwin Hills. Using her personal key, she unlocked the front door and stepped inside.

"Where's Daddy?" Marin asked, walking into her mother's pride and joy—her recently renovated gourmet kitchen.

"He's playing golf with some friends at the country club," Shirley replied smoothly, with no expression on her face. "Why? Do you need money?"

Marin shook her head no. "I don't need any money. I just wanted to see my dad. He's been out of town the last couple of times I stopped by the house."

"I called you earlier to see if you wanted to attend Tyler Perry's new play with me." While she talked, Shirley applied the finishing touches to her roast.

"At the last minute I decided to go to the Entertainment Fellowship meeting. Pastor Warner Brice was the keynote speaker."

"Really?" Shirley replied nonchalantly while opening the oven door to check on the yeast rolls.

Marin sat down at the breakfast bar, watching her mother move about, preparing dinner. "He seems like a really nice man."

Wisps of wavy hair fell casually on Shirley's forehead. "I've never heard anything negative about him."

"I can't believe he's not married. He's so tall and muscular. The man is fine." Marin broke into a grin. "I love that patch of gray at his temple—makes him look sexy."

Shirley looked over at Marin. "Honey . . . why all this sudden interest in Pastor Brice?"

Smiling, she answered, "I think he might be interested in me."

Her mother laughed. "Not hardly."

Marin sighed with exasperation. "I can't believe you just said that to me." Her mother always had something negative to say when it came to her.

Shirley assessed her daughter with a critical squint. "You have to be realistic, Marin. Pastor Warner Brice is not going to be interested in someone like you."

Her mother's contemptuous tone sparked Marin's anger. "What's wrong with me? Why do you always say things like this to me?"

"Do you even go to church?"

"Yes."

"When?" Shirley wanted to know. "You're usually at the club with us having brunch on Sundays."

"I don't go every Sunday," Marin amended. "But I do attend from time to time."

"Dear, I don't want to see you get hurt. Pastor Brice is much older than you and I'm sure he's probably looking for someone more mature and around his own age."

"You're wrong," Marin argued. "You didn't see the way he was looking at me."

"He is a man. With the way you dress he'll look at you, but that's all, Marin. Mark my words."

She felt her flesh color. "Why don't you think I'm good enough for him? I'm not a bad person."

"Do you remember the Benjamin Cason sex tape scandal?" Shirley asked. "That was just a couple of years ago. I'm sure he's heard about it. Everybody else sure did."

Marin stiffened, momentarily abashed. "He taped me without my knowledge. I pressed charges and sued him, remember? *I was the victim.*"

"And then there's the time all those rumors were surfacing about you and Anthony Little. The man's marriage almost broke up."

Her cheeks burned in remembrance. "I was young and stupid. We played lovers in the movie we were working on and . . . things just got out of hand."

"You were barely seventeen," Shirley reminded her.

Marin shuddered in humiliation. "Well, I never said I was a saint. I'm sure Warner Brice isn't one either."

"He was supposed to get married once before, if I remember correctly. His fiancée died a few months before the wedding. Cancer, I think."

"That's so sad."

Shirley agreed. "I'd heard he was terribly grief-stricken. That girl was the love of his life. Some say he never really recovered."

"I get it, Mom." Biting her lip, Marin looked away. "What I don't get is why you always do this to me." She spoke with light bitterness.

"Do *what* to you? Tell the truth?"

As casually as she could manage, Marin asked, "Can't you ever say anything nice to me? Why won't you even try to support me just a little bit? Even when I was a child, you made me feel like everything I did was wrong. None of my choices were ever good enough for you. Cheerleading, dance—nothing."

"You're being dramatic, Marin."

"I'm telling you Pastor Brice is interested in me and you throw his love for a dead woman in my face."

"We have always supported you, Marin," Shirley stated. "Who do you think paid for all those dance lessons, acting and singing lessons?"

"But you're always negative when it comes to me. I can see it on your face. You actually believe that Warner Brice is too good for me—your own daughter. Most women would want their daughter to be with a man like him."

"I'm not saying you're not good enough for him, darling. That's not it at all." Shirley hesitated, measuring her for a moment. "I just think you still have some growing up to do. You're not ready to settle down. A man in Warner's position wants a wife, I'm sure."

"I want to get married," Marin announced. "I'm ready to settle down."

Shirley eyed her daughter suspiciously. "Since when?"

Marin smiled. "Since meeting Pastor Warner Brice. There's something so incredibly sexy about the man. And when he looks at me—I don't know, he just makes me feel special." Her smile disappeared. "Something I never felt with you. You have always made me feel like a big screwup."

Shirley was nonplussed. "Then go to a therapist, dear. You don't get married because you feel slighted by your parents—something that's not true at all, by the way. Your father and I love you. We really do."

"You just don't respect me," Marin said in a choked voice.

Instead of responding, Shirley changed the subject. "Are you staying for dinner?"

"No. I'm having dinner with a friend."

"Male or female?"

Marin regarded her mother quizzically for a moment. "Female. Why?"

"So, where are you going?"

"Harold and Belle's. Why all the questions, Mom?"

Opening the oven door, Shirley asked, "Is it a big secret? I was trying to make conversation."

Marin sighed, then stood up. "I need to get going. I don't want to be late."

"But I thought you wanted to see your father."

"I did," Marin responded. "But I can't wait any longer. So before you ask me again, I'll just tell you. I'm meeting Carol for dinner."

"Carol Leon-Grady?"

Marin nodded. "We're becoming really good friends."

"She's a good little actress," Shirley acknowledged. "I liked the last movie she did. I cried all over the place when she died."

Marin held her temper in check as her insecurities sprang up. Her mother was never as complimentary when it came to her acting skills. Carol was still pretty new to the business and had been in only a couple of movies. Her mother acted like Carol was a much better actor than Marin was.

"Tell Daddy I came by and I'll give him a call later."

"If this is about money, you might as well tell me. He will."

"Mom, I'm fine. I don't need money. See you."

"Let's have lunch sometime this week."

Marin slipped her handbag on her shoulder. "Sure. Just give me a call." She turned away without waiting for a reply, walking briskly to leave the house before she lost her nerve.

As soon as Marin stepped outside the house, she took several deep, calming breaths. All she'd ever wanted was her mother's love and respect. Shirley would never win the Mother of the Year Award, but you could never convince her of that.

Her mouth clenched tight, Marin got into her car and backed out of the driveway.

She couldn't shake her mother's words out of her head.

Her lips puckered with annoyance. What did her mother know

anyway? *She was hardly around when I was growing up. She and Daddy have always been married to their careers.*

Despite his busy life, her father always seemed to have a kind word for Marin. He had always been encouraging and supportive, but Shirley never had anything positive to say to her.

She decided she'd rather remain childless than treat a child the way Shirley treated her.

CHAPTER TWO

M arin was the first to arrive at Harold and Belle's and she decided to wait until Carol's arrival before being seated.

While waiting, she scanned the dining area, checking to see if she recognized anyone.

The New Orleans–style restaurant was a favorite of hers. Warm and inviting, the eatery was bathed in soft lighting. Etched glass and beautiful artwork in vivid hues added to its charm. Fresh flowers placed in vases on every table welcomed the guests.

Carol showed up ten minutes later.

"Sorry I'm late. Got caught up in some traffic near Exposition and Tenth Avenue."

The guests sitting in the dimly lit dining area smiled, pointed and whispered as she and Carol followed the maître d' to their table.

"Everybody's just staring at us," Carol said in a low voice.

Marin loved the attention. "We're actresses. People are going to recognize us."

"I still can't get used to it. I always feel like I'm in a fishbowl."

"You are," Marin replied. "But pretty soon you'll start ignoring the stares, the whispers and even the tabloid reporters. Relax. Just act normal. Oh, and stop making that expression. You never know when you're going to be photographed."

Their waiter came over within seconds after they sat down. He introduced himself and asked for their drink orders. "You sure were eyeing Pastor Brice hard today at the meeting," Carol teased. "What was that all about?"

Marin gave her friend a sly smile. "Carol, the man is fine, don't you think? Tall and bald. That smooth complexion the color of a new penny. Oh, my goodness, he's gorgeous. I bet he gets his eyebrows waxed. Did you see them?"

"He *is* nice-looking. Pastor Brice seems kind of quiet though. I've seen him at a couple of events and he usually just keeps to himself. I don't think I've ever even seen him bring a date."

The waiter returned with their drinks.

Carol sampled her apple martini. "Mmmm . . . girl, this is delicious."

Marin had a one-track mind. "Pastor Brice looks a lot like his father, don't you think?"

Carol agreed. "Garfield—girl, that man talks all the time."

The two women shared a laugh.

"I like him though," Marin took a sip of her martini. Pointing to the glass, she added, "I love their apple martinis."

"I like their cosmopolitans, too."

"Garfield is real down-to-earth. When we were on the *Code Red* set, he was such a professional. He even helped me run lines."

Carol smiled.

The waiter returned to take their food orders.

"Have you been to his church?" Marin questioned when the waiter walked away from their table.

"A couple of times," Carol answered. "I just joined West Angeles. You should come with me one Sunday."

"I will," Marin promised. "I'm still looking for the right church."

Her comment seemed to amuse Carol. "Hmmm, I have a feeling that Pastor Brice will be seeing a lot of you at Victory Baptist Church."

Seeing the amusement in Carol's eyes, Marin laughed. "Tomorrow too soon?" she queried, settling back in her chair and running fingers through her short hair. "I really can't explain it, Carol, but I've got such a good feeling about Pastor Brice."

Their food arrived.

Marin stabbed a shrimp and stuck it in her mouth. She loved the shrimp-and-crawfish étouffée. "I'm telling you . . . I really have a good feeling about this man."

Carol assessed her friend's face. "You're interested in him. Girl, don't you think Pastor Brice is a little too old? He's got to be at least thirty-five."

Marin shook her head no. "I like older men."

Leaning forward, Carol pursued her thoughts, "A preacher though? I'm all for God and everything, but do you really want to date a *minister*?" Her tone held a note of disapproval. "I'm not saying you're not his type, Marin. I don't know if there is a certain type of woman destined to be first ladies—I just think there's a huge responsibility factor involved."

"I can handle it. Carol, all I want is a man who will treat me like a queen. I want a man who will adore me and won't be jealous of my being in the limelight. Pastor Brice's father is an actor and his mother is a Grammy Award–winning singer. Look at him—he's one of the biggest ministers on television. I think we'd make a great team."

Laughing, Carol sliced off a piece of fried catfish and pierced it with her fork. "Girl, wait till Dru hears about this. She's gonna fall out." Laughing, Carol stuck the food in her mouth.

"Don't you dare. I didn't say anything about having a crush on him," Marin snapped. "I simply want to get to know him better. What's wrong with that?"

"You have the hots for him."

Folding her arms across her chest, Marin responded, "So what if I do? The way he was looking at me during the meeting, I'd say Pastor Brice is just as interested in me. I'm sure of it."

"Think about your career for a minute. How will Pastor Brice feel about your acting? And the partying? I've never seen Pastor Brice at any clubs. Girl, you know you love a good party. You ready to give that up?"

"I don't have to give anything up. I can attend a party without getting falling-down drunk," Marin countered. "I know how to carry myself and Pastor Brice will come to see that about me. He knows this is my career and some of the biggest deals are made at parties. I'm a Christian, and the one thing that we do know about Pastor Brice is that he loves the Lord."

Carol nodded in agreement. "Yeah, he definitely loves God. I guess the question you'll have to ask yourself is if you love the Lord as much as he does." Leaning forward, she continued, "Marin, listen to me because I'm being very serious. If you want this man, then you better be able to prove to him that you can be a real first lady. This isn't a role you're auditioning for, Marin. This is for real."

Throughout the rest of her dinner, Marin considered Carol's words. Would life with a man of God be that different?

After they finished eating, Marin decided she wasn't ready to go home to an empty house.

She and Carol stayed for a while longer listening to the live band that played every Friday and Saturday night.

"I still can't see you dating Pastor Brice."

"I can see it clear as day," Marin replied. "There's something special about that man."

She was on a mission.

The next morning Marin dressed with care. She applied her makeup with a light hand for a more natural effect. She chose a taupe-colored dress with a matching four-button asymmetrical jacket.

To finish off her sophisticated look, she selected a simple pearl necklace and pearl earrings, then used her fingers to brush her short, wavy hair away from her face.

Pleased with her appearance, she left for church.

She stuck in a gospel CD to put her in the mood and sang along during the entire drive to Victory Park Boulevard. Marin broke into a smile when she pulled into the parking lot of Victory Baptist Church. She released a deep, cleansing breath and took a moment to morph into her role for today. That of a first lady.

Inside the sanctuary, Marin found a seat two rows from the front, to make sure he would see her. The church held thousands of members and visitors, so she'd left home in plenty of time to arrive early.

Marin heard the soft murmur of voices, whispering about her, but she was used to it by now. She was a celebrity and recently voted one of the top ten most beautiful women in Hollywood by *People* magazine a few months ago.

"Marin . . ."

She turned around at the sound of her name to find one of her closest friends, Dru Wilkerson.

"Carol told me you'd be here this morning."

Marin moved aside to let her friend sit down. "Hey, girl. I didn't know you were back in town."

"I got in late last night." Lowering her voice, she whispered, "So Carol tells me you've met Pastor Brice?"

"What did she do? Call you as soon as we left the restaurant yesterday?"

"She left a message on my voice mail. So c'mon, Marin . . . what's going on with you and my pastor?"

Marin glanced around to see if anyone could hear their conversation. Keeping her voice low, she answered, "Dru, don't listen to Carol. You know how much she loves drama."

"So you're not after Pastor Brice then?"

Marin released a long sigh. "Don't start."

Dru broke into a open, friendly smile. "Hey, it's okay with me. He's a good man, Marin. Seriously, I think he'd be real good for you."

Their conversation changed as more people joined them, filling up the pew.

Church services began twenty minutes later.

As soon as Pastor Warner Garfield Brice stepped up into the pulpit, his eyes scanned the congregation.

Marin resisted the urge to stand up and shout, "I'm here."

His eyes traveled the room once more, this time landing on her.

Their eyes met and she smiled. At that moment, Marin knew that if she played her cards right, he would soon be hers.

After the church service ended, Marin hastily made her way up to the front of the pulpit. She wanted to reconnect with Warner Brice before anyone else had a chance to take his attention away from her.

Marin hadn't wanted to be rude yesterday, but today was a different story. She wasn't about to let him leave without her contact information. Not this time.

She noticed Dru standing a few feet away, watching them, but Marin didn't care. She was a beautiful woman and any man with half a brain would be flopping at her feet. Marin had caught several of the men in church openly gawking at her. Warner was no exception.

He spotted her and stepped down out of the pulpit. Smiling, he greeted her. "I hope you enjoyed the service this morning."

"I did, Pastor Brice. I truly had a wonderful time."

"If you're not in a hurry, I'd like to speak in private with you."

"I'm not in any hurry. I'll be standing over there with Dru."

"Great. I shouldn't be much longer."

Marin gave him a tiny smile before walking over to her friend. In a low voice, she whispered, "So now do you believe me? He wants me to wait here so that we can talk."

"He might want to offer you the gift of salvation."

Marin rolled her eyes at Dru. "I can't believe you just said that to me."

"Why not? You know I'ma tell you the truth."

"Whatever . . ."

Dru laughed. "C'mon, Marin. You know you my girl."

"Well, your girl is about to work her magic on the good pastor. I'll give you a call later."

Dru burst into laughter. "I hope you're right. If you're not—I'm never going to let you live this down."

She spotted Warner walking in their direction ten minutes later.

Marin would soon prove to her mother and her friends that she and Warner were meant to be together.

CHAPTER THREE

Eight Months Later

"I now pronounce you man and wife."

Warner exhaled a long sigh of pleasure. He had been waiting a very long time to hear those words. He pulled Marin into his arms, drawing her close. He pressed his lips to hers, reluctantly settling for a chaste kiss instead of the lingering, passionate one he desired.

Grinning, Warner escorted his bride down the aisle and through the double exit doors located at the back of the church. They escaped into a nearby room, where they waited until it was time to go back into the chapel for the wedding photographs.

His eyes traveled down the length of her, nodding in obvious approval. "You look so beautiful, sweetheart."

Marin broke into a big smile. "We did it. *We're married.*" She held up her left hand to show off the eight-carat emerald-cut engagement ring with its platinum matching band. "This is truly the happiest day of my life."

Warner couldn't take his eyes off his new wife. Marin was stunning in the couture white wedding gown, a 1930s-style dress made of silk charmeuse fabric. From the moment they'd met, he and Marin had spent as much time together as possible. He'd truly found his soul mate and best friend. Warner and Marin found they shared much in common—including their love for the Lord, the theater, reading mysteries and historical fiction, and long walks on the beach.

He loved the sound of her laughter, the way she cocked her head to one side when she was trying to explain something. He loved everything about her. Six months into their courtship, he had proposed and Marin accepted. Now they were man and wife. Warner couldn't have been happier.

Bridesmaids and groomsmen suddenly burst into the room, putting a end to the short time they'd had alone to revel in their newfound joy.

Amid congratulatory wishes, Chanelle pulled her brother off to the side before they headed back into the sanctuary for pictures. "I'm happy for you, Warner."

"Thank you, sis. I have to admit, I'm very happy myself."

She cast a look over her shoulder to where Marin was holding court with members of the bridal party, then turned back to face her brother. "She better be good to you."

"She will. And I'll be good to her as well."

"I just wish she could've chosen another wedding dress. The low back of it is terribly inappropriate. Don't get me wrong—it's a beautiful gown. I love the way the overskirt drapes . . . she's got the perfect body for it." Chanelle looked down at her own body. "I could never wear it."

Warner gave her a reassuring smile. "You're having a baby, sis. When you're not pregnant, you're skinny as a rail."

"That's so sweet. *I think.*" Chanelle glanced over her shoulder once again. Marin was now talking to her parents. "She could've had the designer sew the back up a little higher. I suggested she have a bow attached to the back so it wouldn't appear quite so low, but Marin wasn't interested. I do like the whole idea of the nineteen-thirties theme."

He chuckled. "I'm glad you approve."

"Warner, I'm sorry. I shouldn't be so critical."

"No, you shouldn't. This is Marin's day and I want it to be as beautiful and romantic as she always dreamed. You have to remember, she's not as old-fashioned as you and I."

"Old-fashioned? Warner, I'm not old-fashioned. Not at all."

Marin walked over to join them. "Honey, the photographer's waiting on us."

Chanelle smiled. "The wedding was beautiful, Marin."

"I think so, too." Gesturing toward her sister-in-law, Marin continued. "You look great. Sage is a wonderful color for you."

Chanelle pressed a hand to her swollen belly. "I have to admit I wasn't sure about the color, but you were right, Marin."

Warner took his bride by the hand. "She has exquisite taste."

His sister nodded. "I'm going to go get our parents. You know how our father loves to talk."

When Chanelle walked away, Marin looked up at her husband and said, "I don't think your sister likes me very much. I've done everything I can to be friends with her."

"She's always been protective of me. But once Chanelle really gets to know you, she's going to love you as much as I do," Warner vowed.

"It doesn't matter," Marin responded. "As long as I have your love, I don't care about anything else. Warner, I just want to be a good wife to you."

Marin exhaled a long sigh of contentment. She was married to a wonderful man and she'd landed a role on a new TV series, *California Suite*. Her heart sang with delight.

She was blissfully happy and not even her mother could take that away from her today.

"Darling, you look so beautiful," Shirley complimented Marin for the hundredth time. "You make a beautiful bride."

"Thank you, Mom," Marin murmured. She couldn't remember her mother ever giving her a compliment like this in the past. Not even on her prom night. Shirley had hated her choices in gown and date.

"And that ring is stunning." Shirley grasped her daughter's hand. "Be careful who you're flinging that around. You don't want to come up missing a finger."

Marin laughed. She felt a warm glow spread through her. "I'm sure I'll be fine, Mom. My husband will protect me."

On cue, Warner walked over, joining them.

"Take care of my baby, Pastor Brice." Shirley embraced Marin. "She's a treasure."

Marin glanced over at her mom, not believing what she'd just heard. *Who's she trying to kid?* she wondered silently. They didn't have that kind of relationship. Shirley was probably trying to give Warner the idea that they were close. Too late. Marin had already told him the truth.

The wedding coordinator approached them while they were talking with Dru and her husband, Larry.

"It's time for you two to have your first dance."

"I didn't know you could dance," Marin whispered. "I figured it was against church rules or something."

"I'm having a dance with my wife. There's nothing wrong with that." Warner pulled her close.

She drank in the comfort of his nearness. "I'm so happy, Warner."

He smiled. "I'm glad. I hope that you'll always feel this way."

The bridal party joined them on the dance floor, surrounding the couple.

Marin gloried in their moment, wrapped in a silken cocoon of euphoria. Life just couldn't get any better for her as far as she was concerned.

Two hours later, Warner escorted his bride out to a waiting limo, and Marin couldn't have been happier. She was eager to be alone with her new husband.

They were on their way to the airport to enjoy their honeymoon in Australia.

"The wedding was a dream come true," Marin confessed. "Only so much better."

"Everyone looked like they were having a good time."

"Even your parents and Chanelle. I know they're still not too crazy with the idea of me being your wife."

Warner took her face in his hands, holding it gently. "In time, they're going to love you as much as I do."

Marin prayed that what Warner said was true. Deep down, she really wanted his family to like her.

After their flight landed in Sydney, Warner and Marin were whisked to their hotel by another stretch limo.

"This is so exciting for me. I've never been to Australia before. I've always wanted to come here." Marin reached over and took her husband's hand. "I love you so much, Warner."

Gathering her into his arms, he held her snugly. "I love you too," he murmured. "Tomorrow morning, we're going to board our private yacht. We'll spend the day sailing the Sydney Harbor. I've arranged to have a chef prepare a delicious lunch for us."

"I just assumed we'd be spending the next twelve days of our honeymoon in bed," Marin murmured in a seductive whisper. "I can't wait to start that part of our marriage. I'm so hungry for you."

"I'd like nothing better, but I thought you wanted to see some of Australia."

"I do," she confirmed. She settled back, enjoying the feel of his arms around her. "So what else will we be doing?"

"Wednesday, we'll take a helicopter flight over Sydney and the Blue Mountains. After lunch we can take a driving tour through Megalong Valley to explore the Australian bush. We have reservations at a hotel in the Blue Mountains, so we'll spend a couple of days there."

"You really planned this trip from beginning to end, didn't you?"

Nodding, Warner said, "I want our honeymoon to be a memorable one. Remember when you said you wanted to go to a private beach?"

"Yes . . ."

"Well, on Friday, we fly to the South Coast and we'll spend the weekend on a private beach there. We'll spend the rest of our honeymoon in Cairns."

"This is such a dream come true for me. Oh, Warner, I'm so excited."

He brushed a light kiss across her forehead. "You are my dream come true, sweetheart. The answer to a prayer."

"I hope you'll always feel this way about me."

"I will," Warner vowed. "God laid it on my heart that you were the woman for me. He's never wrong. Ours will be a wonderful love story— one that we'll be able to share with our children."

Marin fell quiet. They'd discussed having children before the wedding and she wanted to be a mother one day, but not anytime soon. Her career was taking off and she wanted to focus on that for the time being. Motherhood would have to wait.

*   *   *

"Our wedding pictures are all over the tabloids and the Internet," Warner complained over morning coffee and breakfast.

"Why are you so upset?" Marin asked. "You allowed *Jet* magazine to send a photographer to our ceremony."

Pointing to the *National Star* newspaper, he responded, "But these people are always looking for some dirt."

"I read it, Warner. It's actually not a bad article. I do think it was tacky of them to mention the differences in our ages though. Not to mention bringing up my past."

"How did they get the pictures in the first place?"

Marin shrugged nonchalantly. "Who knows how they manage to get any of the stuff they end up with. They look amateurish, so I'm sure someone who was at the wedding probably sold us out. You know this comes with being celebrities."

"I know. I just don't like it. I prefer a more normal life."

"Warner, that sounds nice in theory, but you know you're being unrealistic. We are very much in the public eye, honey. People are curious about us."

His gaze met hers. "I intend to keep our marriage a private affair and I hope you'll do the same."

"Of course."

Warner took a long swig of his coffee. "Marin, when we start having children, I want them sheltered from the media. I don't want their faces splashed all over the tabloids."

"You don't have to worry about that. I feel the exact same way." Marin took the newspaper away from Warner, saying, "We're on our honeymoon, sweetheart. Last night was blissful, but I'd like to see some of Sydney. Hurry up and finish your breakfast."

Warner pointed toward her plate. "You haven't finished your own breakfast."

She grinned. "That's because I'm too happy to eat."

"You need to keep up your strength. We've got a lot planned."

"And you're concerned about my strength so that I can do some sightseeing in Australia?" she asked playfully, glancing at him.

He held her gaze. "Well, that's one of the reasons."

Marin laughed. "I don't think I need to ask what the other reason is."

Warner took another bite of his omelet. "No, you don't. I'm sure you already know the answer."

She finished off her glass of cranberry juice. "Okay, I'm ready to go. C'mon, Warner—I don't want to spend another minute here in this suite. It's beautiful and all, but I'm dying to experience Australia."

Warner straightened his glasses, then rose to his feet. "Alright, Mrs. Brice. Have it your way."

Marin stood up and strolled around the table, standing in front of her husband. Bending down, she embraced him. "You are so good to me. My life can only get better from this moment on."

CHAPTER FOUR

He swept Marin into his arms. "Welcome home, Mrs. Brice."
"Warner, put me down," she pleaded. "Sweetie, you really don't have to carry me into the house."

He set her down in the foyer. "I've always wanted to carry my bride across the threshold like that."

Staring in the hall mirror at her reflection, Marin fluffed up her short curls, then turned around to face Warner. "It's funny, I actually expected to feel a little out of place when I first moved in, but I don't. This feels like home to me. More than any other place ever has."

"I'm glad to hear that, because now this *is* your home, Marin. I want to you feel comfortable."

Warner took her by the hand and led her into the formal living room, where they stood basking in their love for each other.

After a moment, Marin looked up at Warner and said, "I hope I don't hurt your feelings by saying this, but I'd like to do some redecorating. I have more eclectic tastes when it comes to furniture and I'd like my personality to be reflected in this house as well."

"I understand. That's fine with me. Just don't get all carried away with flowers and pink."

"I won't. You definitely won't have to worry about pink. I had pink bedrooms most of my childhood. I hate that color." Leaning back against Warner, she confessed, "You know . . . I've always wanted to live in Hancock Park. I just love the houses in this area."

Warner's arms encircled her once more. "I'm exhausted from our travel. How about you?"

"I'm feeling kind of tired, too." Giving him a seductive look, Marin suggested, "Why don't we go up to our bedroom, take a long hot shower together? I'll give you a massage and we can just go from there—what do you say?"

"Why are we still standing here?" he whispered, his breath hot against her ear.

"You think we made a baby last night?" Warner asked the next morning.

Yawning, Marin stretched. "I don't know, honey. Maybe. But don't be too disappointed if it doesn't happen as quickly as we'd like. My doctor says it's going to take time for the birth control pills to leave my system."

"Why were you taking birth control if you weren't sexually active?"

"They regulated my period," Marin lied. "Honey, I was upfront with you. I told you that I wasn't always saved. I was out in the world, but that changed a couple of years ago. After Ben Cason and I broke up, I became celibate."

She was lying through her teeth, but she didn't want Warner to think poorly of her. She was embarrassed by her past.

"I'm not judging you, sweetheart," Warner answered indulgently. "The past is the past."

Marin sat up in bed, letting the sheet fall, exposing her nakedness. "How do you think your church members feel about me?"

"What do you mean?"

"My breakup with Ben was in all the tabloids. I'm sure they read or heard about the tape Ben claimed to have of he and I having sex. He was threatening to sell it. They probably think I'm a tramp."

"Honey, they don't think anything like that. I have some wonderful members. Especially Sister Mollie Ransom and Sister Irma Wooten. Real good people. They were at the wedding."

"So how did they react when you told them we were getting married?

We kept much of our relationship private until a couple of months before the wedding."

"Why are you asking about this now?"

"I guess the reality didn't really hit me until now."

"They were happy for me, sweetheart. Everybody was. I think a few of them were starstruck. You have quite a lot of fans in church." He grinned. "In Australia, too. I wasn't sure we were going to be able to finish our lunch the other day."

"I'm sorry."

"No, honey, it was fine. I enjoyed watching you pose for pictures and sign autographs."

"It was so sweet when a few of them came back with wedding gifts for us."

Warner agreed. "I had to laugh when that one lady told you her son actually cried when he found out you were getting married." Pulling her into the circle of his arms, he quipped, "You're leaving a trail of broken hearts, you know."

"I'm sure some of those women at our wedding weren't crying totally out of happiness—it was because they were devastated." She moved to get out of bed. "I need to go to the bathroom. I'll be right back, hon."

Marin padded barefoot to the bathroom, closing the double doors behind her. She reached into her makeup bag and pulled out a compact containing her birth control pills.

She hastily put the last one in her mouth and made a mental note to call for a doctor's appointment. It was almost time for her annual checkup.

Warner knocked on the door, making her jump. "Hey, you coming out soon? I need to take a shower."

Marin flushed the toilet. "Be right out."

Opening the doors wide, she announced, "It's all yours."

Warner eyed her from head to toe. "Why don't you join me?" he suggested, his voice husky with emotion.

"Oooh, baby, I love the way you think," she purred. Her eyes raked boldly over him.

✳   ✳   ✳

Sitting up in bed, Warner put on his glasses. "I need to call Deacon Thompson tomorrow morning as soon as I get to the church."

"Warner, we just got back from our honeymoon," Marin complained. "Can't you take another day or so to just get settled?"

"I wish I could, but we're getting ready for the men's conference. I really need to get back to work."

Marin cuddled up beside him. "You're no fun, Warner."

"You have to get back to work as well."

She released a short sigh. "I know, but I'm just not ready to leave you. I really enjoyed our time together."

"So did I. But think about it. We get to come home to each other every day for the rest of our lives."

Marin smiled. "That's a nice thought."

Warner climbed out of bed. "I need to get dressed and down to the church. I'll try and come home early."

"I hope so. I miss you already."

Looking over his shoulder, he grinned. "I'll be back as soon as I can."

She lay back in bed, savoring the essence of married life. Warner was truly the type of man she'd always wanted.

Marin was happy.

Twenty minutes later, Warner kissed her goodbye and strode out their bedroom. He was on his way to the church.

She lay in bed for another ten minutes before finally getting up and going into the bathroom. She showered quickly, then slipped on a pair of denim shorts and a tube top.

It was time to make this house her own.

Her mother arrived twenty-five minutes later, just as Marin was finishing half a grapefruit for breakfast.

"So, how was Australia?" she asked, settling down in the family room.

"Oh, Mom, it's so beautiful. I love Sydney. Warner and I had such a wonderful time. It was the perfect start to our marriage."

"There's more to marriage than exotic vacations."

Marin's smile disappeared. "Here you go again. Mom, why do you do that? Just let me be happy. Okay?"

"You need to stop being so dramatic. All I'm saying is that marriage is a lot of work."

"I know that."

"Marin, what is your problem with me?"

"You're negative. Mom, I can't remember the last time you said anything nice about me or my work."

"Marin, how can you say such a thing?"

"It's true. Mom, do you remember when I won Miss Junior Los Angeles?" When Shirley nodded, she continued, "Instead of congratulating me, you made it clear how much you detested beauty pageants and that you thought I could've found a better way to spend my time."

"Marin, you are a smart girl. Beauty fades over time. You need to have something you can fall back on."

Sighing, she responded, "And acting is not it. Right? That's what you're really trying to say."

"Marin, I've always tried to get you to see *all* of your possibilities. You shouldn't limit yourself."

"I need you to see that I'm doing what I love. Mom, all I've ever really wanted to do was act. It's freeing. I love acting. Why can't you respect that?"

"Because I know you can be so much better."

"This is my life, Mom. I'm doing what I love."

"If I thought it made you as happy as you say it does, I'd be thrilled for you—but I don't see it, Marin. I really don't see it."

She frowned. "Mom, let's change the subject. You and I are never going to agree. Let's just drop it."

Shirley glanced around the room. "Are you planning to make any changes to the house?"

Marin nodded. "I've got to put some color on the walls."

"How does Warner feel about it?"

"This is my house, too."

"So you're saying Warner doesn't have any say?" Shirley was challenging her daughter. "This has been his home for a lot longer, dear."

"Mom, Warner is fine with my doing some redecorating." Sighing, Marin rose to her feet. "I need to run some errands," she announced. "There's not much food in the house and I want to make a nice dinner for Warner."

Shirley laughed. "You? You're planning to cook? I don't believe it." She stood up. "You may want to take a few cooking lessons. Warner would certainly appreciate the effort, I'm sure."

Marin held her temper in check. She refused to let her mother dampen her mood. "Mom, I'll walk you out."

While Warner was working in his office at the church, Marin passed the time by going from room to room of the five-thousand-square-foot custom-built house. She critically studied each room, making notes of what needed to be added or changed.

The doorbell rang.

Marin finished writing down her thoughts before rushing off to answer the door. She peered through the tiny peephole and sighed. "Great," she muttered under her breath. First her mother and now her sister-in-law. She was really being tested today.

"Chanelle, what a surprise," she said, feigning a smile. She stepped aside to let her sister-in-law enter. "Please come in."

Chanelle didn't move right away. She stood in the doorway, studying her for a moment before commenting, "You're glowing."

"I'm extremely happy," Marin admitted. "You won't believe how happy I am. Warner is a wonderful man and I'm very lucky to have him in my life."

"*You are blessed.* I hope you'll always feel that way about my brother."

Her eyes traveling to Chanelle's, Marin questioned, "Have you always been so protective of Warner?"

Chanelle seemed surprised by her query. "Yeah . . . I guess I have, but he's the same way with me. When Mitch and I were dating, Warner gave him such a hard time. My brother and I are very close."

Marin became increasingly uneasy under Chanelle's intense scrutiny. "I love your brother with my entire being," she assured Chanelle. "I'm going to be a good wife to him."

"We'll see." Chanelle pointed to the legal pad in Marin's hand. "Did I interrupt something? Looks like you're busy."

"Making notes for the decorator. I'm dying to make some changes to the house. I don't know who decorated this place the first time, but it reminds me of my mother's house. Traditional furnishings and cream-colored walls . . ." Marin made a face.

"I decorated the house," Chanelle stated quietly.

Marin's stomach clenched. Awkwardly, she cleared her throat. "Oh. Chanelle, I didn't mean anything negative by my comment. The color's nice but just doesn't really work for me."

Chanelle shrugged nonchalantly. "It's natural that you'd want to make this house yours. You are my brother's wife, after all."

Marin set her pad down on the sofa table in the hallway. "Yes, I'm Warner's wife and I want you to know that I love him very much. Chanelle, he is my life."

"That's the second time you've declared your love for Warner in the last twenty minutes. I'm glad you feel this way. That is, if you're really being truthful, Marin. Warner's been through a lot and he truly deserves to be happy."

"I can't imagine what he went through when Sherilyn died."

Chanelle seemed surprised. "He told you about Sherilyn?"

"Yes. We don't have any secrets," she responded as casually as she could manage. "He told me they were engaged and that shortly after, Sherilyn found out that she had uterine cancer. Stage four. She died within months of the diagnosis."

Chanelle nodded. "He was devastated. For a while there, we thought he might give up preaching, but Warner's faith is strong. Instead of turning on God or blaming Him for Sherilyn's death, Warner drew closer to the Lord. That's the kind of man you married."

A flicker of apprehension coursed through Marin, gnawing away at her confidence. "Chanelle, I know that you don't really care for me. What I'd like to know is why? I've never done anything to you."

"Marin, it's not that I don't like you. I don't know you. I *know* what I've heard about you, and even you have to admit that it's pretty scandalous."

She sat in the chair, her thin fingers tensed in her lap. "Chanelle, surely you do know that you can't believe everything that's written in the tabloids. Before you decide that I'm all wrong for your brother, why don't you take the time to get to know me? Just give me a chance. I don't want to be a bone of contention between Warner and you."

"That will never happen."

Marin flinched at the tone of Chanelle's voice. "Will you please give me a chance before you judge me?"

Chanelle took her time responding. "Okay. Let's start with you sharing your testimony with me."

Marin was caught off guard by her sister-in-law's request. "Excuse me?"

"*Your testimony.* What is your relationship with God? Do you even have one?"

"Yes, I have a relationship with the Lord," she muttered uneasily. "I got saved a couple of years ago. It was right after I was in a car accident. I don't know if you remember, but I almost died—"

Chanelle cut her off, saying, "I read something about it."

"Well, I know that I'm alive because God was with me. He saved me. I knew that I owed Him big, so I started going to church. I dedicated my life to Him."

Marin stared across at Chanelle, her heart pounding. She worried that she hadn't responded correctly. What exactly does one look for in a testimony?

Feeling unsure of herself, Marin changed the subject. "You don't have much longer," she observed aloud. "You must be very excited."

Chanelle ran a hand over her belly. "Mitch and I can hardly wait for this little guy to come out."

"So it's a boy."

"Yes. He'll be here in about ten weeks."

"Please let me know if I can do anything for you," Marin said. "Maybe I could host a baby shower."

"You don't have to go to all that trouble."

"But I want to do it," she insisted. "I'd really like to do this for you, Chanelle."

"That would be nice. Thank you." Chanelle's eyes traveled the room a moment, then returned to Marin. "Have you and Warner discussed children? I hope I'm not being too personal."

"You're not. And yes, we have. We're waiting on God to bless us with a child."

Chanelle was surprised. "Really? I know Warner can't wait to become a father, but I just assumed you wanted to focus on your career rather than motherhood right now."

"That shows how little you know about me," Marin couldn't resist replying. "Being a wife and having a family is very important to me."

She didn't really care much for Chanelle, but she had to sheath her inner feelings because Warner and his sister were very close. Marin knew that just being nice to Chanelle wasn't enough. She would have to work hard to build her trust.

At least I have Warner under my thumb, she thought silently. He loves me and wants to make me happy. Maybe once he realizes that Chanelle and I just aren't cut out to be friends, he won't push me to have a relationship with her. We don't need Chanelle in our lives to be happy. We have each other. I'll just have to make him see that.

CHAPTER FIVE

Warner met his longtime friend Adrian Reed for lunch the following day.

"I thought only brides walked around with that special glow," Adrian said teasingly once they were seated. "Man, you look like you're really enjoying married life."

"I am," Warner confirmed. "It's great."

Adrian said, "Not for me. Guess I'm not cut out for it. Just ask my ex-wife."

"You have to find the right person."

Shaking his head, Adrian responded, "I'm not interested in finding nobody. I think I'm gonna just focus on my kids right now." Changing the subject, he announced, "After next season, I'm retiring. My knees can't take it no more."

"I won't believe it until I see it," Warner replied with a chuckle. "Man, you've been talking about retiring for a while now."

"I know, but I'ma really do it this time. I need to be home with my son. He's been acting up in school. You know, not doing his work."

The waitress arrived to take their drink order.

"I'll have iced tea," Warner said.

"Me, too."

While they waited for their drinks to arrive, Warner and Adrian scanned the menu, trying to decide on their entrées.

"You know, I never figured you to marry an actress."

Warner glanced up from his menu. "Why not?"

"You strike me as wanting a woman who's ready to settle down and raise a family."

"Marin wants to have a family. We're already trying to get pregnant."

Adrian raised his eyebrows in surprise. "Really? I kind of thought she was focused on her career. It's really taking off."

"I believe she can have both."

"Marin and your family getting along well?" Adrian inquired after a moment.

Warner nodded. "I think Chanelle is still a little wary of Marin, but I'm positive that before long they'll be good friends."

The waiter arrived with their drinks, setting them on the table before writing down their lunch order.

Their discussion transitioned to football while they waited for their food to arrive.

"Looks like the Steelers might be getting rid of me for sure. My bones can't take those hits anymore."

"So you're really thinking about retiring?"

Adrian nodded. "I've made enough money. Now I just need to figure out life after football."

Lunch arrived.

"How is Mama Reed doing?" Warner questioned between bites.

"The same. Mom's still fussy. I hired a housekeeper for her and the poor girl complains that my mom won't let her do her job."

"Have you suggested the condo to her yet? That house is too big for her."

Adrian shook her head. "Man, I don't know if she's ready for that. She really loves her house."

"What about a live-in companion?"

"Warner, she'd lose her mind. You know how funny she is when it comes to having all kinds of people in her house." Adrian laughed. "I told you Mom gives her housekeeper a fit. The poor woman's threatened to quit several times."

Chuckling, Warner reached for his glass of iced tea. "She is a tiny spitfire."

"Mom's just straight-out mean. I love her to death, but that's a mean li'l woman."

"She's opinionated, that's for sure." Warner chuckled.

Adrian nodded in agreement.

"Marin's mom is very opinionated, too," Warner said. "She comes off as being critical sometimes."

"I watched Roy Kelly's trial on *Court TV*. Shirley Miller ain't no joke," Adrian responded. "That's for sure."

"Her father is tough. I've seen him in action a couple of times. He's the type of judge I never want to have to go before."

"Man, I'm with you." Adrian stuck a forkful of food into his mouth. "But Marin, she's a dream come true for me."

Leaning back in his seat, Adrian stated, "Man, I hope you'll feel this way a year from now. Five years from now. Hell, I hope you feel this way tomorrow."

Warner laughed. "Be careful, Adrian. Your bitterness is showing."

Sitting in the second pew, Marin struggled to stifle her yawn. She'd been bored to death listening to Hazel Pittman droning on and on during women's Bible study. As much as it might disappoint Warner, this was definitely not something she wanted to do on a regular basis.

When the study ended, Marin felt like jumping up and shouting, she was so glad it was over. She didn't linger around talking like some of the other women.

She grabbed her purse, slinging it on her shoulder, and slipped out of the sanctuary. Warner met her at the entrance of the administration building.

"Did you enjoy the women's Bible study?" he asked.

"Sister Hazel's a little long-winded."

Warner laughed. "She does love hearing the sound of her own voice."

"I think I'd prefer doing my own study. *Alone.*"

"You can still do that, Marin, but participating in group Bible study gives you a chance to connect with other believers in fellowship and to grow in your understanding of the Bible. You told me yourself that you wanted a better understanding of the Word."

"And I meant it." Marin paused a moment before saying, "I hope you won't think badly of me, but I was so bored in there. Warner, it was horrible for me."

"What made it so horrible?"

Lowering her voice, Marin responded, "Sister Hazel. I know she's married to one of your assistant pastors. I can't tell you the first thing I learned tonight. I didn't get a thing out of what Sister Hazel talked about. Some people may do well with group study, but I don't think I'm one of them."

"Will you at least give this another chance?"

Against her better judgment, Marin nodded. "Sure honey, I'll do it for you."

Deep down, she was resentful. She didn't want to waste her time coming here week after week, but she had no choice. If she didn't, the church members would probably think she wasn't a Christian. They might even judge Warner by her actions, but Marin wasn't about to let that happen.

She was stuck in a situation she wanted nothing to do with. An idea occurred to her.

Maybe she could arrange to work longer hours on Wednesdays at the studio. That way, Warner wouldn't look bad and neither would she. It was a perfect plan.

The following evening, Marin sat quietly, waiting for Warner to finish working on his sermon. She had grown irritated by his refusal to put it away long enough to spend a little quality time with her. This reminded her too much of what her life was like growing up, when her parents had always been too busy for her. She had never come first in their lives and she definitely didn't intend to go through it again in her marriage.

"How much longer?" she asked, trying to hide her irritation.

"Honey, I'm almost done. I just want to finish this one paragraph."

"You said that earlier," Marin said with a huff.

Warner took his eyes away from the computer to look at her. "Marin, I'll be done in a few minutes."

Releasing an impatient sigh, Marin picked up a magazine lying on the end table and opened it. She loved Warner, but right now she felt like choking some sense into him.

She was his wife—she was the woman that men all over the world wanted, fantasized about—so what was his problem?

Marin fumed silently while reading an article concerning the importance of couples' spending time together.

"I'm done," Warner announced before she finished the article.

She put the magazine back down on the table. "It's about time."

"Why are you so upset?" Warner questioned. "I didn't take that long."

"We're supposed to be spending quality time together."

He pushed away from his desk and stood up. "We have spent time together, Marin. What are you talking about?"

"It's not just a one-time thing," she argued. "We have to do it on a regular basis."

Warner walked from around his desk. He pulled her up from the couch, embracing her. "I love spending time with you. I really do."

"I enjoy being with you, too. That's why I'm talking about this now. Warner, I want our marriage to be a good one. I want us to be happy. But that can only happen if we stay on the right track."

"Marin, while I love the time we spend together, I can't just forget or forsake my responsibilities to my church. This is my calling and I'm committed to it."

Stiffening, Marin responded, "I'm not asking you to abandon your calling. I'm just saying that I want you to be mindful of your responsibilities at home as well."

"I hear you. I just didn't think I was overdoing it at work. I assumed things were going well between us."

"I have to come first in your life. I have to know that I matter. That's all I'm trying to say, Warner."

"Of course you matter. Our marriage is very important to me. But I need you to understand that God is at the head of our lives, or at least He should be. Then our marriage comes after that. That's the proper order."

Marin didn't respond.

"Honey," Warner prompted.

"Then take me upstairs and show me how much you love me, husband."

Warner yawned.

"See—you're exhausted," Marin stated. "You work too hard, Warner. I'll run you a nice hot bath and then I'm going to give you a massage when we get upstairs."

"Sounds good to me."

Marin led the way from Warner's office to their bedroom on the second level. She intended to make this a night Warner would not soon forget.

CHAPTER SIX

Warner unlocked his front door and stepped inside the house. He was thrilled to be home and was looking forward to spending an evening with his wife. She didn't have to work today, so for once they were both home at a decent hour.

His eyes searched the living room and then the dining room. His mouth split into a big grin. The roses he'd had delivered to Marin graced the huge table in an elegant display of beauty and splendor.

"Thank you, God, for sending this beautiful woman into my life."

Marin floated down the stairs in nothing but a stretch lace robe with scalloped edging and beaded flower trim. She was a vision of pure beauty, Warner decided. A gift from God.

"When did you get home?" she asked. "I just got off the phone with your secretary to see if you were held up."

Grinning, he responded, "Just walked through the door." Warner leaned down to kiss his wife. "How was your day, sweetheart?"

"Okay. Chanelle stopped by the house earlier. She made a German chocolate cake and brought some over for you."

"Really? Were you wearing this?"

Marin laughed. "Goodness, no. The only reason I'm dressed like this now is because I just finished taking a shower."

He wrapped his arms around her midriff, exploring the hollows of her back. "Uh-huh."

"Oh, you think this is for you?"

"It isn't?"

"Honestly, I just got out of the shower." Laughing, Marin embraced her husband. "Thanks for coming home a little earlier for me. I don't want our jobs coming between us so soon. We've only been married three weeks."

"I'll never let that happen," Warner stated. His kiss was slow, thoughtful.

"I hope you mean it."

"I do. I have my priorities in order, Marin. You won't have to worry about that." Warner brushed a gentle kiss across her forehead. "So how was your visit with my sister?"

"I think it went okay. I invited her and Mitch over for dinner on Friday. I hope you don't mind."

"We don't have anything else planned, so that works for me. I appreciate your doing this. I want you and Chanelle to really get to know each other. We're family."

"We're on our way, I believe."

"Praise God," Warner murmured. He sniffed the air. "Dinner smells delicious. What did you cook?"

Marin shook her head. "I ordered it from Harold & Belle's. You know how much I love their food. You know, with our schedules, we should hire someone to come in and cook. We need to hire a staff, actually."

"A staff?"

"Yes. We need a full-time housekeeper. I'm surprised you don't have one already. We need a cook and I need a personal assistant. I had one, but she quit on me right before I met you."

"I'll let you handle all of that. However, Maria Puente is the woman that's been cleaning my house for years. She also cleans Chanelle's house."

"The girl that cleaned my condo before we got married is good. I'm telling you, Sylvia can clean. I think we should make her our housekeeper. I don't have to worry about her going through my stuff. *I trust her.*"

"Maria is honest and she does a pretty good job. If she didn't, Chanelle wouldn't keep her."

"Warner, I'm really comfortable with Sylvia. She's the one I want."

"Sure. Whatever. It's not a big deal, honey."

Marin gave him a slight push toward the curving staircase. "Honey, why don't you go upstairs and take a shower?" she suggested sweetly. "Get comfortable. When you're done, I'll have dinner on the table. We can eat and then"—she gave him a seductive smile—"have *dessert.*"

Marin chose a slim-fitting, sleeveless dress by Ralph Lauren to wear for her dinner party. She wasn't really thrilled with the idea of spending the evening with Mitch and Chanelle—they were so boring. She hoped Warner appreciated her efforts because she was only doing this for him.

She ran her fingers down the silk and linen fabric, her hand stopping at the narrow belt. She loved the way the simple dress draped her slender frame. It wasn't too sexy or too conservative.

She slipped on a pair of brown leather mules to complement the tan color of her dress.

Chanelle and her husband arrived just as Marin descended the stairs. She groaned inwardly. She'd hoped to have a few minutes alone with Warner before their arrival. He hadn't been home a good twenty minutes. Marin pasted on a smile. "We're so glad you and Mitch could have dinner with us."

Mitch embraced her. "Thanks for inviting us over."

"You guys are family," Marin responded smoothly, her eyes traveling to Chanelle. "We plan on getting together like this often."

Chanelle's gaze was full of remoteness. "We'd like that. *My* family's big on having dinner together—spending time together. We're very close."

"C'mon," Warner urged, joining them in the foyer. "Let's get comfortable in here. Dinner's almost ready."

They settled in the formal living room.

"Marin, you look very nice in that dress," Chanelle said, complimenting her sister-in-law.

She smiled. "Thank you."

"Chanelle, how did your doctor's appointment go?" Warner asked.

"Great," she responded. "The baby's doing well and has already turned. He's in the birth position."

Mitch laid a hand on his wife's stomach. "We can't wait to see this little guy."

"Do you have a name picked out for him?" Marin inquired.

"Yes. Joshua Garfield Foster."

Marin couldn't believe they were going to saddle the poor child with such old names.

"Are you enjoying your role on *California Suite?*" Mitch questioned.

"Actually, I am," Marin answered. "Playing the role of a woman everybody loves to hate—it's so much fun. I love being Brooke Martin because it's freeing. She's the type of person who really doesn't care what people think of her. She says exactly what she feels, good or bad."

"You might not love it so much when one of the viewers walks up and slaps you in the face," Chanelle said. "Some people get so wrapped up in shows that they get the actor and the character confused. It happens more than you know."

"Thankfully, I haven't had to deal with any real crazy people yet."

Chanelle reached over and picked up a small round plate. Using a toothpick, she placed several cubes of cheese on it along with a couple of crackers. "Maria told me that she's no longer working for you, Warner. Was there a problem?"

He shook his head no. "Marin wanted to continue using her own housekeeper."

Chanelle's gaze swung to her. "Oh, I see."

"I don't have anything against Maria. It's just that Sylvia knows exactly how I like things." Marin felt the need to defend her decision.

Mitch struck up a conversation with Warner, leaving Marin and Chanelle in awkward silence.

"Warner tells me that you and I have something in common," Marin suddenly blurted. "We both love plays. Well, Tyler Perry is bringing his new stage play to town. We should go see it together. I love his plays."

Nodding, Chanelle replied, "Maybe we should do a girls' night out."

"It'll be fun."

Chanelle gave her a tight-lipped smile.

I can't wait for this night to end, Marin thought silently. She and Chanelle would never be friends. They would merely tolerate each other for Warner's sake.

Ten minutes later, they were seated around the dinner table.

"Dinner is wonderful," Chanelle said.

"I can't take credit for it," Marin confessed with a tiny smile. "I ordered from Harold and Belle's."

Chanelle laughed. "I usually have my dinner parties catered, too. When I try to cook on my own, I mess up. I guess I'm so focused on everything being good that I end up burning something."

"We have another thing in common." Marin rose to her feet. "I'll bring out coffee and dessert."

Chanelle moved to stand. "Let me help you."

"Oh, no, you're our guest. Just sit back and enjoy yourself."

Warner stood up. "I'll help Marin."

In the kitchen, he whispered, "See, honey? Things are going well."

She and Chanelle had discovered they had a couple of things in common, but Marin wasn't about to rush to the conclusion that the evening had been a success. The tension in the air was still thick enough to slice with a knife.

Sunday morning, Marin got up early and began pulling clothes out of her closet, laying them all over the bed.

"Honey, what are you doing?" Warner asked when he strode out of the bathroom.

"I'm trying to decide what I'm wearing to church. I want to look like a first lady."

He laughed. "Anything you put on will be perfect."

Marin held up a loden green dress.

Standing in front of her full-length mirror, she placed the dress in front of her, eyeing her reflection. The simple sheath was elegant and ladylike, perfect for church.

She showered quickly.

She dried off and slipped on her robe. She styled her hair, fluffing up her curls with her fingers. After applying her makeup, she put on her dress. It fit her body like a glove, but it wasn't tight enough to raise the eyebrows of high-collared conservatives. The box-pleated skirt gave the outfit a timeless chic look.

She assessed herself in the mirror.

Marin ran her fingers through her short hair once more. A double strand of pearls would really set off the dress, she decided.

They left for church thirty minutes later.

Marin sat in Warner's office with him until it was almost time for the service to start.

As soon as she walked into the sanctuary, her eyes scanned the first three or four rows down front, searching for a familiar face. Dru was sitting on the third row with her husband. Marin walked over to join them.

"I was wondering where you were," Dru whispered.

"I was with Warner in his office," she responded.

"You look nice."

"Do I look like a first lady?"

Dru nodded. "I think so. But then again, I'm not exactly sure what a first lady should look like."

"You are so not funny."

"Relax, Marin. Just be you."

The organist began playing, signaling that it was time for the choir to sing their opening song.

Warner, his senior pastor and two associate pastors entered the sanctuary, dressed in flowing black robes.

Marin smiled. It thrilled her being married to the tall, handsome man standing in the pulpit. A man who loved and adored her in return.

Finally, someone who loves me enough to put me first. Someone who actually thinks I'm special. A wave of bitterness flowed through her. Her own mother never made her feel loved.

Marin loved her mother, but she also resented her. Shirley had never been there for her when she truly needed her. She even tried to turn her father against her, but her dad refused to let that happen. It didn't matter anymore. She had Warner. Her husband would always be there for her—she knew it in her heart. He would never let her down.

They stood up for prayer, forcing Marin's thoughts back to the present.

After praise and worship, Warner walked up to the pulpit. His eyes found her and Marin winked.

She knew there was a chance one of the TV cameras caught her on tape flirting with him, but she didn't care. She loved her husband and wanted the whole world to know.

Warner began his sermon by saying, "The King James Version translates First Thessalonians five, verse seventeen to say, *pray without ceasing.* The Living Bible paraphrases it to *always keep on praying.*" He paused for a moment before continuing. "Prayer has both a human and a divine side. We talk with the Father and the Father communicates with us. The most valuable part of the prayer experience is the listening side. That's when the Father speaks to our needs."

Guilt oozed out of Marin's pores as she listened to her husband talk. The only time she really talked to God lately was when she wanted something or was in trouble.

"We should have the habit of prayer because Father God listens to us," Warner was saying. "Our heavenly Father is eager to bestow His gifts upon us."

Marin wrote down his words and made notations in her Bible.

"The Father gives only gifts that are good for us. Turn to Matthew seven, verse eleven. I'm reading from the New King James Version. *If you then, being evil, know how to give good gifts to your children, how much more will your father who is in Heaven give good things to those who ask Him.*"

Warner ended his sermon by saying, "God has placed a hunger in our hearts to fellowship with Him."

His words left Marin with something to think about. Maybe that was why she'd always felt like something was missing, like she was searching. For what, she had no idea.

A couple of women approached Marin at the end of the service. "Mrs. Brice, my name is Mollie Ransom, and this is Irma Wooten. First off, we'd like to offer our congratulations on your marriage to Pastor."

Marin smiled. "I remember seeing you both at the wedding. Thank you so much. It's a pleasure to finally meet both of you."

"I saw you at Bible study a couple of weeks ago, but you left before I had a chance to speak to you," Irma stated.

"We'd like to host a luncheon for you with the women in our church. Sort of a way for them to get to know you."

"When did you have in mind?"

"We know how busy you are," Mollie interjected. "So if we could do it in a couple of weeks—would that work for you?"

Marin pulled her appointment book from her purse. "Were you thinking about a weekend?"

"Yes."

"That'll be fine," Marin responded. "Thanks so much for thinking of me."

"We're looking forward to spending some time with you," Irma gushed. "We're so happy Pastor's found a wife. He's such a good man."

"Is it okay for us to e-mail you or call you with the details, Mrs. Brice?" Mollie inquired.

Marin nodded. "You can call me and please—it's fine to address me as just Marin. We don't have to be so formal with each other."

Mollie Ransom broke into a grin. "You're so down-to-earth."

"I don't know how else to be. I'm looking forward to the luncheon."

"We are, too," Irma responded. "We're very excited."

They talked for a few minutes more before going their separate ways. Marin walked toward the exit doors. She found her friend Dru standing in the last row talking with her husband.

"Hey, you two."

"Hello, Marin." Larry greeted her with a hug. Dru embraced her next.

"Hey, girl. Your husband preached this morning. I really enjoyed the sermon. It was definitely something I needed to hear. Larry and I were just talking about that."

Marin smiled. "He stepped on my toes a little this morning." She chuckled. "I plan to ask him why he decided to tell my business all on national television."

Larry and Dru laughed.

"Ladies, I need to get out of here. I'll see y'all later." He kissed his wife, then walked through the exit doors, leaving Dru alone with Marin.

They sat down.

"I don't think I've ever seen you so happy," Dru observed aloud. "Things must be going very well."

"They are," Marin confirmed. "I've never been happier. The women here are even hosting a luncheon for me. They want to get to know me better."

"I know." Grinning, Dru announced, "I'm on the planning committee."

Breaking into a smile, Marin asked, "Was this your idea?"

Dru shook her head no. "It was actually Sister Mollie's idea. She's a big fan of Pastor Brice. She's a fan of yours, too."

"She seems like a sweet person."

"She is," Dru confirmed. "Most of the women in the group are good people. We usually have a good time together."

Warner approached them. "Hello, ladies."

"Hello," they responded in unison.

Marin rose to her feet. "Are you ready to go home?"

He nodded. "I thought maybe we could stop somewhere and get something to eat. Dru, would you like to join us?"

Standing up, she answered, "Pastor Brice, thanks for the invitation, but I promised to have dinner with my mom. Today is the anniversary of my father's death and I don't want her to be alone. It's only been two years."

Warner nodded in understanding.

"I enjoyed the sermon this morning. You were talking about me."

Marin looped her arm through his. "And me," she added with a laugh.

Warner chuckled before confessing, "I was talking about myself. I'd written an entirely different sermon for today, but God laid this on my heart while I was driving to the church this morning."

Now Marin understood why he'd been so quiet this morning.

They walked outside. Marin gave Dru a hug before getting into Warner's black Mercedes.

A few minutes later, they were driving out of the parking lot and heading to Beverly Hills for lunch.

"Did you know about the luncheon being hosted in my honor?" she asked. "Sister Mollie and Sister Irma talked to me after the service."

"I knew the women's ministry wanted to plan something for you." Warner glanced over at her. "Are you okay with this?"

"Of course. They're doing it for me. I think it's so sweet."

"They want to get to know you."

Marin reached over and took Warner's hand in hers. "I'm looking forward to getting to know them as well."

She was blissfully happy.

Marrying Warner had been the best decision she'd ever made in her life. In the past, Marin had always found a way to screw up, but not this time. She was going to do everything possible not to ruin her marriage.

CHAPTER SEVEN

"Hello, Mom."

Shirley Miller glanced up from her menu, her eyes sharp and assessing. "Marin, what in the world do you have on?" she asked, referring to the black tube top and white cropped pants her daughter was wearing.

Marin chuckled to cover her annoyance. "It's nice to see you, too," she responded.

"Honey, for goodness' sake—you're married to a minister now. Your clothing should reflect such. You're practically naked. I'm sure Warner would want you to dress appropriately when you're not working on a movie set."

"Whatever," Marin muttered under her breath. She sat down in the chair with her arms folded across her chest, facing her mother. "You called me for lunch, so what is it that you want to discuss this time?"

"I just wanted to spend some time with my daughter. Do you have a problem with my wanting to see more of you?"

They stared at each other across a sudden ringing silence before Marin finally responded. "Maybe if you'd stop being so critical of me all the time, we'd spend more time together. Ever since Warner and I got married, all you do is lecture or criticize me. Mom, I'm so tired of debating with you over whether or not I'm a good wife to Warner. He's not complaining, so why should you?"

"Marin, I only want the best for you. Why can't you see that?"

"I have the best," Marin insisted. "I have a wonderful husband, a great career and I'm happy."

Shirley's stare drilled into her. *"Are you really as happy as you're trying to make me believe?"*

"Yes. I'm very happy. I couldn't be happier." Shaking her head, Marin uttered, "I can't believe you sometimes—"

"Marin, tell me something. Do you love Warner? Is that why you married him?"

She gave her mother a sidelong glance of utter disbelief. "Of course I love him. Why would you ask me something like that? Do you think I married him for his money? Mom, I don't need his money. I have money of my own."

"But do you love him?"

"Yes, Mom. I love Warner. He is my soul mate."

Shirley regarded Marin with a speculative glance. "You two are so different. He's very conservative while you . . . well . . ." She gestured toward Marin's outfit. "Anything but . . ."

"What exactly are you trying to say? Do you think I dress like a slut or something?" Marin challenged her mother. "Is that what you're trying to say?"

Shirley lifted her chin, meeting Marin's gaze straight on. "I would never use the word 'slut.' "

"I guess you wouldn't. It's too foul a word to slip between those dainty little lips of yours."

"I didn't call you here to fight. I merely thought we could have a pleasant lunch together."

"Mom, I'm not a screwup," Marin said. "I know you think I am, but I'm not. I've made some mistakes. I'm pretty sure you have, too. I'm not perfect. I'm just trying to live my life."

"Marin, I just want you to use those brains—not that body—to be successful. You're so much more than some pinup girl. You could have been a doctor or a lawyer."

"I can't be what you want me to be," she responded in a rush of words. "Mom, this is me. We're just not the Brady Bunch. Why can't you get that into your head? I'm never going to be the woman you want me to be."

"You're an angry young woman."

Marin laid down her menu. "Let's just change the subject. I think I'll have the grilled salmon Caesar salad." Her voice was firm, final. "Mom, what are you having?"

"Did you enjoy your lunch with your mother?" Warner inquired when Marin walked into the house later that afternoon.

"She was her usual critical self," Marin stated. "It's okay, though. I didn't expect anything different."

Warner studied her for a moment. "Your mother loves you. You know that."

"It would be nice to hear her say it for a change. All she ever does is lecture me. Or tell me that I should've been a doctor, a lawyer—anything but an actor. She hasn't figured out that I'm a grown woman. A married woman."

"No matter how old you get, she'll always be your mother and you'll always be her daughter."

Smiling, Marin agreed. "You're right."

"I have to go to Reno this weekend. I'm preaching at Pastor Bibb's church. Why don't you come with me?"

"I forgot all about that." Marin shook her head. "I can't go. I need to work on my scenes for next week. And I'm meeting with Nancy on Saturday."

"I thought you were going to drop her as your agent."

"We're going to talk Saturday. Then I'll make my decision."

"Pray about it, honey," Warner advised. "You've been with Nancy Maynard a long time. You always said that you two work together well."

"Lacey Kravitz thinks I should get another agent. She left Nancy because she couldn't get her career off the ground. Look at how well she's doing now."

"Just pray about it before you make a move," he said a second time.

Marin followed Warner into their kitchen. She reached into the refrigerator and pulled out a bottle of water. "I'm ready to take my career to the next level. You know? I've done soap operas and now I'm working on my third television series, but I think it's time to do a major film project."

"I understand," he murmured. "Just be patient, Marin. You're a good actress and people are going to see that. Look how well *California Suite* is doing—you're the one getting top billing."

"I know. I love the show and I'm planning on staying on as long as they'll have me, but I still want to do a major movie—something with blockbuster potential."

"You've gotten some offers for films, haven't you?"

"B movies," Marin responded. "That's not what I want. I've worked very hard in this industry. I feel I've already paid my dues."

"There's nothing wrong with wanting to further your career."

Setting the water bottle down on the granite countertop, Marin announced, "I'm going to grab a sandwich, then go up and study my lines. Do you want one?"

Warner shook his head no. "I'll get something while I'm out. Stanley and I have to go over some reports, so I need to go back to my office for a little while."

He could tell that Marin wasn't happy about his going back to the church and he didn't understand her feelings at all. He was going to the church, not to some bar or a club.

"I'm not going to be gone long," he stated. "Maybe an hour or so."

Her back to him, Marin shrugged. "See you when you get back if I'm not asleep." She pulled out a package of deli ham, mayo and mustard.

Warner retrieved a loaf of bread from the pantry and set it on the counter. "Here you are."

"Thanks," she muttered without looking at him.

Marin's mood had changed.

"Is there a problem?" Warner inquired.

"No."

"What's wrong, Marin?"

"Nothing."

"Then why are you acting like this?"

She glanced up then. "I'm not acting any kind of way. I'm fixing a sandwich. You said you were leaving—shouldn't you be on your way?"

Marin was upset over his leaving. That much was clear. Warner just couldn't understand why it bothered her so much. He was going to a meeting that wouldn't last more than a couple of hours. What was the big deal?

Marin didn't know why she got so angry with Warner whenever he left to go to the church. It was his job. She knew it, but the truth was that she didn't like his work cutting in on their evenings or their plans to spend time together.

It was unfair and irrational, but it was how she felt. It didn't bother her when she had to work later or travel—she just didn't want Warner doing it so much.

When Warner came home, Marin was in a better mood. Dressed in a sexy gown, she snuggled up to him, wanting to make up for her poor attitude earlier.

Their making up didn't last long because the next morning Warner announced that he would be leaving for Reno from Sacramento.

"When did you find out about this?" Marin questioned. She swung her legs out of bed.

"I just spoke to Peter Sanford a few minutes ago," Warner responded while buttoning up his shirt. "The original pastor they asked to preach at San Martine Baptist couldn't do it at the last minute."

"They could've found someone else."

"Honey, they asked if I could fill in and I told them I would. Why don't you just come with me."

"I have to work, Warner." Sighing, Marin continued, "You're married now. You can't just go off accepting every offer to preach without consulting me."

Warner slipped on his glasses before responding, "I didn't think it was a big deal."

Marin stood up and slipped on her robe. "It *is* a big deal to me. I expect to be informed of things like this *before* you make a decision. You owe me that much."

"I didn't think you'd mind, Marin."

"Maybe I wouldn't, if you thought enough of me to talk about it first."

"I'm sorry." Warner sat down on the edge of the bed. "And you're right. I should've consulted you."

Marin eyed her husband. "Warner, I know this is what you do. I know that you travel all over the world preaching. I just want to be a part of the decision making when it comes to when and where. Is that too much to ask?"

He shook his head. "No, it's not."

She paused in the doorway of the master bath. "I always miss you when you're gone."

Warner rose to his feet. "Honey, I'm sorry for not consulting you on this. It won't happen again."

Marin pulled him closer to her. "At least you're not leaving for another four days."

"I'll be back home before you know it."

Smiling, Marin responded, "I'm holding you to that."

They spent every waking moment together for the next four days.

Marin was lonely with Warner out of town preaching. He'd wanted her to join him but she refused, citing her work schedule as the reason she needed to remain home.

Now she was beginning to regret her decision. She considered driving over to see her parents but quickly tossed that idea out the window. She was still upset with her mother.

Chanelle had even called and invited Marin to her home for dinner, which she gently turned down. She didn't feel like dealing with her sister-in-law this evening.

"Warner, I miss you," she murmured softly. "I'll be so glad when you get back."

She picked up the script she'd been studying and tried to go back over her lines.

An hour passed. Then another.

She put the script away in the drawer of her bedside table.

She went downstairs and into the kitchen. She made herself a cup of tea.

Warner called while she was still downstairs.

"I miss you," she told him.

"You should've come with me. We had a good time earlier. The spirit was really moving."

"I'm sorry I missed it," Marin murmured. She was sincere when she said that. She wanted to truly share in that part of his life. She was a little jealous of the relationship Warner had with God. It was the kind of connection that she desired to have with the Lord. "Warner, when you get back, I want us to study together," she blurted. "And I want to take my prayer life to the next level."

"Honey, I'd like that too."

She could hear the pleasure in Warner's voice. He hadn't put any pressure on her, but she knew this was a desire of his as well. "I bet you're over there doing a praise dance."

Warner laughed. "I won't deny that I have been praying about it. I want us to grow in the Lord together."

"I think you're way ahead of me, sweetie. I'm not a heathen or anything like that, but I know I've not been as committed as I should. I'm going to do better."

She and Warner talked for the next hour.

"I hate to end this call, but I have to get up at the crack of dawn, honey. I miss you, Warner."

"I should be there by the time you get home as long as my flight isn't delayed. I love you, Marin."

"I love you, too. See you tomorrow. Rest well."

"That's no longer possible since I married you. I don't sleep well when we're not together."

"Neither do I," Marin confessed. She laughed. "We're pathetic."

"We're in love."

Marin sighed. "Good night, baby. Have a safe flight home."

They ended the call.

Smiling, Marin cleaned up, then went back upstairs to her bedroom. Warner would be home tomorrow and this dreadful loneliness she felt would disappear.

CHAPTER EIGHT

Marin didn't expect that over three hundred women would be attending the luncheon in her honor. She'd met so many women—there was no way she'd ever remember all of their names.

"Girl, they came out for you," Dru whispered. "Everybody wants to meet the woman who stole Pastor's heart."

"Think I need to watch my back?"

"I would," Dru replied with a chuckle. "I'm sure some of them had their eye on Pastor Brice."

"I felt like I was interviewing for a job. These women practically wanted to know my entire life story. Especially that Hazel Pittman. I get the feeling that she'd like to be first lady of Victory Baptist Church."

"I'm sure she would like her husband to be Pastor's right hand."

"I'm not sure she approves of me," Marin responded. "You should've seen some of the looks she gave me."

"Maybe it makes her feel better to think that she's in charge or something." Dru shrugged. "I don't know about Sister Hazel sometimes."

"So you don't think they're trying to make sure I'm the right woman for Warner then?"

"Oh, they were definitely checking you out to see if you're first-lady material."

Marin swallowed hard. "You're kidding, right?"

Dru chuckled. "You should see your face. Relax, Marin. They love you."

"As an actor or as Warner's wife?"

"Both, I guess." Dru looped her arm through Marin's. "C'mon—chill."

Irma walked over to where they were standing. "I hope you two enjoyed yourselves."

"We did," they responded in unison.

"Everything was lovely," Marin said complimenting her. "I really had a good time. You all made me feel very welcomed."

Irma clapped her hands in glee. "I'm so glad you had a nice time. I know this is probably not as nice as some of the events you've attended, but we wanted it to be special."

"The luncheon was very nice, Sister Irma."

"Your mother is sweet. And so funny."

Marin smiled. "She's a card alright." Her eyes traveled to where Shirley was standing, a few yards away. Her mother may have them fooled, but Marin knew better. Shirley had stood up and pretended she was so proud of her when she was anything but. "That's my mom."

Warner was waiting for her when she arrived at home an hour later.

He greeted her with a kiss. "So how did it go?"

Marin set her purse down on the table in the foyer. "Great," she responded. "I think everyone approves of our marriage. Except Hazel Pittman."

"Excuse me?"

"Warner, they wanted to meet me so that they could see if I fit their image of a first lady."

"That's not why they held this luncheon."

Marin broke into a grin. "Yes, it is and it's okay. I don't mind that they wanted to look me over." Wrapping her arms around him, she added, "I think they all approved, honey. Everybody can see how happy we are. That's all that matters."

"Why do you feel Sister Hazel didn't approve?"

Marin shrugged. "It was just a feeling. She just kept grilling me. She wanted to know everything about my life."

"She's harmless."

"I'm not worried about Hazel. You and I are married and there's nothing she can do to us."

"This is not exactly what I had in mind when I said we should do something special to celebrate being married for one month."

Marin straightened Warner's bow tie. "I know, but it's important that we attend this party. We don't have to stay the entire time, but I'm auditioning for a role in Bobby Marshall's new movie and this party is my one chance to connect with him."

"You must really want this part. You know I'm not one for Hollywood parties."

"This one is not quite like that," Marin explained. "This is Dru's birthday party and the real reason we're going, but I know Bobby Marshall will be there and being in one of his films will definitely take my career to the top." Marin reached out, lacing his fingers with her own. "Warner, you understand that, don't you?"

He nodded. "I do. I just thought we could have a romantic dinner somewhere special. Maybe Marino's, since you love the restaurant so much. Afterward, we could come back here and . . ."

"We can leave the birthday party right after I talk to Bobby. Okay?" Standing on tiptoe, Marin touched her lips to his. "Can you do this for me?"

He stroked her arm sensuously. "Anything for you, my beautiful and very talented wife."

She kissed him a second time. "You are so good to me."

"When are you getting dressed?"

"In a few minutes," she responded. "I need to finish my makeup."

Warner slipped on his glasses. "I'll go downstairs to my office. I need to make a couple of phone calls before we leave."

"I'll be down shortly."

Warner did a double take when Marin glided down the stairs fifteen minutes later. She was going to dominate the evening in the silken gown draping her body with a head-turning effect.

"So what do you think?" she asked, twirling around slowly. "It's not too much, is it?"

Warner silently assessed her. The dress featured a plunging wrap V-front with spaghetti straps that tied behind the neck and a V-back. "You look stunning."

"Then you approve?"

"Would you actually change clothes if I didn't?"

"Warner, what's wrong with this dress?"

He chuckled. "Nothing. It's fine."

Marin visibly relaxed. "Good. I just didn't want it to be too over the top for the wife of a pastor."

"Honey, just be yourself."

"You say that now," Marin responded. "I hope you remember later."

"Do I seem wishy-washy to you?"

"I'm not saying that, baby," she quickly assured him.

"Then what is it that you're trying to say?"

"Nothing. C'mon, honey. We need to get out of here. We don't want to be late."

Marin eyed her husband. "Are you sure I look okay?" She wanted to look sexy but not to the point that it would embarrass her husband.

"You're stunning."

They were soon on their way.

"Dru's house is so beautiful," Marin told Warner on the drive over. "She and Larry bought it a couple of years ago and they've totally renovated it. The master bedroom has his and her bathrooms. Can you believe it?"

"Sounds nice."

"It fits them. Dru has a craft room—she's really into scrapbooking—and her kitchen is huge. Warner, wait until you see it. You'd love it. My mom would go crazy if she saw it. You know how much she loves her kitchen. Dru has an indoor grill."

"Sounds nice. I've been thinking of us getting one of them."

"Me, too," Marin stated. "I think we should screen in our deck, too. I cherish our privacy. We can add more trees in the back of the house."

Warner agreed. "We can look into all of those things."

When they arrived, Dru and Larry greeted them at the front door.

"Happy one-month anniversary. I'm glad you two could make it." Dru stepped aside to let them enter the foyer.

Larry and Warner stood to the side talking, while Dru and Marin headed to the kitchen area.

"Everything looks beautiful," Marin told Dru. "Looks like everyone you invited came."

"A couple of people couldn't come, but that's okay. We're still going to have a good time." Dru handed Marin a glass of wine.

"Thanks," Marin murmured.

Warner and Larry joined them a few minutes later.

She noted the expression on Warner's face when he saw her with the wineglass, but he didn't say anything. Marin didn't think anything was wrong with having a glass of wine every now and then. She was a social drinker.

Bobby Marshall, one of Hollywood's hottest African American directors, was standing near the fireplace, looking bored. Seizing the chance for a one-on-one conversation, Marin breezed past Warner, Larry and Dru.

"Bobby, how are you?" she asked with a smile.

He smiled back. *A good sign,* Marin thought to herself.

"I'm great. How are things going on *California Suite?*"

"Good," she responded.

Bobby eyed her from head to toe. "You're looking good. I guess marriage to the pastor ain't too bad."

"It's wonderful," Marin gushed. "He's such a sweetie."

Bobby laughed. "That's the first time I've heard that said about Pastor Brice."

Marin stole a peek over her shoulder. Warner was still standing in the same spot, watching her. She waved.

He waved back, but his signature smile wasn't in place. Before she could excuse herself, another person walked up.

"Hey, gorgeous," he greeted.

Marin recognized the man as Kevin Jeffrey, another hot director. She hugged him, saying, "I haven't seen you in a while. I sent you an invitation to my wedding but never heard from you."

"I'm sorry I missed it. I was in France. But from all the pictures I saw it looked like it was nice. Things have been so crazy with me."

"Well, it's good seeing you."

"I saw your husband a few minutes ago."

"Yeah. He's over near the door. I guess I'd better go over and join him."

Dru walked over. "Hey, guys. Can I steal Marin away from you for a minute?"

"Sure," Kevin responded. "I need to speak to Bobby anyway." He embraced Marin. "Good seeing you again, gorgeous. Can't believe you up and got married on me."

Marin laughed. "You're crazy."

Dru pulled her off to the side. "Pastor Brice doesn't look like he's having a good time. Maybe you should go talk to him. You kind of just left the man at the door."

"Warner knew I came to network. He's fine."

"Marin, go talk to your husband. It won't hurt to just check on him."

"You are so bossy." Marin strode over to where Warner was standing.

"Having fun?" he asked her.

Marin didn't care for his dry tone. "Okay? What's wrong with you? Are you ready to leave?"

"Are you?"

"No," Marin answered. "What's wrong, Warner?"

He straightened his glasses. "We'll discuss it later."

Marin gazed at him for a moment before walking away. She didn't know what Warner's problem was, but she was having a good time and wasn't about to let him ruin the evening for her.

Warner stood in the background while Marin continued to work the entire party, laughing and at times flirting with different men. In his mind, he knew what she was doing was harmless, but he couldn't tell it to his heart.

He was jealous. He didn't like the way some of the men were eyeing his wife. He especially didn't care for the way they hugged her or touched her arm in such a familiar way. It seemed almost intimate.

Marin had told him that she'd been celibate for the past couple of years. Warner knew about the so-called sexual escapades of his wife, but one couldn't really trust what was written in supermarket gossip magazines. The truth was that he didn't want to believe any of it.

"Pastor Brice," a young lady greeted him, interrupting his musings. "I thought it was you standing over here. I met you last year at the Focus on the Family conference. I wrote *Family Sins.*"

"You're Virginia Best. I enjoyed your book."

She seemed surprised to hear that he'd read her memoir. "I just wanted to say thank you for supporting me. I really appreciate it."

"It's a great book. I think all women should read it."

They talked for a few minutes more. Warner looked up and found Marin watching them. He wondered if it bothered her at all to see him in a deep conversation with another woman.

Warner had a feeling it did because she kept looking over at them. Virginia caught Marin watching them and quickly moved on.

Larry came over and offered to give him a tour of the house. They were joined by a couple of the other men who had been abandoned by their wives.

When they returned, Marin went to him, asking, "Where have you been? I was looking for you."

"Larry gave me and a few of the other guys a tour of the house."

"Oh. I thought maybe you'd left me here."

"Why would I do that?" Warner questioned. "We came together."

Marin shrugged. "You didn't seem like you were having a good time."

"I would probably enjoy it more if I could actually spend some time with my wife."

"I'm *your* wife, Warner. You have me all the time." She gave a little laugh. "Don't be so selfish."

Warner didn't crack a smile. He wasn't in the mood for her teasing.

"It was a joke, honey." When Warner didn't respond, Marin added, "Why are you acting this way?"

"I'm tired."

"Are you ready to leave?"

"If you don't mind," Warner responded. "It's been a long day."

"Okay, fine," Marin muttered. "Let's go."

They said goodbye to Dru and Larry, then walked out to the car in silence.

"Warner, honey, what is going on with you? Why are you so quiet?" Marin queried when they were back at home. "Is something wrong?"

"Yes, as a matter of fact there is," he responded. "Marin, I'm uncomfortable with the way you carried on earlier."

"Carried on? What are you talking about?"

"I don't appreciate the way you were flirting with the men at the party. It sends out a wrong message."

"And what message is that?" Marin demanded, her mouth taking on an unpleasant twist.

"You're my wife and you should act like a married woman."

Marin dismissed his words with a wave of her hand. "Warner, you're being silly. Everyone knows I'm married and no one intruded upon that. We were just having a good time tonight. That's all. I've worked with Michael and Richard on a couple of movies and we've become good friends. They were at our wedding, remember?"

"What about the other one? The one you couldn't keep your hands off. Isn't he a movie director or something?"

"Oh, you're talking about Kevin Jeffrey. He's directing that new Dana Witherspoon film."

"The one you're getting ready to audition for?"

Marin nodded. "If I don't get to work with Bobby Marshall, maybe I'll be able to get this one."

"So that's why you were practically hanging off the man?"

"I was doing no such thing," Marin snapped. "He has a great sense of humor and we were laughing and just having a good time. Honey, you don't have to act so jealous."

"Marin, you should always keep in mind that you're married to me. We have a church filled with people who watch our every move. We are held to a higher standard—"

She cut him off, saying, "You mean *you* are held to a higher standard. I'm not a preacher."

"But you are my wife," he continued. "If I can't control my own family, they will begin to wonder if I can lead my church."

"You're overreacting, Warner. Everybody in your church knows that I'm an actress. Your membership's increased since we got married partly due to the fact that I'm your wife. I support you in everything you do, but I need you to do the same for me."

"It's not that I don't support you, sweetheart. I just want you to be mindful of what is expected of a minister's wife."

"First, you tell me to be me and not stress out about being a pastor's wife. Then you get mad at me when I do just that." Marin folded her arms across her chest. "Warner, make up your mind. You can't have it both ways."

"Marin, I support you. I really do. But as in all things, we have to use wisdom."

"I don't just jump into anything," Marin stated. "I'm very picky about the roles I take on. Warner, you don't have to worry. I'm not going to do anything to jeopardize my marriage."

The next day, Warner came home to find Marin preparing a romantic candlelit dinner for them.

"What's going on?"

Wiping her hands on an apron, she answered, "I wanted to do something nice for you. My way of saying I'm sorry. I never want to do something that will embarrass you, Warner."

He embraced her. "Honey, I love you. We just need to sit down and talk about our expectations, I think."

"Can we do it over dinner?"

Warner nodded. "It smells delicious. Beef Stroganoff. Where did you order it from?"

"I actually cooked dinner this time," Marin announced proudly. "I don't think it turned out too badly either."

"This is a pleasant surprise. I didn't think you knew anything about cooking."

"I never said I *couldn't* cook. I just don't like cooking."

Marin fixed plates for both of them and carried them to the dining room.

Warner gave a quick prayer.

Pointing with her fork, Marin urged, "Try it."

He sampled the meal. "Honey, this is delicious."

She smiled. "I found the recipe in one of my cookbooks. This is my first time trying it." She took a bite. "Mmmm, this is good."

"How are you doing on the shower plans for Chanelle? It's tomorrow, right?"

Nodding, Marin responded, "Great. Everything's pretty much done." She reached for her water glass and took a long sip. "I think even your sister will be pleased. Maybe she'll ease up on me after the shower. I'd really like for us to get along."

"Chanelle is a good person," Warner stated. "I know she's a bit protective where I'm concerned, but once she gets to know you, everything is going to be fine."

"What about your parents? Your dad acts okay with me, but your mom—she's still a bit frosty, for lack of a better word."

"It takes my mother a while to warm up to people. I'm telling you, Marin. Before you know it, my family's going to be as crazy about you as I am."

"I'm glad you're not still upset with me," Marin replied. "I don't like fighting with you."

"I don't like it either. But I don't like watching my wife flirt with other men."

"I wasn't flirting, Warner. Besides, it wasn't like I was going home with somebody other than you. You know that. I was simply making nice so that he would consider me for his next film."

"We're having a nice dinner. Let's not ruin it," Warner stated after a moment. "I think you know where I stand on this discussion."

She nodded. "Yeah. I certainly do. I'll make sure to act like the perfect first lady from now on."

Warner eyed her, as if trying to gauge her sincerity.

"I'm being serious. I won't embarrass you again. You have my word."

CHAPTER NINE

Marin placed the cake in the center of her table. The guests for Chanelle's baby shower would be arriving soon and she was nervous.

"The place looks beautiful," Millicent told her as soon as she walked into the house. "Marin, you did all this yourself?"

"Yes, I did." She was thrilled by her mother-in-law's words. Marin wanted nothing more than to win Millicent over. She cared what Warner's parents thought of her and wanted their approval. "Do you think Chanelle will be okay with this? Mitch told me that they were going with a Winnie the Pooh theme."

Smiling, Millicent responded, "She's going to be so pleased. You've done a wonderful job, Marin."

The first guest arrived.

"Could you please answer the door for me?" Marin asked.

"Sure, dear." Millicent strode elegantly across the gleaming hardwood floors toward the doorway. She was a born hostess, Marin decided.

More guests arrived and finally the guest of honor, Chanelle.

She glanced around. "Marin, this is so nice. Thank you. You didn't have to go to so much trouble for me."

"We're family."

They gathered in the sunken living room to enjoy the festivities. Everyone participated in the games, including her mother, which truly surprised Marin because Shirley had never been the type to play shower games.

For the first time since they'd met, Chanelle seemed to let down her guard as the afternoon wore on. Even Millicent acted a bit giddy.

The baby shower was a success.

Marin was on cloud nine by the time Warner arrived home. He found her in the family room talking with Millicent and Chanelle. She got up and began packing up the gifts while Warner spent some time with his sister and mother.

Her housekeeper was still cleaning up from the shower, so Marin stayed out of her way.

Millicent joined her. "Let me help you, dear. Chanelle drove the SUV so that she could get her gifts home." She glanced around. "But she's received so many—I will probably have to take some of them in my car." Marin agreed.

Warner helped to pack the cars. Chanelle and Millicent left, with the housekeeper leaving a few minutes behind them.

Marin and Warner settled down in the family room.

"Mom and Chanelle kept raving about the shower," he said with a smile. "From what they told me, they really enjoyed themselves. Mom said you were a very gracious hostess."

Marin grinned. "Good. I'm glad they had a wonderful time. I really wanted everything to be perfect." She rested her head against his chest and murmured, "Being a part of your family is very important to me. You guys are so close. I never had that. Being the only child of two busy parents is extremely lonely."

"You're not alone anymore, sweetheart. You never have to feel that way again."

Marin had a lunch date at Marino's Italian Restaurant with Dru.

"I don't know if I can do this," Marin said as soon as she sat down at the table. "I'm not sure I can be the type of wife Warner wants me to be."

Dru handed her a menu. "Why would you say that?"

"We had an argument the other night, after your birthday party."

"Over small stuff or something big?"

"Warner said I was flirting with the guys at the party."

Dru cracked up with laughter. "You *were* flirting, Marin."

"No, I wasn't. All I was doing was laughing at Bobby's stupid jokes. I admit I was doing some behind-kissing because I desperately want him to consider me for his new film. Warner acts like he doesn't understand how this industry works. I'm sure Garfield did that and a lot more for his career."

A waitress arrived with two glasses of ice water.

"I ordered one for you," Dru explained.

"Thanks," Marin mumbled, picking up her glass. She took a long sip.

"Marin, Garfield is Warner's father, *not his wife*. Believe it or not, there's a big difference. Besides, I doubt that he even knows everything Garfield went through."

"According to Warner, I have to be mindful of my place as his wife. He knew when he married me that I was an actress. Nothing has changed since then, so why is he acting a fool now?"

"Because the man is a pastor, Marin. You knew that before you married him, too," Dru pointed out.

"Whose side are you on?" Marin demanded.

"You have a good man. You want him to support what you do, then you need to support what he does. Look at me and Larry. My man plays for the Clippers, and I can't tell you how much I detest sports, but it's my job to go out there anyway and support him. I sit at those long, boring games because I love my man. You see, it works both ways."

"You're right," Marin conceded. "But I can do sports with no problem. Sitting through Sister Hazel's Bible study—girl, that's pure torture."

Dru laughed. "She doesn't always teach the study, Marin. The women take turns."

"Every time I go, Sister Hazel's giving the lesson." Marin crossed her legs, knocking her purse off the chair to the floor. She muttered a curse under her breath. "My stuff is all over the place."

She pushed her chair back and bent down, picking up the items that had fallen out.

After lunch, Marin stopped at the pharmacy to drop off the prescription for her birth control pills.

Her cell phone rang.

Marin recognized her mother's phone number and groaned. *I wonder what she wants,* she thought to herself.

Marin answered the call. "Hello, Mom."

"I'm glad you picked up," Shirley began. "Your dad and I wanted to invite you and Warner over for dinner on Sunday."

Marin's attention was on searching through her purse. "I can't find it," she exclaimed.

"What can't you find?" Shirley questioned.

"Nothing," Marin responded.

She went through her purse once more. The prescription had been in it when she left the doctor's office this morning. She'd made sure to get it from the nurse.

Marin checked her watch. It was too late to call. Dr. Harris' office was closed. She would have to try and reach her tomorrow morning.

"Dear, you still there?"

She struggled to hide her frustration. "I'm here."

"Dear, what's wrong? You sound a bit out of sorts."

"Just lost something I really needed. It's okay, though. I can get another one tomorrow."

"What is *it?* Why are you being so secretive?"

"Mom, it's not a big deal. Nobody's being secretive about anything. Now what were you saying about Sunday?"

"I was checking to see if you and Warner can join us for dinner?"

"I'll have to talk to him, then call you later." She ended the call within a few minutes.

Completely annoyed, Marin left the pharmacy and drove home. She didn't want to have a baby right now.

She tried to reassure herself that she'd been on the pill for so long that missing a couple wouldn't cause her to become pregnant, but she needed to get another prescription as soon as possible.

Her mood brightened when she saw a thick package from Bobby Marshall's office. If this was what she thought it was, Marin was on her way. Starring in a Bobby Marshall film would give her career the boost it needed.

*   *   *

"The script came today," Marin announced excitedly when Warner came home. "Bobby's movie. It's the one that I've been waiting on. I didn't expect to get it so fast though."

"So what do you think?"

"I'm so perfect for this part, Warner," she told him, her mind a crazy mixture of hope and fear. Marin needed her husband to understand just how much a role like this could pay off for her in the end. "It was written for me."

He gave her a big grin. "Good. I'm happy for you."

"Warner, this role is exactly what I need. Which means that . . ." Marin paused a moment before continuing. "I'm going to have to step out of my comfort zone." She paused for a moment more, searching for the right words. "This role calls for frontal nudity." Marin quickly added, "It's not a very long scene though."

Warner straightened his glasses. "What did you just say?"

Marin led him over to the sofa. They sat down side by side. "Warner, there's a short scene where I have to strip down to get into the shower. It's not a love scene."

"I don't care what it is. I don't want my wife showing her body for the world to see."

She detected a hint of censure in his tone. With both hands on her hips, Marin confronted him. "Warner, this is *my* body." She'd figured he would be against it, but she had hoped to make him understand that it was just for a few seconds—not long at all.

"You're *my* wife, Marin. How did you think I'd feel about this? Better yet, what did you think my church members will say?"

"They're the same people who'll be in the movie theaters, Warner. I'm pretty sure they're not as rigid in their faith as you are."

"Your body is God's temple, honey."

Marin clenched her mouth tighter. "Fine. I'll see if they'd be willing to use a body double. Will that make you happy?"

A hint of annoyance hovered in Warner's eyes. "No. That's just as bad, Marin. People will still assume that they're seeing your body."

"I can't believe you're so worried about what others think. Warner, you and I will know the truth."

"What about my parents and Chanelle? What about your parents? How do you feel about them seeing you like that?"

"We can tell them the truth. Warner, it's really not a big deal."

A shadow of irritation crossed his face. "It *is* a big deal, Marin. A very big deal."

"Warner, this has nothing to do with the church. This is my career. I don't want to be known as a Christian actor. I want to be known as an actor who happens to also be a Christian."

Warner's stare drilled into her. "I understand what you're saying, sweetheart, but there's a much better way to do it. You don't have to compromise your values."

Her lips thinned with irritation. "I don't feel like I'm compromising anything. Movies are simply an imitation of real life. What we depict on-screen is what's really going on out there."

"Movies have been doing that for years," Warner countered. "And there were some wonderful movies. Movies without all the profanity and graphic sex scenes. Nothing is left to the imagination anymore."

Releasing a long sigh, Marin stated, "Warner, we're never going to agree on this subject."

"So what are you planning to do?"

She hesitated, torn by conflicting emotions. "I'm going to audition for the part and if I get it, I'll ask them to take out the nudity."

Warner's gaze burned through her. "And if they refuse? What then?"

Shrugging, Marin responded, "I honestly don't know."

They stared at each other across a sudden ringing silence.

"Since you don't want to listen to me, all I can tell you to do is pray about it, honey. Seek God's wisdom and allow Him to show you what's right."

Marin bit down hard on her lower lip to keep from screaming. Warner was such a prude. But what bothered her more was that he didn't trust her judgment.

He was not going to ruin her career though. She would never allow it. She had worked too hard to get where she was. There was no turning back now.

She wanted more than anything to be a Hollywood superstar. She wanted to prove to her family—her mother especially—that she could be a successful actor.

Being married to a well-known and much-sought-after pastor wasn't enough for Marin. She wanted to achieve a certain level of stardom for herself. Only then she could be happy. Happier than she'd ever been in her life.

She just needed Warner to support her dreams and her career. In a way, Marin even understood his reservations about her showing her own body. What she couldn't understand was why he wouldn't compromise when it came to using a body double.

Marin was already in bed when Warner came upstairs a couple of hours later. She'd turned in early because she had to be at the studio shortly after four a.m.

"I thought you'd be asleep by now," he told her.

She sat up in bed, her back resting against a set of goose-down pillows. "I wanted to talk to you."

Warner removed his glasses, then took off his shirt.

"I'm not going to do any nude scenes. Out of respect for you—and for God. I thought about what you said and you're right," Marin stated with an ease she didn't feel. She felt the screams of frustration at the back of her throat.

"Thank you," Warner said in response. "I appreciate it."

"I love you, Warner. You're my life."

"I love you, too."

Mixed feelings surged through her. She didn't want to lose the role. If Bobby decided he didn't want to change the script, then she would probably be fired.

She would never forgive Warner if that happened. Bobby had hand-picked her for the role.

The next morning, Marin went through her purse once more, looking furiously for her birth control prescription. "Where is it?" she whispered.

She retraced her steps in her mind.

Let's see. After I left the doctor's office I met Dru for lunch.

She recalled her purse falling and the contents spilling out onto the floor.

"Oh, no," she uttered as she realized the prescription was probably somewhere in the trash by now.

Marin called the restaurant, just to see if someone had turned it in. She'd been off her pills for a week because of her delay in getting the refill. She'd been too busy.

She and Warner had made love last night. Marin worried briefly if she could've conceived but then remembered that someone had told her the longer a person stayed on the pill, the longer it took to get pregnant.

"I've only missed five days. I should be okay," she said out loud.

After she showered and dressed, Marin called her doctor to get another prescription.

She prayed that none of the staff at Marino's ended up calling the house to announce that they'd found the prescription—especially if Warner was home.

Marin didn't want him discovering her lie.

CHAPTER TEN

"Nancy just called. I didn't get the part," Marin announced a few days later. "Bobby's not looking for prudes—his words, according to my agent."

Warner reached out for her but Marin moved out of his reach. "I'm sure something else will come your way. You're a good actress. Hollywood loves you."

Irked by Warner's nonchalance, Marin snapped, "I'm sure my losing that role makes you very happy."

"How can you say that?" Warner demanded. "The only thing I didn't want was my wife's naked body splashed all over movie screens and television. I'm sorry, but I'll never change my mind about something like that."

"So you don't care what happens to my career. That's why I didn't get the part. Because I said I wouldn't get naked."

"I never said I didn't care about your career."

"You might as well," she countered. "If I can't fully commit to any role that I do, I might as well give up acting."

"Maybe it's something you should consider," Warner insisted with impatience.

"How can you say that to me?" Marin demanded. "What if I asked you to give up preaching?"

"I don't want to argue with you. Marin, I'm not against your acting, but I would like for you to look for better roles. Roles where you don't have to take your clothes off. More family-centered roles."

"You're crazy," she muttered without thinking. "I'm not that kind of actress."

His mouth dipped into an even deeper frown. "Excuse me?"

Walking off, Marin responded, "I don't want to discuss this anymore. Just drop it."

She headed up the stairs.

Warner followed her to the staircase. "Honey, let's calm down. C'mon down here."

"Leave me alone, Warner," she responded over her shoulder. "I can't talk to you right now."

Marin rushed into her bedroom, slamming the door shut. She put a fist to her mouth to keep from screaming.

Her heart started to race, her chest felt tight and she felt as if her breathing was cut off.

I'm having a nervous breakdown, she thought to herself. *I can't do this. I'm not cut out to be Warner's wife.* She felt like a volcano on the verge of erupting.

She climbed into her bed and lay down in a fetal position, a war of emotions raging through her.

My life should be fulfilling. Why do I still feel like something is missing? But what? I have a wonderful husband. I live in a beautiful home, but I still feel empty. I feel alone. Her mind reeled in confusion. *Maybe something's wrong with me.*

Marin wished she could share her feelings with Warner, but she couldn't. He would never understand. Maybe he would just tell her the same things her parents always did. That she was nothing but a spoiled, ungrateful and selfish woman.

An hour passed.

Marin was surprised that Warner hadn't come up to their bedroom by now. She'd half expected him to follow her when she'd stormed up earlier in anger.

He hadn't come because he didn't care about her feelings. Warner was responding the exact same way her parent responded—by ignoring her feelings.

She was tired of being ignored. She needed someone to acknowledge her. She needed someone to actually take the time to understand what she was going through.

The knock on the bedroom door made her jump because it was unexpected. Warner stuck his head inside, asking, "Honey, are you still upset with me?"

Marin shook her head no. "I'm not upset."

"You sure?"

"Warner, I'm not mad with you."

"Marin, you know how much I love you, don't you?"

She nodded, tears filling her eyes. "I love you, too. I really do." Marin reached out for him. "I don't mean to be such a screwup."

"Screwup? Where did that come from?"

"It's the way I feel. Mom just came here telling me what an embarrassment I am to them and to you. Warner, I'm so sorry."

The silence lengthened between them, making Marin feel uncomfortable. Warner felt the same way her mother did—he just hadn't said the words yet.

"Honey, you are not a failure or a screwup."

She clenched her hands until her nails left indentations on her palms. She took a deep breath and tried to relax.

Warner captured her eyes with his. "I mean it. You're not a screwup."

She gave him a tiny smile.

"You okay?"

"I'm just very tired, Warner."

"Will I disturb you if I do some studying in the sitting room?"

Marin shook her head no. "In a few minutes, I probably won't even realize you're in here."

He kissed her forehead. "You are not a failure. Always remember that. God doesn't make failures or mistakes."

She heard what Warner said, but she wasn't so sure. If God didn't make screwups, why did she always find a way to mess up her life?

Marin parked her car beside Carol's brand-new Mercedes.

"You're late."

Looking over at her friend, Marin responded, "So are you. You just got here, too."

"How are things with you and Warner?"

"Okay."

"You sure? You look kind of down this morning."

Dru walked up from behind them. "Leave her alone, Carol. Apparently, Marin doesn't want to discuss her personal business with us."

"That's not it," Marin countered. "Just got a lot of stuff on my mind right now."

"Well, we've got this photo shoot to do for *Essence*. We need to get a move on. I'm glad Shanika's the hairstylist. She can do wonders and I need a miracle." Dru removed the scarf from her head. "My hair looks a hot mess."

Marin patted her head. "You're not the only one, girl. I meant to cover mine with a baseball cap, but I was rushing to get here. I forgot to grab one."

"I keep one in the car," Carol said. "You never know when you'll need one."

After getting their hair and makeup done, the three women sat waiting for the art director and photographer to call them.

"Okay, I need to talk to somebody," Marin blurted. "Carol, how does your husband feel about you doing nudity?"

"He'd lose his mind," she responded. "But I wouldn't do it anyway."

"Even if it's a part that could really boost your career?"

"I wouldn't do it."

Marin looked across the table at Dru. "What about you?"

"Nope. Not interested in flashing my boobs all over a screen. Larry probably wouldn't care, but I'd have a problem with it."

"I don't see anything wrong with it. It's art."

"Surely you don't really believe that mess? But then, this is coming from someone who was taped by her ex-friend having sex."

"I didn't know he was taping me."

Dru laughed. "Don't give me that. I know you too well, Marin. We grew up together, remember?"

Her eyes narrowed and hardened. "Yeah. And what's that supposed to mean?"

"That's always been one of your fantasies. You told me that when we were freshmen in college. Right after you snagged that part in Haywood's film."

Marin blinked, then focused her gaze. "That's because it was a scene in the movie. I didn't really mean it."

Carol finished off her bottle of cranberry juice. "I remember *that* movie."

"It was my first," Marin announced proudly. "I had that one-liner, but it led to bigger and better projects for me."

"Your career has really taken off," Dru acknowledged. "Have you considered maybe taking some time off?"

"For what?"

"To enjoy your marriage. Maybe."

"I don't need any time off."

"What about your husband's church?"

"What about it? Am I supposed to start preaching the Word to everybody because I'm now first lady of Victory Baptist Church?"

"No. Your faith can be a personal thing for you. I know mine is for me. But if people want to talk about it, I will."

Carol agreed. "I'm not a preachy person either, but I am a believer and I want everything I do to reflect that, including acting. But, then, it's easy with a lot of the movies I do. Most of them have that spiritual element in them. That's the thing with black people. We have the Lord all up in everything we do."

"But what about when we step out of our comfort zone?" Marin asked. "I know that many of the black actors in the industry label themselves as Christians but they aren't pushing their religion on people."

"I don't either," Dru countered.

"But that's what I would be doing if I turn down good parts because I'm married to Warner."

"I've turned down parts because of my faith," Carol admitted. "I'm even careful about what I audition for because I want to be comfortable with what I'm doing. If you notice, I don't ever have parts when I have to curse. I just don't want to compromise my faith."

"Marin, you and I have had this discussion before," Dru interjected. "And we've talked about it at the Entertainment Fellowship meetings. Actors are sometimes placed in uncomfortable situations because of our faith. That's why you have to pray about it and keep God first."

"But don't you agree that we sometimes have to separate our beliefs from our characters? What about the time you had to play a prostitute, Dru?"

"I didn't have a problem with the role because it didn't cause me to compromise my beliefs. I didn't have to be nude. It wasn't about the act of prostitution but about the woman herself."

Marin turned to Carol, saying, "I'm amazed you've made it this far by turning down stuff. There are so many girls out there wanting to act."

"If I listen to the enemy, he'd have me believing that my career is over. I refuse to think that way. See, I believe that God can work through the movie and television industry."

"Pastor Brice says that all the time," Dru contributed. "He's always saying that we should consider Hollywood a mission field."

Marin had to agree. "Warner just said that to his father last week. I guess he's right. But I still don't think God is going to hold our jobs against us."

Carol chuckled. "I told you it was gonna be interesting being married to a preacher."

"I love my husband dearly. I just want him to let me do my job—no matter what it is. Warner has to trust me."

"What about *his* job, Marin?" Dru queried. "Do you support Pastor Brice?"

"Yeah. I do. Dru, it's not like I'm going to make porn movies. I'm willing to do only brief nudity or use a body double if it's that much of a problem for my husband. It doesn't have to be my body that people see on the screen."

"But they will think what they're seeing is your body," Carol pointed out. "I clearly understand what Pastor Brice is saying."

"I can't believe you people are such prudes. You're never going to make it in Hollywood with that kind of attitude," Marin said flatly.

Carol shrugged. "But I'll be able to live with my decision. Can you say the same?"

After the photo shoot, Marin stopped by Victory Baptist to see Warner. She found him in his office.

"I just left a message on your cell," he told her when she walked in and sat down.

"I know. I got it when I pulled into the parking lot."

"How did it go?"

"Great," she responded. "They took some great shots of us. We're going to grace the October issue. I'm going to have to buy up a bunch of them. It may be the only time I'm featured in *Essence*."

She could sense that Warner was still thinking about their discussion the night before. "Why don't we talk about it?" Marin suggested. "I can tell it's still on your mind."

"I think we should just agree to disagree on this, Marin."

"Warner, just for a moment, put aside the fact that I'm your wife. If I were just any other actor coming to you about this, what advice would you give me?"

"I would say that I feel a person who has any real faith in Jesus Christ will live his or her life accordingly."

"Even if it means that it could cause problems for them in the industry?"

Warner nodded. "A born-again Christian actor will turn down a sexually explicit script and he won't take off his clothes and jump into bed with someone. Regardless of the fact that it's just pretend. That it's a movie."

"Any kind of holdup in production such as revising or rewriting scripts can be expensive, Warner. You could easily be labeled a troublemaker because of your beliefs."

"My father once told me that he'd been offered this great movie deal for a lot of money. I think it was something like two hundred and fifty thousand dollars back then, but it didn't matter. He turned it down."

"Why?"

"He had a problem with something in the script."

"Did he have to do a sex scene?" Marin couldn't imagine her father-in-law in a role like that. He always seemed to take on more family-type parts.

"The story line called for my father to kiss his on-screen lover passionately."

"That's it? A kiss?"

"Passionately," Warner repeated. "Father said the overall story was wonderful, but he just couldn't kiss a woman who wasn't his wife like that. He said he couldn't help but wonder what Chanelle and I would think but also how Mother would feel. Father said to do something like that would undermine his testimony."

"Wow." Marin was impressed.

"I have always respected Father for making a stand not only for my mother but also for God. He wasn't going to compromise his faith for two hundred and fifty thousand dollars."

Marin sat quietly, thinking over Warner's words. "I guess I never looked at it that way really. My faith is priceless and I don't want to compromise that. I really don't, Warner."

"Most people try to separate their faith from the rest of their life, but the truth is you can't. Our spiritual walk affects every facet of our lives."

CHAPTER ELEVEN

Marin was still in a foul mood over losing the role in Bobby Marshall's movie, although she was trying to pretend otherwise.

Warner had done everything he could to cheer her up, but it was a losing battle. It didn't help that she was turned down for another role earlier today.

Why did it have to happen today of all days? The very day they were supposed to celebrate their two-month anniversary.

Warner suggested on the phone, "Let's go to dinner, Marin. We've been married for two months now. That calls for a celebration by Hollywood standards." He chuckled.

"I'm not in the mood to celebrate anything," she responded dryly.

The June weather was nice enough for Marin to take a midday swim. But even swimming from one end of the pool to the other couldn't smooth her ruffled feathers.

She was a good actress. She was beautiful. She was the perfect leading lady for Bobby's new film. It wasn't fair that she'd had to give up the role for Warner.

Marin's attitude was cool toward Warner when he arrived home that evening. After a few attempts to engage her into conversation, he left her alone.

Marin stayed up in their bedroom sulking while he worked in his office.

The phone rang an hour later.

"Mitch is on the phone," Marin announced on the intercom. "Your sister's in labor."

Warner rushed into their bedroom minutes later. "I'm going to the hospital. Would you like to go with me?"

Marin nodded after a moment. "Give me ten minutes."

He released a short sigh of relief. He hadn't been sure she would be interested in joining him. Marin still wasn't very comfortable around his family.

"Thank you," he told her when they were in the car. "I appreciate your coming with me."

She glanced over at him. "I'm your wife—where else would I be?"

"I hate seeing you look so unhappy, Marin."

She didn't respond.

"There will be many other roles for you to tackle, sweetheart. Your career is not over."

"There won't be if I suddenly start being picky about what I will and won't do," she responded. "I want to be considered a professional, Warner. Someone who isn't afraid to do what it takes."

"I understand that. I just don't believe you have to take off your clothes to do it."

"Realism sells."

"Sex sells," Warner countered. "Marin, you have to stand for something in this world."

"Honey, I know what you're saying. Really I do. It's not like I wanted to do a pornographic movie. It was a split second of nudity—it wasn't even going to be *my* body."

"Even that shouldn't be okay. We don't need all of that for entertainment. I don't need to see a woman's naked glory to make a movie enjoyable. I don't need all the profanity to make it real for me. I'm sorry, but I just don't need all that."

Warner stole a peek at his wife. "Marin, do you understand where I'm coming from?"

"I do. I get it. But the reality is that I'm an actor and in order to make money and be successful, I have to act. *It's a job*. Once I leave the set, I don't bring that stuff home with me."

"I still believe you can be just as successful without taking your clothes off and cussing."

"The next time *Sesame Street* does a casting call, I'll be sure to be one of the first in line."

Warner chuckled. "Why don't we just agree to disagree on this subject?"

Joshua Garfield Foster made his way into the world shortly after midnight.

Marin and Warner spent a few minutes with Chanelle, Mitch and the baby before returning home. She had an early call in the morning.

"I thought we'd be pregnant by now," Warner said as they readied for bed.

Marin didn't respond. For the moment, she didn't feel guilty for taking birth control. She was still a little upset with Warner.

"Maybe we should see a fertility specialist."

Irritated, she glanced over at her husband. *"For what?"* Softening her tone, she continued, "Warner, it's only been two months. Sometimes these things take time."

"It's just that holding Joshua . . . I can't wait to see and hold my own child. Marin, I really want us to have our own children soon."

Marin didn't really care what he wanted. She deserved to have a career of her own and for the moment that's where her focus was. It was abundantly clear to her that Warner didn't care about her work. He was focused on her getting pregnant. Well, she would have children when it suited her and not before, Marin decided.

In bed, Warner tried to pull her closer to him, but Marin stiffened and moved away from him.

"Not tonight," she said. "I'm exhausted."

He sat up in bed. "Is something wrong?"

"I'm just tired and I want to go to sleep." Marin knew her tone was cool, but she didn't care. She could barely conceal her feelings of resentment toward Warner at the moment.

Marin could feel the heat of his gaze on her, but she pretended otherwise.

"Sweetheart . . ." he prompted.

Marin refused to turn to look at him, for fear she would feel guilty over the way she was acting.

Sighing in resignation, Warner lay back down. "Good night, Marin."

She pretended to be asleep.

He didn't touch her, but Marin could tell he wasn't sleeping. They lay side by side, eyes closed, but sleep didn't come for either of them easily.

The next morning, Warner wasn't in bed when she woke up. Marin went running downstairs looking for him.

She found him in the kitchen drinking a cup of coffee.

"I'm sorry about last night," Marin blurted. "I didn't sleep that well."

"Neither did I," Warner admitted. "I don't like going to bed with tension between us. From this moment on, I'd like us to be able to settle any differences we have before we go to sleep."

"I agree."

"What did I do to upset you?" Warner inquired.

"I was still peeved over losing that role in Bobby Marshall's film. I really wanted that part, Warner. It was perfect for me and it definitely would've sent my career shooting to the stars."

"I know how much it meant to you, Marin. But I believe if you'll just be patient the right role will come your way."

Marin considered his words. "Maybe you're right. I'm not exactly known for my patience though."

Warner embraced her from behind. "That's because you're human, sweetheart."

Turning in his arms, Marin wrapped her arms around Warner. "I don't know what I'd do without you. I don't even know why you put up with me. You could've had any woman you wanted. Why me?"

"Because I followed the call God placed on my heart. He chose you as my mate and I have no regrets."

Her gaze met his. "Neither do I. I don't have a single regret about marrying you, Warner."

*   *   *

The honeymoon was definitely over.

Two weeks later, Marin was feeling neglected and hungered for Warner's attention. He'd preached at a couple of churches two nights already; then there was men's Bible study on Wednesday and a business meeting on Thursday.

"Honey, come up to bed. I'm lonely."

"I'll be up soon," he responded without looking up from his computer monitor. "I just need to finish the notes for my sermon on Sunday."

"I thought you finished it a few days ago. You may not have noticed, but we haven't spent much time together lately. You've been too busy for me the last couple of weeks."

"That was another sermon, Marin. God just spoke into my spirit earlier that this subject is what I need to preach on."

"Why can't you finish it tomorrow?"

Warner glanced over at her. "Honey, I'm almost done."

Marin rose to her feet. "I'll see you tomorrow. I have to be at the studio early."

"Okay," Warner responded nonchalantly. "I'll try not to wake you."

Her mood veered sharply to anger. "If you're not happy with me just say so, Warner."

"Where is this coming from?"

Marin paused in the doorway of Warner's office. "You never want to spend time with me anymore."

"I've had a lot going on, sweetheart."

"So have I, but I'm still trying to keep everything in perspective."

"I'll get this done tonight and we'll do something tomorrow night," Warner promised.

"Just forget it," Marin replied. "I already have plans."

"Marin—"

"Forget it, Warner. I'm going out with Dru and Carol tomorrow night. Don't bother to wait up."

Marin left for girls' night out with Dru long before Warner got home. She didn't want to see him right now.

"You look like you're in a bad mood," Dru said.

"Warner loves that church more than he loves me," Marin complained. "He spent most of last night in that office of his working on a sermon. Dru, can you believe that? He couldn't spend a few minutes with me. *Me.*"

"You married a minister. What did you think was going to happen? He's going to put God first in all things. Remember: God first, family second."

"Is that in the Bible?"

"Not exactly in those words, but it does say that you have to seek God first."

"Humph," Marin grunted.

"Warner loves you," Dru responded. "I hope you know that."

Folding her arms across her chest, Marin responded, "I'm not so sure."

"C'mon, girl. Marin, you can't be serious," Dru declared. "You know that man adores you."

"Then he needs to act like it."

"Girl, you need to grow up. Marin, the world doesn't revolve around you. I'm your friend and I love you, but I have to be honest with you."

"I'll remember that the next time you start complaining about Larry not being around."

"Marin, don't mess this up," Dru told her. "You have a good man."

"You sound like my mother."

"I don't mean to," she responded. "Marin, you and I have been friends for years. You've been wanting a man who'd treat you like a queen and now you have that."

"Warner has a good wife, too," Marin reminded her. "He's fortunate to have me. I'm sure I bring something to the table in our marriage."

Smiling, Dru agreed.

After her evening out, Marin was in better spirits, motivated by her talk with Dru and two glasses of wine.

It was past midnight and Warner was up waiting for her when she got home.

"Have a good time?"

She nodded. "I did. Dru says hello."

"Still mad at me?" he queried.

Marin dropped her purse as she crossed the room in quick strides. She sat down on Warner's lap. "Honey, I'm not mad. Sometimes I just get lonely here in this big house. I enjoy spending time with you." Grinning, she added, "You've spoiled me, Warner."

He held her close. "Marin, I love you. Don't ever forget it. But I have to honor my commitment to the church. Getting married doesn't change anything."

Marin kissed him, putting a halt to further conversation. She didn't want to spend another minute talking.

A bright flare of desire sprang into Warner's eyes. Marin felt passion rushing in her like the hottest fire, clouding her brain.

Without saying a word, she led Warner upstairs to their bedroom. She didn't want to think about anything; instead she wanted to show her husband how much she loved him.

CHAPTER TWELVE

"**I** think the chicken I had for dinner last night was bad," Marin moaned, her hands pressed to her abdomen. "I really feel sick." She and Warner had attended a Fourth of July barbecue at a friend's house.

"Are you going to be able to make it through the photo shoot?" Dru inquired. Studying her friend, surveying her face, she added, "Marin, you don't look well at all."

"I'm not," Marin admitted. "I feel terrible, but I'm not missing this opportunity to be on the cover of *Ebony*." Giving Dru a weak smile, she added, "Even if I do have to share it with you and Carol."

"I'm so psyched about doing this," Carol interjected. "First *Essence* and now the cover of *Ebony*—wow!"

Marin felt a wave of nausea sweep through her and placed a hand to her mouth. "I'm going to be s-sick—"

Carol rushed off to get a bottle of water and a packet of saltines.

"Here, try some crackers," Carol said when she returned. "Maybe this will help." Holding out the bottled water, she added, "And drink a few sips of water."

Marin dropped into a nearby chair. "I hate getting food poisoning."

Dru agreed. "It's definitely no fun."

They were summoned over to makeup.

"Let's go get ourselves stunning," Dru murmured.

Carol glanced over her shoulder at Marin. "You gonna make it?"

"I have no choice. I want to be on the cover of *Ebony*. This may be my only chance." Marin swallowed the bile that had risen to her throat. She prayed for the strength to get through the photo shoot.

It was by the grace of God that she managed to make it through the session without throwing up. She couldn't make it all the way home, however.

Two miles from home, she had to pull over and park to keep from getting sick in the car.

Marin sent up words of gratitude when she finally made it to her house. She went inside and sought the comfort of her bed.

I must have caught some type of bug, she decided. A couple of actors on the set of *California Suite* had been ill with a stomach virus. They must have passed it on to her.

Great, thought Marin. She had two fund-raisers coming up this week and she didn't want to cancel out at the last moment.

Marin prayed she'd feel better in a day or so.

"This can't be right." Marin re-counted the days on the calendar. "I'm late." After suffering from the stomach virus for a whole week, she had decided to check the date of her last period.

She sat down on the edge of her bed. "I can't be pregnant," she whispered. "I'm not ready to be a mother."

She knew Warner would be thrilled with the idea of parenthood. He was looking forward to becoming a father.

It wasn't that Marin intended to wait forever to be a mother—she just wanted to hold off for a couple more years.

"This is not happening to me," she told herself. She couldn't be pregnant. She'd been on the pill for such a long time—how could this have happened so quickly? *What do I really know about being a mother? It's not like I had a good example to follow.*

A wave of nausea swept through her. Marin considered buying a home pregnancy test, but she didn't want to chance Warner's finding out, so she called her doctor and made an appointment.

Warner was out of town but would be back tomorrow evening. For once, Marin was glad to be home alone. Her mood right now wasn't the best. She didn't feel well and she was stressed out over the possibility that she might be pregnant.

What will I do if the test comes back positive? She had no idea how to answer that question.

"Mom, what are you doing here?" Marin demanded when she opened her front door around nine thirty the next morning. She hadn't slept well and still wasn't in the best of moods.

"I came to see you. Why else would I be here?"

"I just didn't expect to see you today. Do you know what time it is?"

"Are you saying I should've called first?" Shirley brushed past her daughter into the house.

Marin followed her mother into the living room. "Well . . . Warner and I could've been . . . busy."

"He's out of town. You told me, remember? I wouldn't have just popped over like this if he were home." Shirley studied Marin's appearance, scanning her from head to toe. "Dear, you look sick. What's wrong with you?"

Shrugging, Marin answered, "I don't know. Maybe a virus or something."

"Have you been to the doctor?"

She shook her head no. "I'm sure I'll feel better in a day or so. There's been some type of virus going around the studio. It was bound to hit me sooner or later."

"I still think you need to see a doctor. You really look pale. Better to be safe than sorry."

"Mom, you worry way too much." Marin headed toward the foyer. "I need to eat a piece of toast or something."

Shirley was right behind her as they navigated to the kitchen. "When I see you looking like this—yes, I worry. You look dreadful."

Marin whirled around, facing her mother. "Thanks so much for that. You've said it over and over again. I get it. I look horrible." Marin pulled out a loaf of wheat bread from the pantry.

"All I'm saying is that you don't look well. Marin, you've got to stop being so sensitive, for goodness' sake."

"Why do you always do that?" she snapped in anger. "You dismiss my feelings as if I shouldn't feel the way I do."

"I don't do that," Shirley replied, taking a seat at the breakfast bar. "You've always overreacted. Even when you were a child. Your father could tell you the exact same thing and it would be fine coming from him. But me . . ."

"That's not true," Marin countered. "Look, this is getting us nowhere. And I'm not in the mood to argue, but I have feelings too. Very valid feelings, Mom. One day you're going to have to acknowledge them, whether you like it or not."

Marin held the folds of her robe together, prompting her mother to ask, "Why aren't you dressed?"

"You knocked on my door at nine in the morning," Marin replied. "Remember?"

"You're so dramatic." Shirley sighed.

Marin shook her head sadly. She wasn't in the mood for a fight. "Did you ask Daddy about dinner on Saturday?"

Her mother nodded. "I did. We're on. Are we meeting at Marino's?"

"Sure, that'll work." Marin popped a piece of bread into the toaster. "I've got to put something in my stomach."

"Where's the coffee?" Shirley inquired. "You always have coffee on."

Marin couldn't stand the smell of coffee right now. It made her feel nauseous.

"Would you like me to put on a pot?" her mother offered.

"No," Marin answered quickly. "I'm in the mood for herbal tea this morning."

Shirley made a face. "You sure you're okay?"

Rolling her eyes heavenward, Marin responded, "You didn't worry about me this much when I was a child."

"I worried a lot over you, Marin."

"When? Between high-profile cases? Mom, c'mon, be honest. Your clients were more important than I was."

"Marin, I really wish you'd stop telling these lies. I was a working mom—like any other mother. I did the best that I could. You know that you have a part in this as well, Marin. You could've been a better child."

She was blown away by her mother's words. Shirley was actually trying to blame her for the way she was raised. Marin clenched her teeth as she buttered her toasted bread.

"Don't you think that's way too much butter?" Shirley inquired.

"I like lots of butter on my toast."

Distracted, Marin nibbled on her toast and tried to focus on what her mother was rambling about. At the moment, she didn't care about attending some upcoming luncheon.

". . . and can you believe they're giving me the Woman of the Year Award?"

"Huh?" Marin ran her fingers through her hair. "Mom, can we do this on another day? I've got a lot on my mind right now."

"You're really acting very strange, Marin."

"I don't feel well and I'm tired, Mom. I've been working long hours. I'm up late some nights—"

"Then I guess you're too busy to have a spa day with your mother."

Frowning, Marin asked, "Can I have a rain check?"

Shirley hugged her. "Feel better, dear. Well, I need to get going. My toes are begging for a pedicure, my nails need work and my pores are dying to be vacuumed."

"Bye, Mom. Have fun." Marin escorted her mother to the front door.

"Sure you don't want to join me?"

"Not today," she responded.

Marin waved her mother off, then went back up to her room and crawled into bed. "God, please help me find the best way to handle this situation," she prayed. "Please . . . I need you."

She stayed in bed for almost two hours.

Then, after a shower, Marin felt better, strong enough to get dressed.

Every time she thought of the possibility that she might be pregnant she was moved to tears. This was so unfair.

She wasn't ready to be a mother and she definitely didn't want to put a child through what she'd had to deal with. Nobody deserved that.

Marin blamed her mother for her insecurities. Shirley wasn't affectionate, had never been. She was cold. Her father wasn't much better, but he always tried to make some time for her. He tried to be supportive, even though he agreed with her mother that Marin should've gone to college for something other than drama.

CHAPTER THIRTEEN

"**M**rs. Brice, you're six weeks pregnant," Dr. Harris announced on the last day of July. "You're going to have a baby."

Marin sat there for a moment, tongue-tied and shaken by the news. When she found her voice, she responded, "But I'm on the pill. I've been on them for a long time. I didn't think getting pregnant so soon was possible."

"Have you missed any?"

"I missed a week because I was too busy to request the refill in time. Then I lost my prescription and had to get another one from you." She ran trembling fingers through her hair. "I can't believe this. Are you absolutely positive? Any chance the test can be wrong?"

"You can become pregnant after missing two or more pills if you don't use another method of birth control."

"We weren't planning to have a child so soon," Marin blurted. "Wow . . ."

Dr. Harris went on to explain what she could expect over the coming months, but Marin wasn't really listening. She was still trying to digest the news.

I'm really pregnant.

She left the doctor's office in a daze. She barely remembered stepping on and off the elevator.

Outside, she sat in her car for a moment and then suddenly burst into tears. She didn't want a baby. At least not right now.

Looking upward, she asked, "Why are You doing this to me? I don't know anything about being a mother. What about my career? I'm an actress. I finally have a chance to really make it. Why now, God? Why would You do this to me now?"

Marin wasn't ready to go home. There was no way she could face Warner right now. There was a chance that he wouldn't be home—he'd mentioned meeting his best friend, Adrian, for lunch somewhere.

She didn't want to risk it. Not while she was in such an emotional state, because Warner would ask questions.

She drove to the Beverly Hills Hotel and strolled into the bar.

"What would you like to drink?" the bartender asked as soon as she sat down.

"A shot of Jack Daniel's," Marin said, then changed her mind. "Wait—just a mineral water, please. With lemon."

The thought of getting an abortion entered her mind a second time. She'd considered this option before when she realized that pregnancy was a possibility. Marin didn't take this decision lightly. There was so much at stake. Namely her marriage. But if she had an abortion, she wouldn't have to tell Warner about the pregnancy at all. He was scheduled to speak at some church in Indiana in a couple of weeks. She could do it then.

Marin hated deceiving her husband like this, but she had no other choice. "Please forgive me for what I'm about to do."

She finished her mineral water, then left the bar.

In her car, she made a call on her cell phone and arranged to terminate her pregnancy.

She hung up, satisfied.

Her purse fell to the floor of her car. She bent down to pick up the items that had fallen out. "I can't lose these again," she murmured, picking up her birth control pills. "This is how I got into this mess in the first place."

The house was empty when she arrived. Warner had left her a voice mail message saying that he had to run some errands. Marin released a sigh of relief. She needed some time to be alone.

She sat curled up on the sofa in the family room, lost in her thoughts. For how long, she didn't know. She'd lost track of time from the moment Dr. Harris had told her about the baby.

Marin heard the front door open and close. Warner was home.

"Honey," he called out. "You home?"

"In here," she responded.

"Are you feeling any better?" Warner inquired as he strode into the family room.

"Some," Marin answered. "I think it was just a bout of food poisoning. My stomach's been cramping something terrible," she lied. Marin prayed that Warner wouldn't figure out that she was pregnant. That would ruin everything.

"You think that it's food poisoning?"

Nodding, Marin answered, "I'm sure of it. Warner, it can't be anything else."

He didn't press her. "Can I get you something?"

She refused his offer. "No, I think I'll just rest here for a while."

"You mind if I join you on the sofa?"

Their eyes met. "Warner, there's nothing I'd like better," she responded after a moment.

Marin lay in his arms, hiding her tears of guilt against his chest.

Warner didn't think Marin was sick because of food poisoning. He'd eaten the same foods she had from the barbecue. He suspected Marin was pregnant.

He couldn't believe that she hadn't come to the same conclusion. Each time he tried to bring it up, she would adamantly declare that it was food poisoning.

Maybe she just didn't want to get her hopes up or maybe this had to do with him. Marin knew how much he wanted a child.

She doesn't want to disappoint me, he decided.

Her nausea could be due to a number of things, but deep down

Warner knew it was because she was pregnant. He couldn't explain how he knew—he just did.

We're going to have a baby.

Warner felt like shouting out his joy, but until it was official, he had to be cool. He glanced down at his sleeping wife. She looked so beautiful and even though she wasn't feeling well, she had the glow of impending motherhood.

Warner couldn't contain his excitement. He couldn't wait to be a father and to hold their baby for the first time.

While Marin slept, he gently laid her down and decided to run out. He wanted to do something special for her, in honor of their unborn child.

He hoped it would make her feel better.

Marin opened her eyes and sat up.

She did a double take. There were presents all over the love seat.

"What's all this?" she asked. Marin glanced up at the clock on the fireplace mantel, estimating that she'd been asleep for almost three hours.

While she was napping, Warner must have slipped out to run an errand.

Her mouth dropped open when she realized that a couple of the shopping bags were stuffed with baby items.

He knows. But how did he find out?

Marin stared wordlessly at him, her heart pounding. "Baby gifts? Warner, what is going on?" she asked after finding her voice.

"You really haven't considered it?"

"Considered what? Warner, what's going on?" she asked again.

"I went shopping. For the baby," Warner said. "*For our baby.* Honey, you're pregnant. That's why you've been so sick. Food poisoning doesn't last this long."

Marin wanted desperately to lie about the pregnancy, but her heart wouldn't let her. "We're going to have a baby."

"Thank You, Jesus," Warner said softly at first, then again much louder. "Thank You so much for blessing us with a child."

Marin chewed on her bottom lip, waiting for the question that was sure to come.

"Why didn't you tell me that you were pregnant?"

"Because I wanted to make sure I wasn't going to have a miscarriage. I told you I was cramping."

Warner placed a hand on her stomach and began to pray for a safe pregnancy and a healthy delivery.

"Most gracious Father, You have blessed us with a life that is so tiny, fragile and vulnerable. Father God, we want this baby so much. Please grant us favor so that our child will be born alive, healthy and safe. He is a gift from You, Lord, and a blessing to our family. Amen."

Warner opened his eyes and smiled. "We're having a baby. I can't believe it."

"I can't believe it either," Marin mumbled. There would definitely be no abortion now. She was going to be a mother in seven and a half months.

Warner was so excited about becoming a father that he wouldn't let Marin get up for any reason other than to take a bath and get into bed.

"I'm not helpless, honey. I can—"

Warner interrupted her. "If you're threatening a miscarriage, then we have to be especially careful. I want to go to the doctor with you."

Marin wished she'd had the courage to deny her condition. This pregnancy was still not good news as far as she was concerned. The director of *California Suite* would have to decide whether to write her pregnancy into the show or to hide her growing belly behind huge arrangements, big purses or coats.

Two of the other actresses on the show were pregnant and while one had been written in, the other spent less time on-screen. Marin didn't want that to happen to her. Her story line was on the front burner right now.

A baby would ruin all that for her.

The timing just wasn't right for motherhood, but she knew Warner would never agree. Besides, she'd led him to believe she wanted a child as much as he did.

I lied and now I'm being punished.

CHAPTER FOURTEEN

"Marin, why do you look so sad?" Warner questioned a few days later. "Aren't you happy about this baby?"

"It's not the baby exactly. Warner, you're always at that church of yours. I have a career, too. I don't want my baby raised by a nanny, but I can't do it alone."

"You won't have to," he promised. "I intend to be a full participant when it comes to parenting. I've always wanted children and I don't take that responsibility lightly."

"I hear what you're saying, Warner, and I believe you mean it, but the truth is, your schedule is full."

"I'll slow down after the baby comes. You won't have to do this alone."

"You promise?"

"I give you my word, Marin."

She hugged him. "Thanks so much, honey. You don't know how inadequate I feel right now. I really needed to hear you say that you're going to be around. The poor kid is going to need you. I have so much baggage from my childhood."

"Marin, you're going to be a great mother."

She wanted to believe him. Deep down, she hated feeling so insecure at times. There were days she felt like she could take on the world, but at other times she was scared to death and on the verge of a mental breakdown.

"Are you up to having dinner with your parents tonight?" Warner asked out of concern. "You don't look well."

She nodded. "I'll be fine."

Marin stood up and strode over to the walk-in closet. "I guess I need to find something to wear."

"Have you told them about the baby yet?" he asked.

She glanced over her shoulder at him. "No. Did you tell your family?"

Warner shook his head no. "You told me to wait."

"I know you're excited about the baby, but because I'm still having some cramping, I really don't want to say anything yet."

"What did your doctor say?"

"He said it might just be a sign of my uterus stretching and growing. Or it could be a sign that something else is going on. For now he's just watching me carefully."

Warner walked up behind her, embracing Marin. "We're having a baby!"

She pressed a hand to her stomach. "I know."

"I wish you were as happy about your pregnancy as I am."

"Honey, I am happy. I just have so much going on inside my head. You know my hormones are out of sync right now. I'm very moody and emotional."

An hour later, Marin was dressed and ready. Warner joined her downstairs a few minutes later.

They drove to Marino's Italian Restaurant on Sunset Boulevard.

Marin sat in the car for a moment, meditating. She needed to put herself in a calm mood before going inside.

Warner held the car door open for her. "Think positive—we're going to have a good time with your parents."

Marin stepped out of the Mercedes. "I don't know why I let my mother stress me out so much."

"That's not going to happen tonight. I'm not going to let her upset you."

Her parents were already seated in the private dining room when they walked inside.

They greeted her parents, then sat down.

The waiter came and took their drink orders.

Marin sat quietly, listening to her husband's conversation with her parents. She didn't contribute much because she didn't want to make herself sick. Since the drive over, she'd been feeling nauseous.

As soon as their drinks arrived, Marin reached for her ginger ale, hoping it would settle her stomach. She ignored the curious looks her mother kept sending her way.

She ordered a light meal but found she couldn't really eat when it arrived to the table.

"Marin, you're not eating," her father observed aloud. "Are you feeling well?"

She took a tiny sip of ginger ale. "I'm fine."

Her mother stopped eating. Shirley stared, silently surveying Marin.

After a moment Marin said, "Mom, will you please stop staring at me? I said I was fine."

"We should tell them," Warner whispered.

She shook her head no.

Warner apparently wasn't listening to her. He suddenly rose to his feet and blurted, "Marin and I have an announcement."

"Warner, no!" Marin exclaimed. She wasn't ready to share the news of her pregnancy yet.

"C'mon, sweetheart. Let's tell them. They're your parents—they won't leak it to the press until we're ready."

Her mother looked from her to Warner. "Tell us what?"

Grinning from ear to ear, Warner practically shouted, "We're going to have a baby!"

Her mother's gaze traveled to hers. "This is wonderful news, darling. You must be so excited."

"We are," Warner responded. "Aren't we, honey?"

Marin could only nod.

"You don't seem very excited, Marin."

"Mom, don't start. I'm not in the mood."

"I'm not starting anything. I'm merely stating a fact: that you don't seem very happy about being pregnant."

Marin pasted on a smile. "See . . . I'm grinning like a Cheshire cat. I'm thrilled, Mom."

"You can't fool me, Marin. You're my daughter. I know you."

"I'm happy. Trust me, Mom." Marin released a soft sigh when her mother backed off. Abortion was totally out of the question now. Warner would be telling his parents next.

Throughout dinner, Shirley and Robert talked about Marin's childhood, exposing skeletons she didn't want out of the closet.

Warner seemed thrilled to hear the stories of her youth, while Marin, deep down, just wanted to scream. Could her life get any worse?

"Tell me something, Marin. Why didn't you want us to know about the baby?" Shirley asked the following day when they were out shopping. "I would've assumed you'd be pleased. Warner was certainly excited."

"I knew you couldn't just let that go," Marin responded with a sigh. "It was just that this was something I wanted to keep between me and Warner for a little while. Can't you understand that?"

"Are you sure this is the truth?"

Marin cast a look in her mother's direction. "Why would you ask me something like that?"

"I'm asking because you don't look the least bit thrilled about being pregnant."

"Did it ever occur to you that I look this way because I can't keep any food down and I'm always tired? Mom, I'm pregnant."

Shirley selected a linen blouse and held it against her body. "I've always figured your career was more important to you than motherhood or marriage."

"And I've always told you that you don't really know me, Mom. Now will you please stop trying to analyze me? I'd like to enjoy this day with you." Marin took the blouse from Shirley and stuck it back on the rack. "That's definitely not you, Mom."

"Marin, sometimes it's so difficult trying to talk to you. Honey, I'm not your enemy."

"*Really?* Well, it's so funny to hear you say that. Because that's exactly the same way I've always felt. Mom, you and I see things differently, that's all. We will always disagree."

"You are so negative," Shirley uttered.

"Humph. I think you've got that the other way around." Marin looped a pair of jeans across her arm.

"I don't want to fight with you, Marin."

"Then let's not," she replied. "No more talk about me or my pregnancy—oh, and not one word about my marriage. Let's just focus on shopping. Deal?"

Shirley rolled her eyes heavenward, sparking laughter from Marin.

The following Sunday after church Warner stood up and signaled to his family that he had something to say.

"Marin and I wanted to share our good news with you all. She and I are having a baby," he announced.

"Congratulations," his parents said in unison.

Marin's eyes traveled to Chanelle, who said, "Looks like Joshua will have a playmate soon."

She smiled but said nothing. Chanelle ran hot and cold, Marin had come to understand. Some days she was warm and friendly. Other days she was cool as a cucumber. Today was one of those times.

Marin decided to just leave Chanelle alone. She was a bit surprised and a little hurt by the way Warner's parents responded to the news. They seemed very nonchalant about it.

"I don't think your family's real happy about the baby," Marin told Warner as soon as they arrived home. "I wish we hadn't told them now."

"They're happy, honey. They're thrilled."

"Were we at the same house? Because I didn't see any of that."

"You don't know them like I do."

"I expected them to at least show a little bit of excitement."

Warner placed both hands on her shoulders. "Honey, I'm telling you—my parents are thrilled to be having another grandchild. You'll see."

"I did notice that Chanelle was in one of her moods."

Warner shrugged. "She was probably tired."

"You don't have to make excuses for her, Warner. It's really okay. We're never going to be friends and I'm fine with that." As far as Marin was concerned, Chanelle was the one missing out.

*   *   *

Marin was scared. In fact "terrified" was more the word for what she was feeling. Warner had vowed to be there for her and the baby, but she knew his commitment to the church. Victory Baptist would always come first.

Her career would be placed on the back burner and she was feeling resentful about it. She was entitled to have a life of her own. She regretted not having the abortion, but she wasn't sure she could've gone through with it—she truly loved Warner and didn't want to hurt him that way. However, it would've made things so much easier.

There was so much responsibility that came with motherhood. Marin wanted to be everything to this child that her mother wasn't to her. She just truly had no idea where to begin.

She walked slowly up the aisle in the bookstore, looking for books on pregnancy and childbirth.

"Mrs. Brice?"

Marin glanced over her shoulder. "Sister Mollie. Hello." She turned away from the books, hiding the section she'd just been perusing. Folding her arms across her chest, she asked, "What are you doing here?"

"Looking for a good book to curl up with," Mollie replied. "I guess you're doing the same thing."

Marin smiled and nodded. "I was actually looking to do some research for a role I'm preparing for. The character is diagnosed with . . . with heart disease. I figured I'd read up on the condition."

Mollie seemed to buy her story. "How exciting."

"I love my work."

"I can tell. Acting seems to come so natural for you."

They talked for a few minutes more before Marin excused herself. She headed over to the wellness section and waited for Mollie to leave the store.

Marin picked up a couple of books on pregnancy, paid for them and quickly left the store.

At home, she fixed herself a sandwich and settled down in the family room to read. The books covered the changes her body would go through but very little in them prepared her for the emotional roller coaster she was riding.

Marin placed a hand on her belly, whispering, "Okay, little one. I don't have a clue about mothering, but I'm going to give this my best shot. I just hope you don't come to regret it. I'm giving you fair warning that I'm selfish at times and a little self-absorbed, but I'm basically a good person. Now your daddy—he's a wonderful man. You're going to love him. So don't worry, little baby. He's going to keep me on the right track."

"Who are you talking to?" Warner inquired when he entered the room.

"The baby," Marin responded. "I heard that it's good to talk to them."

"You're going to be a wonderful mother." He picked up one of the books she'd purchased earlier. "You won't need these."

Marin laid down the book she was reading. "You really think I'll be good at being a mom?"

Warner nodded.

"I don't believe having a baby makes you a mother. Look at my mom. She never should've had a child. Mom isn't really maternal or supportive— at least not the way I needed her to be. I can't ever remember her giving me a hug." Marin searched her memory. "I don't even recall seeing her and my father hugging or kissing."

"Sweetheart, some people just aren't affectionate."

"I know that now. But try explaining that to a child. I don't ever want my baby to feel unloved."

"He or she won't. We'll make sure of it."

"Having a baby is a huge responsibility, Warner. This child's happiness is in our hands. And I'm still trying to deal with my own issues."

Warner sat down beside her. "We're a team. You and I will get through this phase of our life together."

Laughing, Marin covered his hand with hers. "How are we ever going to survive the teenage years?"

"With much prayer."

CHAPTER FIFTEEN

"You almost didn't make it," Marin fussed when Warner rushed into the examination room. "We're almost done."

"Honey, I'm sorry I'm late. The meeting went longer than I anticipated it would."

"Well, you almost didn't get here to meet your son."

"I—" He stopped short. Gazing at her, Warner replied in disbelief, "My s-son? I have a son?"

Smiling, Marin nodded. "We have a little baby boy in there."

"Would you like to see him?" the lab technician questioned.

Warner practically shouted his response. "Yes!"

"She's making us a tape. The best part is that we can see him in 3-D. We'll really get to see him clearly. Like looking through a window."

Warner seemed amazed by it all. When he teared up upon seeing his son on screen, Marin's own eyes got watery. She was just as fascinated as Warner by the little person growing inside her. She was really having a baby.

Marin had never counted on feeling this excited about her pregnancy. She'd never thought it was possible for any person to be so incredibly happy.

She loved this baby more than she loved her own life.

*　*　*

It never failed.

Marin woke up feeling nauseous. She groaned and shifted her position, turning over to her left side. "When is this going to end?"

Warner sat up in bed. "Have you discussed this with your doctor?"

"She said that it should taper off around the second trimester, but it hasn't. Dr. Harris says that some women actually go through this the whole nine months."

Getting out of bed, Warner asked, "Can I get something for you?"

Marin shook her head no. "I just need to stay here for a few minutes. I feel terrible."

Warner climbed out of bed and walked barefoot into the bathroom.

She could hear the shower going as she lay still with her eyes closed. She was afraid if she moved too much, she would throw up.

Before Warner could finish his shower, Marin was in the bathroom, her head hanging over the toilet.

He helped her back into bed.

Marin settled against the pillows, moaning.

"I think you should go see the doctor," Warner announced, buttoning up his shirt. "I'm going to call and try to get an appointment for today."

He picked up the telephone and dialed.

"My wife isn't feeling well at all. She's still feeling nauseated and she's almost six months along."

Warner hung up a few minutes later, saying, "You have a ten o'clock appointment."

"There's probably not much she can do about it."

"I'd feel better if Dr. Harris checked you out."

Marin slowly made her way out of bed. She stood up and then had to sit back down, she was so dizzy.

Warner was instantly by her side. "Let me help you."

"I don't know if I can make it." Marin groaned. "I feel so sick."

When the dizziness passed, she attempted to stand up a second time. "I'm going to be sick," she muttered. She rushed across the floor to the bathroom.

She barely reached the toilet before she had to vomit.

"You're going back to bed," Warner said. "Don't even think about getting out until time for you to go to the doctor's appointment."

Marin was in no condition to argue and she was way too sick to care.

"Mrs. Brice, we're going to admit you to the hospital. You're very dehydrated, and we need to get some liquids into you," Dr. Harris announced after a few tests and an examination. "You've also lost some weight since your last visit, which really concerns me."

"I can't really keep anything down. I think it's stress."

Warner pushed up his glasses. "Stress? Honey, why are you so stressed? You cut your hours at the studio some."

"It's not really work," Marin explained. "I've just been worried about the baby—if I'm going to be a good mom, things like that."

"You're going to be a wonderful mother," Warner assured her. "You don't need to stress yourself out, sweetheart."

Dr. Harris patted Marin's hand. "Your husband's correct. Mrs. Brice, your condition is known as nausea and vomiting of pregnancy—we call it NVP. I want you to start eating small meals every two or three hours, and don't lie down right after eating. It might be a good idea to keep a pack of saltine crackers beside your bed."

"I didn't know it could last this long," said Marin. "I thought after the first trimester, I'd feel a whole lot better."

"In most of the cases I see, it usually ends between the fourteenth and sixteenth weeks of pregnancy. However, there are some women who have NVP throughout their entire pregnancies."

Marin groaned. "I hope I'm not one of those women. I don't think I can take much more of this."

Warner asked Dr. Harris, "When will she be able to go home?"

"In a couple of days, but that may change after I see the results of her blood work."

Walking Dr. Harris into the hall, Warner said, "I have one more question. What are the effects of nausea and vomiting of pregnancy on Marin and the baby's health?"

"There are short-term dietary deficiencies, but they don't seem to have any harmful effects. Mrs. Brice came in just in time and we were able to control the condition by giving her fluids and vitamin supplements. The nurse will give you some material on controlling NVP once your wife is released from the hospital."

Marin's parents arrived just as Warner finished his conversation with the doctor. He told them that Marin was being admitted to the hospital.

"There are a bunch of reporters outside," Judge Alexander announced. "Are you going to tell them anything?"

"I don't think they need to be privy to our personal lives during this time. I'll make a few calls and see if I can get somebody to call off the hounds."

"I'll call in some favors myself," Shirley offered. "I don't want Marin stressed out."

Warner agreed.

They headed into her room.

Marin actually seemed thrilled to see her parents. Warner stood back, giving them some room to spend time with their daughter. Now that she was about to become a mother, she seemed to really care more about family than about her career, which pleased Warner no end.

"Well, you look like you're feeling a lot better," Chanelle stated from the doorway of Marin's hospital room.

"I am," she confirmed. "Hopefully, they'll take me off this thing today. I hate being on an IV. Look at the way it's bruised up my arm."

Chanelle sat down in the empty chair beside the hospital bed. "Warner said you were really dehydrated."

Marin nodded. "I was so sick—some days I couldn't tolerate anything, not even water. Did you feel nauseated when you were pregnant?"

Chanelle shook her head no. "I guess I'm one of the lucky ones. I had a good pregnancy. Didn't get sick at all."

Pointing to the door, Marin responded, "Get out of my room. Just leave right now."

Chanelle laughed.

"How is Joshua doing? He's such a little cutie."

"My little honey bear's doing great. He's getting so big."

Rubbing the tiny bump that was her stomach, Marin said, "In a few months, he'll have a playmate. I just hope I can make it until then. I'm so scared of losing my baby."

"You will," Chanelle stated. "Be careful what comes out of your mouth. Always speak life over your situation."

"You and Warner are definitely brother and sister. He says that all the time."

"That's where I got it from. But he's right. Words are powerful things."

Marin continued to rub her stomach. "I love this little person already and I haven't even met him."

"I felt the same way." Chanelle met Marin's gaze. "I have to be honest with you. I was a little worried when I found out you were pregnant. I didn't really think you'd put having a family over your career—especially since it was going so well for you."

"Warner really wanted to have children as soon as possible." Marin chuckled. "He thinks if he waits any longer he'll be too old to play ball with them."

Millicent Brice stuck her head inside. "May we come in?"

Marin smiled. "Sure."

Her mother-in-law walked through the door, followed by Garfield. Millicent carried a beautiful bouquet of flowers in an array of colors. "I bought these to cheer you up," she said.

"Thank you. They're gorgeous."

"We saw Warner in the hall. He told us to make sure you knew he was back."

Marin relaxed. Warner had gone home to shower and change. She was grateful that her in-laws cared enough to visit her, but she still felt uncomfortable around them. They were polite to her, but there was still a wide gap between them. Maybe the baby would bridge that gap.

The room settled into silence.

Warner, please hurry back in here, Marin silently urged. She didn't know what to say to Millicent and Garfield. At least she and Chanelle could discuss pregnancy and babies.

"Have they decided when they're releasing you?" Millicent inquired.

"Not yet. I'm hoping it's tomorrow though. I really want to go home."

Chanelle stood up, saying, "Mama, sit down in the chair. I'm going to have to leave in a few minutes."

Millicent sat down. "I was sick for six months when I was pregnant with Warner. With Chanelle, I was nauseous the whole nine months almost. I decided then, two children would be enough for me. I love my children—I just never liked being pregnant."

"I loved being pregnant," Chanelle gushed.

Marin laughed when Millicent glanced up at her daughter and said, "That's because you didn't get sick or anything. Trust me—if you'd had to go through what I did, you wouldn't consider doing it again."

"I certainly haven't enjoyed being sick," Marin confessed truthfully. "I'm praying the rest of my pregnancy is an easy time."

Millicent patted her hand. "Dear, I do understand your feeling this way. One thing that worked for me was to keep a pack of saltines beside my bed. Each morning before I even got up I'd eat tiny bites of a cracker to help settle my stomach. I always kept a bottle of water with me and I would try to eat very small portions of food."

Warner strode into the room. He planted a kiss on Marin's forehead before saying, "I just finished talking to your doctor. She wants to keep you here for another day. After that, you can go home."

Marin broke into a grin. "YES! I'm so ready to get out of here."

She managed to enjoy the rest of her visit with her in-laws. It was almost four when they finally took their leave.

Warner walked them to the door of the hospital room, then returned to his seat beside Marin's bed. He pulled out a book.

"I saw this on the nightstand. It didn't look like you'd finished reading it, so I thought I'd bring it out here."

Marin broke into a grin. "Thanks. I was just getting to the good part."

Warner opened the book to the page with the folded-down corner. He began reading aloud.

She settled back, listening.

He read to her for the next half hour.

Feeling sleepy, Marin stretched and yawned.

Warner closed the book. "Honey, why don't you take a nap? I can tell you're getting tired."

"You're too good to me," Marin murmured softly. "Sometimes I don't think I deserve you."

She yawned a second time. She didn't want to sleep right now though. Instead, she wanted to just enjoy the pleasure of her husband's company. "You're my best friend, Warner."

His gaze met hers. "I feel the same way about you, sweetheart. I can't see my life without you in it."

"You'll never have to worry about that," Marin promised. "You're stuck with me until death."

Straightening his glasses, Warner responded, "I wouldn't have it any other way."

CHAPTER SIXTEEN

"Hello, diva," Dru said in greeting. "Look at you—lying around in that hospital bed wearing designer lingerie, watching television and reading magazines."

Marin made a face. "Not exactly how I planned to spend my Labor Day weekend."

Carol walked over to the bed and gave Marin a hug. "You know she's jealous, don't you?"

"Yeah," she agreed. "She can't stand it that I'm not having to get up at the crack of dawn and spend long hours on some studio set."

"Hey, I admit it. I'd like to lie around for a couple of days."

"If it wasn't for this baby, I'd be out there going from audition to audition; trying to land another role somewhere so I can get paid."

Dru dropped into the bedside chair. "I love what I do, but, girl, I'm tired. Larry's been talking about having a baby, but I'm not ready. Right now I just want to focus on my career."

"How does Larry feel about it?" Marin inquired.

"He understands. It's not like he's home much anyway. Besides, we're young. We still have time for a family."

Those had been Marin's thoughts exactly. Until she got pregnant. She loved her baby more than she could ever imagine and she hadn't really met him yet. They'd formed a bond through sharing her body over the past six months. Marin would lose her mind if anything ever happened to her child.

"What are your parents doing here?" Marin asked when they pulled into the driveway of their home.

"Mom offered to make us some dinner," Warner replied. "She's really been concerned about you."

"Yeah?"

Nodding, he answered, "I think you two are bonding."

"She understands what I'm going through."

Warner parked the car and turned off the engine. He got out and walked to the passenger side, where he opened the door for Marin.

"I'm so glad to be home."

"I'm glad to have you home," Warner said. "I really missed you."

They walked hand in hand into the house.

Millicent greeted her with a warm hug. "Warner, take your wife upstairs and get her settled in bed."

"I've spent the last three days in bed," Marin protested. "I can lay on the sofa in the family room."

"The doctor said that you have to—"

Millicent cut him off by saying, "If Marin doesn't want to get in bed right now, it's okay. Take her into the family room. She knows what's best for her at this point."

Marin hid her chuckle behind her hand. Some parents just refused to let their children grow up. Millicent and her mother were a lot alike, she was beginning to notice.

Placing her hand on her belly, Marin promised, "I'm never going to do that to you, sweetness."

She drifted off to sleep listening to Warner and his mother debating what was best for Marin.

A week had passed since Marin's stay at the hospital. So far, she hadn't experienced too many problems with keeping food or liquids down as long as she followed the doctor's instructions to drink small amounts of fluids and to eat small portions of soft or bland foods.

Marin had even taken Millicent's suggestion to eat a saltine cracker in the mornings before getting up.

Her mother-in-law checked on her at least once a day, which thrilled Marin. She felt like they were becoming close.

Marin showered and dressed. Her mother was planning on stopping by this morning. After the Roy Kelly case, Shirley had decided to leave the district attorney's office, citing burnout.

She arrived shortly after eleven.

"How're you feeling, hon?" she inquired when they settled into the family room.

Holding up a tabloid magazine, Marin answered, "I was feeling much better until I read this in the *National Star.* They are saying that I nearly lost my baby. It's all over the Internet."

Shirley took the magazine from her and tossed it into a nearby waste-basket. "Honey, you know what kind of trash they publish. They just want to sell newspapers. It doesn't matter if the story is true or not."

"I know. That's what I keep telling myself. I just wish they'd leave me alone."

Shirley smiled. "That's the price you pay for being famous."

"Why can't people understand that we're just like them? Our lives are not any different—we're just people. I'm sure they wouldn't like to have strangers in their personal lives, and we don't either."

"Honey, if you'd listened to me in the first place—"

Marin held up her hand in dismissal. "Mom, don't go there, please. I'm not in the mood."

"I'm just saying that you wouldn't have to deal with all this if you weren't . . ." Shirley's voice died. "Oh well, it really doesn't matter, does it?"

Marin lay back against her pillows. "I'll be so glad when I can keep something down. I hate feeling so sick all the time."

"When you see that baby, it's going to be so worth it."

Marin smiled. "I can't wait to see this little person. I never really thought I'd feel so excited over having a baby."

"To be honest, I wasn't sure you would ever have a child. I never fig-ured you were a candidate for motherhood."

"Neither did I," Marin confessed. "It's interesting how life can change for a person. One minute you're on a path to the right and then before you even realize it, you're going in an entirely different direction."

Shirley agreed.

"I'm going to enjoy every minute of my baby's life. I want us to be close."

"It's a nice thought, dear. But life has a way of getting in the way."

Marin shook her head. "Not for me. Mom, nothing will ever come before my family. Warner's right. God first, family second and career third. I get it."

Marin's morning sickness stayed with her through the first month of her third trimester, but thankfully she was able to continue working through it.

"Shawna, I really like this purse," Marin said one day on the set. "Do you think they'd let me keep it? After I have the baby, we're not going to need to hide my belly on-screen."

"I don't think anybody will care. I bought it at a flea market for about ten bucks."

Marin broke into a grin. "Cool." She shifted in her seat. "These director chairs are not exactly comfortable for a pregnant woman," she complained.

Shawna agreed. "Girl, when I was pregnant, I had to bring in my own chair."

"Maybe that's what I should do." Marin felt a sharp pain in her abdomen. "Ooooh," she moaned and pressed both hands to her belly.

"You okay?" Shawna inquired.

"I don't know. I'm in pain."

"She could be in labor," Marin heard someone say behind her.

"Are you in labor?" another person questioned.

"I don't know. I've never been in labor before, but it's too soon. The baby's not due for another four weeks." Marin felt another sharp pain— or was it a contraction? She didn't really know. "I think I'd better call Warner."

"Call nine-one-one," someone yelled.

"Just sit back and relax," Shawna advised her. "I'll call Pastor Brice. Anybody else you want me to call right now?"

Marin shook her head no. "I just want my husband. He can meet me at the hospital."

Shawna stayed by her side, coaching her through the contractions.

"It's too soon," Marin whispered. "I still have four more weeks to go."

"I guess your little man decided to come early."

Marin tried to push away the fear she felt. "Maybe it's false labor." She bent forward in pain as another contraction hit. "Ooooh, man, that hurts."

By the time they made it to the hospital, Marin's contractions had stopped. The doctor decided to keep her there for a couple of hours before releasing her.

Both she and Warner were relieved. It was too early for their baby to arrive. As a result of what had happened earlier, though, the doctor placed Marin on partial bed rest.

CHAPTER SEVENTEEN

Two weeks later, Marin was sure her pregnancy was doomed. She began experiencing headaches and swollen feet, and her blood pressure was high.

Concerned, Warner and Marin decided to have an emergency room doctor check her out.

She was admitted immediately. She was afraid for her unborn son. She never gave a single thought to her own health.

"Is the baby okay?"

"We're going to have to deliver the baby via cesarean section," the doctor told her and Warner. He explained that the baby was fine but Marin's blood pressure was still going up.

After he left, it seemed like the nurses came in every five minutes to check her blood pressure.

Marin's platelet count had dropped to the point that she needed a platelet infusion. They ran one line for the platelets and plasma and one line for magnesium sulfate. She was transported by a gurney to a labor and delivery room around midnight.

Her arms were strapped down, her body positioned on the operating table and the oxygen mask placed over her face.

Marin was told, "Count back from one hundred . . ."

When she opened her eyes, her mother was sitting beside her bed in the hospital room.

Marin licked her dry lips. "Baby . . ."

"He's a beautiful little boy," Shirley gushed.

"Where's Warner?"

"He and your father went to get some coffee. They'll be back shortly. Oh, Marin, your son looks like a little angel."

"I guess that's why Warner wants to name him Gabriel."

"Marin, I love that name."

"It's okay. I wanted to name him Cayden. Warner says it can be his middle name."

"Gabriel Cayden Brice. I love it."

"Why couldn't we call him Cayden Gabriel Brice?" Marin asked. "There's nothing wrong with that."

"Let Warner have this, darling. It's a small gesture. Besides, you both are getting what you want."

"Why don't you ever support me, Mom?"

"Honey, you just had a baby. This is a happy occasion. Let's just enjoy the moment."

"Whatever," Marin muttered. She'd nearly died giving birth to this child. She should be able to name her baby whatever she wanted.

Marin glanced over at the bassinet, her resentment melting away at the sight of her son. *He's so beautiful,* she thought to herself. *He is an angel created from my love for Warner.*

"I called Rob and scheduled your first session with him two weeks from today. That should give you enough time to recover."

"You've hired a personal trainer for me?" Marin asked incredulously. "Mom, we have a gym right in the house."

"I know that. But Rob can whip you back into shape in no time. You have no discipline."

"I work out three days a week—at least I did before I got pregnant."

"I'm telling you, Rob is the way to go. Just look at me. I don't look as if I've ever given birth to a child."

"You look great, Mom," Marin admitted. "But you do have some flaws—you just hide them well." She chuckled at her mother's expression. "Relax, Mom. I'm just teasing you."

* * *

"I can't believe you let Mom talk you into moving the baby shower here from the Beverly Hills Hotel."

"Your mom didn't think you should be out so soon," Dru explained. "And to be honest, I'm not about to go against Miss Shirley."

"I keep telling her that women don't stay in the house for six weeks these days. She gets upset if I'm not wearing sleeves. She says my pores are open and I'm still recovering from childbirth."

"I heard one of my aunties say that." Dru chuckled. "See why I'm not ready to have babies? Too much work."

Marin laughed. "They're worth it though. I love this little one to death."

Dru glanced over at the tiny bundle in Marin's arms. "Gabriel didn't want to miss the baby shower, I see. He's so tiny."

"I'm just glad my little sweetie is healthy."

"He's so cute," Carol said when she joined them in the living room. She gently brushed his cheek. "Hello, cutie."

Marin beamed with pride. Gabriel was a good baby and while she knew all mothers were biased when it came to their children, she was positive her son was the most beautiful baby ever.

Chanelle and her mother arrived ten minutes later, bringing in two huge shopping bags loaded with presents.

"Let me hold my grandbaby," Millicent demanded as soon as she sat down.

Marin handed Gabriel over. "He's awake for the moment. I just fed him and changed him, so he'll probably fall asleep soon."

"He looks a little like Joshua did when he was first born," Chanelle said. "Don't you think?"

Marin agreed.

More guests began to arrive.

Chanelle glanced around. "Dru did a wonderful job of decorating. Everything looks nice."

"She loves stuff like this." Marin smiled when Gabriel stretched and yawned in his grandmother's arms. Millicent was singing to him softly.

"You hardly look as if you had a baby two weeks ago. You look great."

"Tell that to my mother. She's still trying to get me to use her personal trainer."

"I think you're doing well on your own." Chanelle gestured toward her mother. "She loves babies. I'm telling you now, Mom is going to spoil Gabriel rotten. You see how she is with Joshua."

Shirley arrived loaded down with baby shower gifts. "Hello, everybody," she said in greeting.

Dru and Carol relieved her of her burden.

She sat down in the empty chair beside Marin. "Honey, why don't you put on a sweater? Remember, you've just had a baby. You don't want to get sick."

"Mom, I'm fine. It's nice and warm in here."

"It's February and it's cold, Marin. You could develop something."

Marin's eyes traveled around the room, landing on Chanelle, who gave her a sympathetic look.

Shirley was pushed to the back of Marin's mind as she enjoyed being queen for a day. Dru was a wonderful hostess and kept things moving along.

They enjoyed delicious fare of blackened salmon, mushrooms stuffed with crabmeat, seafood scampi, ravioli stuffed with portabella mushrooms with a garlic herb sauce, salad and rolls.

After eating, Dru and Carol handed out pads of paper and pens. It was time to play the first shower game.

Chanelle acted like a giddy schoolgirl when she won.

Shirley leaned over and whispered, "Marin, if you want to return to your pre-pregnancy size, you really need to give Rob a call. I told you I'll be paying for the sessions."

"Mom, I don't need Rob and I don't need your money. If I feel I need a trainer, I'll get one myself."

"Well, from where I'm sitting, you could stand to lose another ten or fifteen pounds."

"I'm going to put the baby to bed," Marin blurted out. She needed to get away from her mother before she cussed her out.

Upstairs, Marin placed Gabriel in his bassinet and turned on the monitor. Her mother thought she should hire a nanny, but Marin and Warner had decided they didn't need one. They preferred to care for their son on their own.

Marin picked up the handset, then stopped by her bedroom to check herself in the full-length mirror. Her mother's words had gotten to her and she needed to see if Shirley was right. Did she need to lose more weight?

Marin studied her reflection. She didn't think she looked overweight at all. But maybe losing a few more pounds wouldn't hurt. The longer she stared, the more flaws she found. *I need to tone up some and lose some of these hips.*

When she went downstairs, Marin pulled her mother off to the side and whispered, "I'll give Rob a call tomorrow. I want some help in toning up my body."

Shirley smiled. "That's more like it. You should always put your very best foot forward."

When six thirty rolled around, the party that had lasted four hours began to wind down.

Warner returned home just as Dru and Carol were about to leave.

"How was the party?" he asked.

"Great," Marin responded. "We had a nice time. Even my mom behaved herself, although I thought she and your mother were going to have a tug-of-war over Gabriel."

Warner chuckled. "I can believe that."

"We won't need to buy Gabriel a thing. He got everything a baby could need from the shower. Dru bought him some stock. Can you believe that? Gabriel has two shares of Disney stock. Your mother brought Gabriel the most beautiful train bank, in pewter. She also gave him a pewter rattle."

He pulled a gift out of his pocket. "Gabriel's not the only one receiving gifts today. This is for you."

"What is it?"

"Open it," Warner urged.

Marin ripped off the gift paper. She opened the black velvet box. "Oh my goodness. This is beautiful." She fingered the sapphire and diamond necklace. "It's exquisite. I love the earrings, too. They're not too big or too small." Marin looked up at Warner. "What did I do to deserve such a beautiful gift?"

"You gave me a son."

*　*　*

When Dr. Harris announced she was pregnant again three short months after Gabriel was born, Marin wasn't at all surprised. She hadn't been taking her birth control pills because she was breast-feeding. She was actually looking forward to having another baby.

She left the doctor's office and drove straight to the church to see Warner.

"What's got you smiling so much?"

"I have something to tell you and I hope you'll be happy about it."

"What is it?"

"You and I are having another baby."

Warner's eyes widened in surprise. "Really? Are you sure?"

"I just left the doctor's office. You're okay with this, aren't you?"

"Of course. Honey, you know I want as many children as God will bless us with."

"I hope we're having a little girl this time."

"I'd like that too, but as long as the baby's healthy I don't care."

"I told you that I was going to be pregnant again."

"Marin, you look so beautiful right now. You're glowing. I can tell you're really happy about this pregnancy."

"I am," she confirmed. She missed acting, but she had no regrets about putting her career on hold for a few years. When the children were older, she would resume her acting career. For now, she just wanted to enjoy her family.

The next day, Marin called and invited Dru to lunch. She couldn't wait to share her news with someone.

"So what's this big announcement?" Dru asked when they were settled at a table in Marino's.

"Warner and I are going to have another baby."

"You're pregnant again?"

"Yes."

"And you're happy about it? The last time you were so upset when you found out you were pregnant."

"I love Gabriel to death. And we want him to have a little sibling. Besides, I'd rather go on and get my babies out of the way. This way I can take a couple of years off now, then focus on my career when they're older."

"Wow! Larry is still trying to get me to consider having a baby. You're really getting into this mothering thing."

"I am," Marin confirmed. "I'm really enjoying this time in my life."

"I never would've imagined it."

"Shows that you don't know me as well as you think you do."

"I know you well enough," Dru responded. "But I'm happy to see you look so . . . so at peace with everything."

Marin smiled. "I'm totally happy. Dru, being a mother is wonderful. Give it a try. I want our babies to grow up together."

CHAPTER EIGHTEEN

Marin's second pregnancy was a little smoother, although she suffered from bouts of nausea and headaches from time to time. She went into labor around four in the morning on her due date. They dropped Gabriel off with Chanelle before heading to the hospital.

Eight agonizing hours later, the doctor determined that this baby would also have to be delivered via cesarean section. She had really wanted to experience a vaginal birth this time.

Warner went into the operating room with Marin and sat at her head while the doctors worked to deliver their son. He and Marin had both wanted a little girl this time around, but they were just as thrilled that they were about to meet their new son.

Strapped onto the operating table, Marin eyed Warner. "What's on your mind?" she asked.

"You doing okay?" he asked her.

There was no response. She had dozed off. Warner bowed his head, praying that God would guide the hands of the doctors and nurses surrounding his wife.

He heard a tiny whine and opened his eyes.

The whine turned into a cry.

His son was here. "Praise God," he whispered. "Thank You, Father."

Warner's eyes strayed down to Marin's face. She was still asleep. He glanced over at the anesthesiologist sitting on the other side of her.

No one seemed panicky, so he supposed everything was going as planned.

Warner watched the nurse as she gently cleaned the baby, dressed and swaddled him.

"Would you like to hold your son?" she asked him.

His mouth split into a grin. "I can't wait," he responded.

His son tucked safely in his arms, Warner walked back over to the chair and sat down. He wanted to be there if Marin woke up.

She was moved to recovery, where she slept peacefully for another four hours from the pain medication the doctors administered through her IV.

He had dozed off himself while the baby was in the nursery with the doctor. When he opened his eyes, he found Marin watching him.

"The b-baby," she managed. "Where is m-my baby?"

Warner sat up in his chair. "The doctor is checking him out. He's beautiful."

"He's okay?"

He nodded. "Don't try to move. You had a spinal. The doctor said you might get a headache."

"I hurt," she moaned. "I need pain medication."

Warner rose to his feet. "I'll let the nurse know."

Almost on cue, a woman walked through the door. "How you feeling, hon?"

"Hurt," Marin moaned.

The nurse checked her vital signs and administered another shot of pain medication.

It didn't take long for the medicine to work, enabling Marin to doze off without pain.

When she woke up four hours later, she asked for her son. "Bring him to me, Warner. I want to see him."

He gently laid the baby in the crook of Marin's arm.

"Hello, little one," Marin murmured. "You are so beautiful. We're going to name you Rylan Warner. How do you like that?"

She laughed when the baby squirmed in her arms. Marin was too sore to hold him as close as she'd like. She couldn't wait to cuddle with her baby. She glanced over at Warner and asked, "Are you very disappointed, honey?"

"About what?"

"That he's not a little girl."

Warner shook his head. "No. I love my son—both of my sons."

"So do I," she acknowledged. "We have two beautiful little boys. My babies . . ." She lifted her lips to Warner. "We have our children."

"Is this your way of saying that you don't want any more?"

"Not anytime soon. Honey, I do want to go back to work eventually. I love being a mom, but to be honest . . . I miss acting."

Warner nodded in understanding. "Are you thinking about going back right away?"

"No. I'm not changing my mind about staying home with them for couple of years. I'm still going to do that."

Warner spent the next three days going back and forth to the hospital to spend time with Marin and the baby. He always felt like a part of him was missing whenever Marin wasn't sleeping beside him. She was truly the other half of him and Warner couldn't imagine life without her.

Marin was glad to be home.

She wasn't crazy about hospitals or the food they served there. Warner had arrived around eight that morning to take her and the baby home. He helped her dress Rylan and then assisted her in getting dressed.

She was still in a lot of pain from the C-section. She eased her body into bed and lay back against the pillows. "I hope my parents will stay home today," she told Warner. "I'm not up to any company."

"I'll let everybody know."

"When is Gabriel coming home?"

"Chanelle was going to bring him later this afternoon, but I think maybe he should stay with them another night. That way you can get some rest. I can take care of Rylan."

"I'm breast-feeding. You can't do that for me." Marin smiled. "The way my body's aching, I wish you could."

He left her alone to rest.

Marin tried reading a novel, but fell asleep after a couple of pages. When she woke up, almost two hours had passed.

Warner strode into the bedroom, carrying a tray of food. "I thought you might want a sandwich or something. I know you need to take some medication for your pain."

Marin still had trouble believing just how blessed she was. Warner was a doting husband, although Marin still had her moments when she felt he cared more for his church than their marriage.

Since Gabriel's birth, Warner had kept his promise to her and cut back on his travel and speaking engagements. She hoped that with Rylan's birth, he would cut back even more.

The boys had to come first. Marin refused to settle for anything less.

"It feels so good to be out of the house," Marin declared when she met Carol and Dru for dinner. "I love my babies, but I was beginning to get a little stir crazy."

Dru assessed her up and down. "I have to give it to you, Marin. You look great. It doesn't take you long to lose your pregnancy weight at all."

Carol agreed. "I hope I'm as fortunate when I have my baby."

Marin and Dru exchanged glances.

"Are you pregnant?" they asked in unison.

Carol broke into giggles. "Yes. I'm going to be a mom in about eight months. Cameron and I have been trying for three years to get pregnant."

"I didn't know that," Marin murmured.

"We didn't really tell anyone. I didn't need the added pressure of people always asking if I was pregnant yet."

Dru nodded in understanding. "I get that all the time and Larry and I aren't even trying. I don't understand why people think that every couple should be trying to have children."

"And don't let a photographer catch you looking bloated," Marin contributed. "The first thing they print is a rumor that you've got a pregnancy bump. I think the public knew I was pregnant with Rylan before Warner and I did."

"I'm trying to keep my pregnancy out of the news for as long as I can.

We haven't told Cameron's family yet because I'm sure his brother will call up the *National Star* and sell us out in a minute. He was the one who sent them the pictures from Cam's bachelor party."

Dru's mouth dropped open. "Are you serious? His own brother?"

Carol nodded. "He did. It almost broke us up. I couldn't believe he would . . ." Her voice died. After a moment she continued, "I get mad every time I think about it."

"Then don't think about it," Marin said with a chuckle. "Let's move on. The last thing you need to do is go home mad at Cameron."

Dru ordered a bottle of nonalcholic champagne for them.

"Motherhood is really agreeing with you," Carol told Marin. "You seem so happy."

"I am ecstatic. I don't think my life can get any better than this."

"Carol's right," Dru said. "You are absolutely glowing. I don't know if I've ever seen you this happy. I guess you made the right choice to focus on your family right now."

"I did," Marin confirmed. "I have no regrets whatsoever. Warner, the children and I are going to live happily ever after. I just know it."

CHAPTER NINETEEN

Four years later

Marin stood outside the door of Rylan's classroom. This was
the first day of preschool and she wanted to make sure he was
okay with being away from her. Gabriel was in kindergarten
and had been looking forward to it all summer.

Rylan was already making friends and following his teacher around
the room.

My baby's growing up . . .

She wiped away a lone tear and made her way out to the parking lot.

When she arrived home fifteen minutes later, Marin walked into her
empty house and wandered from room to room. She stood in the doorway of Gabriel's bedroom for a few minutes, and then lingered in Rylan's
room, thinking back to the time when they were babies.

The house was too quiet.

She walked back down to the kitchen and took a seat at the breakfast
bar, trying to think of something to do with her time. Rylan wouldn't
be home until one—five hours from now.

She considered going up to the church and helping out with whatever
needed to be done. She usually did that whenever Rylan and Gabriel
were with her parents or spending time with her in-laws. She made a

mental note to put the box of books that had arrived for the women's Bible study in her car.

Since the birth of her sons, Marin had placed her career on hold to focus on her children, but now that they were older and starting school, she would be bored to death if she had to just lie around the house doing nothing. She still had her duties in the Women of Purpose group and with the drama ministry at church, but it wasn't enough for her.

She desired something more in her life now that her children didn't need her as much. Instead of sitting around the house feeling sorry for herself, Marin decided to take the books over to the church. Maybe she could talk Warner into having an early lunch with her.

Hazel and her husband, Pastor Elijah, pulled up beside her in the parking lot. Marin greeted them when they got out of the car.

"Why don't you let me carry those for you, Sister Marin?" Elijah offered. Without waiting for a response, he relieved Marin of her burden.

"Thanks. Just leave them in the room across from Warner's office. That's where we'll be meeting on Wednesday night."

When he disappeared through the double doors of the church administration building, Hazel turned to her, saying, "Pastor Hilliard announced he was leaving to take a position in Nashville."

"Warner told me. I'm going to hate to see him and Martha leave."

"The church is going to need another associate pastor with him gone. Elijah would probably have a fit if he knew I was saying this, but God put it in my heart. Sister Marin, there isn't a man more grounded in the Word than my husband. He's been here at Victory for almost seven years now. He deserves to be associate pastor."

"Has he spoken to Warner?"

"Elijah . . . he's just not going to do something like that. If you could talk to Pastor . . . my husband really wants to be associate pastor."

Marin had a feeling Hazel wanted it more than Elijah did, but she kept the feeling to herself. "I'll mention it. Mostly, I stay out of stuff like this, however."

Hazel smiled. "Thanks so much. God bless you, Sister Marin."

She went to Warner's office after her conversation with Hazel. After knocking softly on the door, she stuck her head inside. "You busy?"

Warner gestured for her to enter. "What are you doing here?"

"I dropped off the books for the women's Bible study."

"How did Rylan do when you took him to preschool this morning?"

"He was fine. I was the nervous wreck." Sitting down in one of the visitor chairs, Marin broke into a short laugh. "The boys are growing up so fast."

Warner nodded in agreement. "I've been thinking that maybe we should try for that little girl we've been wanting."

"Honey, we've been trying for four years now. I think God has blessed us with two beautiful boys and the shop's no longer open."

"I haven't given up," Warner stated. "I have faith that all things are possible."

Marin checked her watch. "How about a quick lunch?"

"Honey, I can't today. I just arranged to meet with Reverend Nixon for lunch. I'm sorry."

"It's okay. I probably should get back across town. Traffic is heavy and I don't want to be late picking Rylan up. Especially on his first day." She glanced at her husband. "So, is this a short day for you?"

"Since Hilliard's leaving, I need to take over some of his duties. He could preach up a storm, but he wasn't a very organized man."

"Oh . . . Warner, have you considered promoting Elijah to associate pastor?"

Warner sat back in his chair. "It's crossed my mind a couple of times. He's never said anything, so I wasn't sure he wanted the responsibility."

Marin rose to her feet. "Talk to him. You can't run this church alone, honey." She blew him a kiss. "I'll see you later."

Maybe it's time I went back to work, she silently considered on the way to the preschool.

In a couple of days, she would be turning twenty-nine. She was still fairly young and her body was in great shape, thanks to her daily workout. Marin mulled over the idea of making a comeback, getting more excited by the minute.

By the time she picked Rylan up from preschool, she'd made a decision.

Warner guided Marin outside the house, his hands on her shoulders. "Keep your eyes covered," he instructed.

"What have you done?"

"You'll see in a minute." When they were on the porch, Warner said, "Okay, you can open your eyes now. Happy birthday, sweetheart."

Marin let out a scream when she saw her present. He'd bought her a BMW Z4 Roadster. "I love it! I love it!" she exclaimed over and over.

She slipped her arms around Warner. "Thank you, baby. I love it."

She wanted to take her new car for a test drive, but they were meeting their parents soon for her birthday celebration dinner at Marino's.

The babysitter arrived an hour later.

Her parents were already at the restaurant by the time they arrived.

"Happy birthday, sweetness," Robert said, then kissed Marin on the cheek.

Her mother embraced her. "My darling, you look fabulous." In a lower voice, she whispered, "It looks like you've put on a little more weight though. You might want to forgo the pasta tonight."

Marin stiffened. "Why do you have to always try and ruin things for me?"

Shirley glanced around before responding, "Keep your voice down. I wasn't trying to ruin anything. I was simply suggesting that—"

"That I'm getting fat," Marin finished for her. "Today is my birthday. Let me enjoy it, please."

Warner wrapped his arms around her, holding her close to him. "Marin, I'm sure your mother didn't mean any harm."

"Your husband's right," Shirley stated. "I—"

Chanelle and Mitch came in next, cutting off any more conversation. They were seated in a private dining room after Millicent and Garfield arrived.

Marin was able to enjoy her celebration by keeping her distance from her mother. She did get a chance to spend a few minutes with her father before he had to leave.

She was a bit disappointed that he had to run out on her dinner party, but she was grateful that he'd come at all. He'd missed most of her childhood parties—too busy working.

"I had a pretty good time," Marin murmured as she readied for bed later that evening. "My mother got on my nerves though."

Warner shut his Bible. "How are you enjoying Bible study?"

"It's great when Sister Hazel isn't facilitating."

"Your suggestion to rotate really is working for the group, I see."

"Hazel fought it initially, but she eventually saw our side of things."

"I need the budget for Sunday School by Friday," Warner stated with a smile.

Marin nodded. "Sure. No problem, Pastor Brice."

He laughed. "Seriously, I'm so proud of you. You've really jumped right in helping out at the church like that."

"Just doing my first-lady duties."

"I'm very pleased. You make me so happy, Marin." He embraced her. "I love you so much."

"Not as much as I love you," she responded. "Honey, I'm glad we're talking because there's something I want to discuss with you."

"What is it?"

"Gabriel's five years old now and Rylan's four," Marin began. "Since they're both in school, I think it's time I went back to work."

Warner laid down his Bible. "Sure. If that's what you want to do."

"I do," she replied. "I'm ready. We can hire a nanny for the boys to get them ready for school and make sure they're okay until I can get home. I spoke to Dru earlier and she was telling me that a part is coming up in Seth Munson's new TV movie. I really think I'm right for it."

"You sound excited."

"I am. Warner, I still want to have a career. I love acting—it's all I've ever wanted to do. And don't worry. I'm still going to be the dutiful mother, wife and first lady of Victory Baptist Church."

He laughed.

"I'm not going to do any nude scenes either. I know how you feel about it."

"You should feel the same way, sweetheart."

Marin held her tongue. She didn't want to have an argument with Warner. Not tonight. Not after the wonderful day they'd had. She wanted to end the evening on a high note.

"Are you done with your reading?" she asked.

Warner met her gaze. "Actually, I am. Why?"

She eased down on his lap. "I thought maybe we could have a private celebration."

"Oh really?"

Grinning, Marin nodded. "Yeah. The boys are asleep. We have some alone time. Let's take advantage of it."

Two weeks after Marin's birthday, the month of April rolled around, prompting her to think of ways she and Warner could celebrate their sixth wedding anniversary. They'd survived the five-year mark. "Thank You, Jesus," she whispered.

She picked up the phone and called Dru for suggestions. "I don't know what to do about our wedding anniversary," she told Dru. "I want it to be special, so I really need your help."

Dru and Larry were always running off to exotic locations.

"You've got to take him somewhere special," Dru said. "You guys could go to a private island. I'd planned to do something like that for our anniversary, but looks like Larry and I might be in the hospital having this baby."

"Maybe not. The baby could come early or late."

"I know, but I have this feeling that this little girl will be coming around our anniversary—if not on that day. Just because."

"You and Larry won't be thinking about your anniversary when that baby comes. She's going to become your whole world." Marin felt a thread of guilt over ever considering abortion with her first pregnancy. Gabriel had been nothing but a complete joy to her.

"I'm taking three months off and then I'm going back to work," Dru said. "I'm not doing what you did."

"I don't regret it. My family needed me. I'm ready to get back to work now, though. I've already called Nancy and told her to let everybody know that I'm back and ready to work."

"So, have you gotten any calls?"

"I don't have anyone from the major studios knocking down my door, but I'm okay with it. *California Suite* wants me back and they're planning this big comeback. It's a nighttime soap opera, but it's still a job."

"Good for you. At least you have steady work."

"I'm looking forward to going back. But back to my current dilemma—I need to find the perfect place to take Warner. I love him so much and I just want to do something special for him."

"Being married to Warner Brice has changed you. I can see it."

"He's so good to me."

After Marin hung up with Dru, she went into Warner's office, surfing the Internet, looking for somewhere to take her husband.

After an hour, Marin found the perfect place. It was a house located on a secluded oceanfront property of the Portlock area in Honolulu. She placed a quick phone call to the agent listed.

After Marin rented the property, she called the airlines and booked flights for her and Warner. She was sure that either her parents or Warner's would watch the children while she took Warner to Hawaii.

CHAPTER TWENTY

"This place is beautiful," Warner stated. "Honey, you did a wonderful job finding this house." He wandered from room to room with Marin following close behind. "Very nice."

"I'm glad you love it. Happy sixth anniversary," Marin said. She wrapped her arms around him, snuggling up to him. "I'm so glad you were able to get away for a few days."

He agreed. "Me, too. I think we needed this little vacation."

"Honey, I've told you this before," Marin began. "You work too hard at the church. Let Pastor Elijah and Pastor Kenny take over some of the duties. The kids and I would like to spend more time with you."

"I'll think about what you said." Warner kissed her on the lips. "I love you, Marin. I want you and the boys to be happy."

"I love you too, baby."

They spent their first night in Hawaii making love.

The next morning, Marin and Warner woke up early and ate a delicious breakfast prepared by a chef hired to cook for them during their stay.

Afterward, they wasted no time before exploring the picturesque island of Oahu.

Throughout the day, they were sprinkled with raindrops, but it didn't last long or deter them from enjoying their vacation.

"I'm going to have to spend a lot of time at the gym," Warner stated over dinner. "Where did you find this guy? The man can cook."

"Dru told me about him." Marin put a forkful of crab cake into her mouth, savoring the spicy flavor. "Mmmm, this is so good."

Warner picked up his water glass and took several sips. "Too bad we can't take Chef Marques home with us."

"What? My cooking's not good enough for you?" Marin inquired with a chuckle.

"I'm not saying that at all, sweetheart."

"It's okay," she assured him. "I know I'm not the best cook. If I could get Chef Marques to come home with us, I would." Marin wiped her mouth with the edge of her napkin. "But then I'd be as big as a house, too. I don't think either one of us wants that to happen."

They laughed.

Warner and Marin spent the next day swimming and playing in the ocean. She was having the time of her life. While she missed the boys, she was thrilled to have this week alone with her husband.

Warner loved seeing Marin so happy.

Going away together was the best thing they could've done for their anniversary. It was the perfect way to reestablish the bond between the two of them.

"Can you believe we only have two more days left?" Marin said. She sat down on the towel beside him, running her fingers through her wet hair. "I love it here."

Warner shifted to his side, facing her. "You look like you're having a good time."

"I am," Marin confirmed. "I am having the time of my life, honey. I really needed this getaway." Stroking the side of his face, she amended her statement. "*We* needed this getaway."

"The church retreats didn't do it for you?"

Laughing, Marin shook her head no.

She lay down on the towel and closed her eyes. Warner sat there watching her, his heart overflowing with love.

"Why are you staring at me like that?"

"How do you know I'm staring? Your eyes are closed."

"I can feel your eyes on me," she explained.

"I was just thinking about how lucky I am to have you in my life. Marin, I love you so much."

She opened her eyes to look at Warner. "I love you too, baby."

"I want more times like this with you."

Marin sat up. "We're going to have a lifetime of memories, Warner. I promise you."

A week after Warner and Marin returned from Honolulu, he had to leave for Dallas for a speaking engagement.

Marin was upset at first, but she settled down once she reminded herself that Warner was only doing his job. She was just tired of all the traveling he had to do lately.

He would get back home exactly one day before she had to leave for Toronto. She was starring in a made-for-TV movie to air on Lifetime in the fall.

She and the children would be gone for almost three weeks. Warner would be joining her for the last week. Marin had planned on hiring a nanny to travel with her, but her mother had suddenly decided that she would join them.

Marcus Fisher, her *California Suite* costar, approached her after work, stopping her at her car.

"Hey, you got any plans for tonight?" he inquired.

"I'm not doing much except going home to pack for Toronto. I leave tomorrow evening."

"Any chance of you changing your mind?" He handed her an invitation. "I'm throwing a little get-together tonight. Why don't you consider coming by? It could do wonders for your career. You've been off the scene for a long time. Everybody on Hollywood's A-list—the black A-list—will be there."

Marin checked the invitation. "I just might do that." She needed to get back out there and start networking. It was time to get her career back on the fast track.

Using her cell phone, she called to see if her nanny could spend the night with the boys. She had a feeling that she'd be coming home late.

Her next stop was a boutique on Rodeo Drive. She needed the perfect outfit to wear to the party.

An hour later, mission accomplished. Marin rushed home to spend some time with her boys before their bedtime.

She read them a bedtime story, then went to her room to get dressed for the party. It had been years since she had attended a Hollywood party and she felt a rush of excitement. She had a strong feeling that this party was going to change her life forever.

"Marin, I didn't expect to see you here," Dru declared when she followed Marcus into the spacious dining area where most of the guests had gathered.

"I need to find out what's going on in the industry. I've been away for a while and it's time I put myself back in view of the directors." Marin placed a hand on Dru's swollen belly. "How is my godchild?"

"She's fine. At times it seems like she's about to kick her way out." Dru glanced around. "So, where's Warner?"

"Out of town. He's in Dallas preaching at some revival."

Surprised, she asked, "So you're here alone?"

Marin glanced around. "And where's your husband, Dru?"

Lowering her voice, Dru advised, "Look, I know you and Marcus work together but, Marin, be cool. Don't do nothing you'll regret. I know he's attracted to you."

She laughed. "It's not even like that, Dru. Marcus and I are cool. That's it. Don't you start believing the tabloids."

"Girl, if I believe that trash, Larry and I wouldn't be together today. They always trying to offer proof that he's being unfaithful or I'm cheating. They were so bad—they published a picture of him leaving a hotel with a woman: ME."

Marin laughed. "I remember that. You had on a hat and some dark glasses—they didn't know it was you. When I saw the picture, I didn't even recognize you."

They found an empty seat on the sofa and sat down to talk.

Checking her watch an hour later, Dru said, "I think I'm leaving. I'm tired. What about you?"

"I think I'm going to hang out a little longer. I need to talk to Danny."

"Anderson?" Dru asked. "That drug pusher?"

Marin leaned toward Dru, whispering, "You might not want to say that too loud."

"Why are you talking to him?"

"I need to get into the head of a drug user for the role I'm doing. Remember the one I told you about? I leave tomorrow evening for Toronto. I think it'll help me really flesh out this character if I talk to Danny."

"Be careful. I don't like that man."

"I'll be fine, Dru," Marin assured her. "Will you please stop playing mother hen? Just be my friend."

Dru lowered her voice to a whisper. "They do drugs at these parties sometimes. You should just put in an appearance and leave. People like us don't hang around, Marin."

"I know what I'm doing, Dru. You don't have to worry about me. I'm not some weak-minded wannabe actress."

Dru embraced her. "Okay. I'll see you later then."

Marcus came up behind them. "Marin is gonna be fine, Dru."

"You just make sure you look out for her."

He laughed. "Girl, go on home and get some rest. Be careful you don't have that baby outside."

Dru rolled her eyes at Marcus before turning to leave.

"Where's the preacher man? He back in town yet?"

"No," Marin responded. "He'll be back tomorrow morning. He was supposed to come home today, but . . ." She shrugged. "He's not."

Danny Anderson walked over to them. His father owned Xenox Records, giving Danny entrée to some of Hollywood's most exclusive parties.

Wrapping an arm around Marin, Danny said, "I'm glad to see you here with yo' fine self. I saw you the other night on *California Suite*. You're good."

"Thank you, Danny. That means a lot coming from you." They were joined by a man Marin recognized as a director. He introduced himself as Hamilton Barnes.

"I keep telling your agent, we need to work together."

"I'd love it, but it has to be a role where I can keep my clothes on. I'm married to a man of God, you know."

"We should talk," he responded. "I'll give your agent a call."

He and Marin shook hands.

She was ecstatic. "Did you just hear that? Hamilton Barnes just said that he wants to work with me. This has got to work out, Marcus. I need this opportunity."

"It's in the bag," he predicted.

"Marcus, do you think I can get Danny alone long enough to get inside his head? I need to know what it's like to be addicted to drugs for my role."

"He's up in my bedroom now. Why don't you go on up. Y'all can talk in privacy. One thing though—don't call him an addict. Danny doesn't like that."

"I don't know about going up to your bedroom, Marcus. Maybe Danny could come down here."

Marcus cracked up. "Danny's harmless. He won't bother you, Marin. Your precious virtue is safe."

Marin gave him a hug. "Thanks, Marcus." She went up to the second level.

She assumed the room with the double doors at the top of the stairs had to be the master suite. Marin knocked on the door. "Danny."

"Come in," he responded.

She stepped inside.

"The preacher's wife," Danny muttered with a chuckle. "What are you doing up here?"

"I wanted to talk to you." Marin's eyes strayed to the rows of white powder lined up on a mirror. An American Express credit card lay nearby.

"Want to do a line?" he asked. "I know you married to that preacher man and all, but I figure you might wanna party a li'l bit."

Marin shook her head no. "I'll pass."

She sat down across from Danny. "I have an upcoming role for a film. I leave tomorrow for Toronto and I'm supposed to be a drug user. The thing is, I've never tried cocaine, marijuana—nothing. I'm hoping you'd be willing to share your experiences with me. Like how it feels when you're high."

Danny cracked up with laughter.

"I'm serious."

"It's hard to explain, but I'll try." Danny bent over and snorted a line of white powder, using a small straw. "I feel a burst of energy—I feel good. It feels like you versus the world." He pointed to the mirror. "Try it. That's the best way for you to know how it feels."

She considered his words. She didn't think trying a line of cocaine just this once would hurt her. Not this one time.

"C'mon," Danny urged. "Try it."

"I'm only doing this for my role."

He shrugged.

Marin followed his instructions. She inhaled the powdery drug in her nostril. Wiping her nose, she sneezed and coughed.

It took a moment for her to feel anything except a thread of disappointment.

She opened her mouth to speak, but didn't. Her heart began to beat faster. She was suddenly filled with a powerful sense of euphoria. She was in the clouds.

One line led to another.

Then another.

CHAPTER TWENTY-ONE

Within two weeks of her first experience with cocaine Marin was hooked. As her coke-induced euphoria faded, she got the urge to do more, and she began doing it almost every day. She was snorting in the mornings before she went to the set, between scenes and right before she went back to the house she'd rented during their stay in Toronto.

One day when she arrived at the house, Warner was waiting for her.

"What are you doing here?" she asked, trying to hide her surprise. They hadn't planned on his joining her for a few more days.

"I told you I'd be here for the final days of shooting, remember?"

She noted his set face, his clamped mouth and fixed stare. "I just didn't expect you until next Monday."

"I thought we should talk."

Marin pressed her lips together, wondering what was going on in Warner's mind. Did he know about the cocaine?

"About what?"

Warner sat down on the sofa beside her. "Marin, is there something going on with you?"

Shaking her head no, she answered, "Why would you ask me something like that?"

"Since you've been here filming *Basic Black,* you've been acting different. You sound strange on the phone sometimes."

"I'm just tired, honey. I've been real tired, but I don't sleep well. I guess it's because I'm not home with you."

"From all the weight you've lost, it looks like you're not eating either."

"I eat," Marin countered. "They feed us well at the studio. If I ate like that all the time, I'd be as big as a house, so I have to keep my weight down. Remember, I have to look the part of a drug addict."

"Honey, the reason for all the questions is because I'm very worried about you."

"Why? There's no need. I'm fine." Marin rubbed her skin against her shirt. She was itching for the drug, literally.

"I don't agree. Marin, I know you and I can tell something's going on with you and I'm going to find out what."

"I'm fine," Marin insisted.

"I was invited to speak at a church in Miami, but I turned them down. I know how you feel about me being gone back to back."

"Warner, if you want to do it, it's okay."

He was surprised by her words. "It's right after I go to Atlanta. I'd have to fly straight to Miami and come home afterwards."

Marin nodded. "Honey, that's fine. Call them back and tell them you'll do it."

"What's gotten into you?" Warner queried. "This doesn't sound like you at all."

She embraced him. "I realize that I've been real selfish, but honey, I'm feeling very secure in our marriage now. Besides, I have to travel for my job. I can't be unfair."

"Are you sure about this?"

Marin nodded. "The boys and I will miss you like crazy, but at least we have each other."

"Why don't you come with me?" Warner suggested. "We could use another little getaway."

"I wish I could, but you know I'm working every day that week. We're shooting on location in Santa Barbara for *California Suite* then."

"I forgot about that."

Marin stood on tiptoe and kissed him. "I'm going to check on the boys. Why don't you run a nice hot bath for us?"

Warner watched Marin sashay out of the family room, wondering what was really going on with her.

The third Friday night in June, Marin got all dressed up in a black dress that used to hug her curves to attend Dominic Evans's black and white party on the last day of shooting *Basic Black*. She and Dominic played starring roles. Marin felt she'd been a convincing recovering drug addict who'd gone on to make something out of her life.

"Marin?"

She looked up. "Adrian! What are you doing here?"

"What are *you* doing here?" He glanced around.

"I starred in *Basic Black*," she responded, pointing to a poster of her and Dominic.

"Where's Warner?"

She pretended not to understand his look. "He's out of town on business. As usual. He left yesterday." Marin struggled to focus her eyes. She'd just done two lines of coke and was feeling pretty good.

Adrian sat down beside her. "You look a little strange. Why don't I give you a ride home?"

Marin boldly met his accusing eyes without flinching. "Why? I'm not ready to leave."

"This is not the type of party you should be at. You should be home with the boys."

"Adrian, I have a career. I work with these people. Why are you acting this way?"

"Warner wouldn't approve."

"He's not my daddy, Adrian," Marin responded sharply, abandoning all pretense. "And tell me something—why are *you* here?"

Triumph flooded through her when he winced at her words.

"Marin, did somebody give you something? Did you take anything?"

She laughed.

"You must think I'm stupid or something."

"I'm not trying to upset you."

Her hands placed belligerently on her hips, Marin snapped, "Then leave me alone."

Adrian watched her for a moment before moving on.

Marin struggled to hide her nervousness. What if he told Warner that he'd seen her tonight? Their host was known to have drugs at his parties.

Warner would most likely be furious with her, but right now she didn't really care.

She wanted to escape. She'd been looking forward to Dominic's party all week, but now that she was actually here, her initial excitement had vanished into thin air.

Warner was surprised to see Adrian waiting for him when he arrived at the church. "I didn't expect to see you."

"I need to talk to you."

He invited Adrian inside his office. "What's up? Did something happen?"

"There's something I feel you should know. Warner, I saw Marin the other night," Adrian told him. "She was at Dominic's party."

"Dominic Evans?"

Adrian nodded.

"Dominic usually has drugs at his parties, I've heard," Warner said. "Is it true?"

"I've only been to two of them," Adrian began. "I saw him doing lines with some of his guests. I don't know if Marin did any. I tried to get her to leave with me but she refused."

"Did she look high?"

Adrian shrugged. "To be honest, I couldn't really tell."

"What I don't understand is why my wife was there in the first place. Was she there with Dru or Carol?"

"I didn't see Carol, but Dru was there for a minute. She left before I did. I know why Marin was there, but I don't think she should mess around with folks like that. Especially since she's married to you."

*   *   *

"Adrian told me that he saw you at Dominic Evans's party the other night."

Marin swallowed hard, lifted her chin, and boldly met his gaze. "And?"

"Excuse me?"

"What's the problem, Warner? Dominic and I starred in *Basic Black* together. We're friends. He's the 'It' guy in Hollywood right now."

"He's also a drug user. *A known drug user*. Dominic stays in trouble."

"What's that got to do with me? To be invited to one of Dominic's parties—it places you on the top rung of Hollywood's social ladder. If you're not invited, it's because you don't matter."

"Marin, don't you ever worry about appearances? If a photographer snapped a shot of you there—you can only imagine what the media would make of all this."

"I don't care what people think," she huffed. "I know and God knows I didn't do anything."

"That's not going to matter. You—"

"Warner, let's not do this right now. I'm not in the mood for an argument."

"Don't walk away from me."

"Warner, leave me alone. I'm tired and I'm going to bed."

Marin moved without haste, but with unhurried purpose.

I should've known Adrian Reed was going to open his big mouth.

"Marin, this isn't over," Warner yelled from the foot of the stairs. "We've got to discuss this further."

She didn't respond.

Upstairs, Marin saw the stack of mail on her dresser. She quickly scanned through, noting the past-due letters from her credit card companies.

She couldn't remember the last time she'd paid any of her bills. She pulled out her checkbook and looked at the balance. She was spending practically five hundred dollars a day on her habit.

Marin heard Warner outside their bedroom. She quickly stuck her mail in the top dresser drawer. She didn't want Warner to find out that she hadn't been paying her bills. She made a mental note to mail out checks first thing in the morning to bring her accounts current.

Another thought occurred to her. *I can pay them online.* She turned on her computer, her fingers moving furiously over the keys.

In less than fifteen minutes, all of her bills were paid. Marin was slipping. She'd never been late with her payments.

She lay down on her bed, hoping her headache would go away.

An hour later Warner entered the room carrying a bowl of soup. "I thought maybe you could try and eat something."

Marin shook her head, saying, "I'm not hungry right now."

"Just try to take a few sips," Warner coaxed. "Honey, I'm worried about you. You're too thin."

She patted the empty space beside her on the bed. "C'mere."

Marin took his hand in hers, saying, "Sweetie, I love you so much for caring, but you really have nothing to worry about."

"I have to be honest with you, Marin. I'm concerned that you're either overwhelmed with working and trying to take care of our children or there's something else going on."

"Something like what? What are you trying to accuse me of?"

"I'm not accusing you of anything, sweetheart." Warner straightened his glasses. "Marin, have you tried anything? Marijuana? Cocaine?"

"I can't believe you just asked me that."

"Have you?" Warner pushed.

"I took something at the studio for my headache and I think I might have taken one too many," Marin lied. "That's it."

"What was it?"

"Tylenol 800 . . . Warner, I don't know. I had a headache and so I took a couple of pills. I think I was only supposed to take one."

"You've been having quite a few headaches lately."

"I used to have migraines as a child," Marin explained. "Maybe they've come back."

"I want you to see a doctor. But right now, I want us to get on our knees and pray. We are not going to give in to those migraines."

Marin swallowed her guilt. Silently, she climbed out of bed and fell to her knees beside her husband.

While Warner prayed, Marin said a prayer of her own. She prayed God wouldn't punish her for her lies.

CHAPTER TWENTY-TWO

Warner continued to worry about his wife. Marin still wasn't sleeping and she hardly ate. She was losing weight.

It wasn't like she was going around shouting or laughing like a lunatic. She wasn't doing anything. Apart from her dazed expression and the slight flush to her skin, Warner couldn't really say there was a problem. She still complained of headaches from time to time, but he couldn't get her to see a doctor. Her pace was a little slower than usual and her speech seemed a bit slurred at times, sounding sleepy.

He stood in the doorway of the playroom, watching Marin play with their sons. A few times he caught her staring off into space in a daze.

"Mommy," Gabriel called, "look at me."

Marin snapped out of her reverie. "I'm looking, baby."

Her voice was flat and expressionless, almost like she was reading from one of her scripts.

Was Marin taking drugs? Warner couldn't be sure. He'd gone through her dresser yesterday while she was at an audition but, to his relief, had come up with nothing.

Warner glanced up when Marin walked out of the bathroom, came over to the sofa in their sitting area and sat down beside him. She looked tired and worn out. Her eyes were sleepy-looking and her face pale.

"Honey, you feeling okay?" Warner asked out of concern.

"I'm drained."

"I can imagine. You didn't sleep well."

"I'm cold," Marin said, hugging herself. "And my skin is itchy. I think I'm allergic to the new detergent Sylvia's using."

He didn't want to think any more of it. He went down to his office to go over his sermon for Sunday. Deep down, Warner couldn't face the truth.

Marin crossed his mind, distracting him to the point that he couldn't concentrate. He gave up after a few minutes.

"Father God, I need Your help. There's something not right with Marin. Help me figure out what it is and how I can help my wife."

She was sitting in bed reading when he entered their room. "That was quick," she commented.

Warner began removing his clothes. "I wasn't in the mood to study."

He climbed into bed a few minutes later. "I need to know something, Marin."

"What is it?"

"Are you doing drugs?"

Marin laughed in response. "Warner, no. I don't take drugs."

He released a sigh of relief. He wasn't sure he believed her, but she had told him what he desperately wanted to hear.

Dru came by the house for a surprise visit.

Marin opened the front door. "Hey, girl."

"Marin, what's going on with you?"

Folding her arms across her chest, Marin demanded, "Why does everyone keep asking me that? *I'm fine.*"

"You're so thin. Are you losing weight for a role?"

"No. What's the big deal?" Marin questioned. "I haven't lost that much weight."

"Yes, you have," Dru responded. "Girl, you look anorexic."

Marin glared at her friend. "If you can't be nice, you should leave."

Dru dismissed Marin's words with a wave of her hand. "I wouldn't be here if I didn't care about you." She sat down on the couch. "Marin, you may have Warner fooled, but I know the deal."

"What are you talking about, Dru?"

"What is it? Crack, cocaine . . . heroin?"

Marin bristled in indignation. "Dru, you are so out of line."

"You have an addiction. I know who your new best friends are. You need to get help, Marin."

"Get out of my house, Dru. Maybe you're the one on drugs. And if you tell Warner these lies, I'll never forgive you."

"Let me help you." Standing up, Dru pleaded. "Marin, we love you."

"How can you say that you love me and then accuse me of being a drug addict?"

"Honey, you can't kick this habit alone. You're not strong enough. I told you about my cousin Lola. Honey, you need to let us get you some help."

Marin walked over to the front door and opened it. "Please leave my house, Dru."

"Let me help you, Marin," she pleaded one more time before leaving.

A week later, there was no denying the addiction.

Marin came home to find Warner rummaging through her clothes and drawers.

"What are you doing?" she yelled.

Holding up a tiny packet of white powder, Warner replied, "I'm looking to see if you have more of these stashed around here somewhere."

He glared at her. "You brought cocaine into my house. How dare you?"

"I can explain," Marin began. "Honey, it's not what you think. Don't listen to anything Dru's told you. She doesn't know what she's talking about."

"Are you really going to try and tell me that what I'm seeing is not cocaine? I'm not stupid. For your information, Dru really cares about you. She's worried about you. So am I." Warner was livid. "What if the children had walked in here just now? Worse, what if they had gotten hold of this?"

Marin began to cry. "I'm sorry."

"I don't want an apology, Marin. I want you to get some help. You need help."

"I'm not addicted, if that's what you're thinking. I was only trying it for a role. You know that I'm starring in that Lifetime movie. I needed to experience it firsthand."

"Stop lying," Warner yelled, stunning her. He'd never raised his voice to her in all the time they'd been together.

"You're an addict," he screamed.

He strode to the bathroom, Marin on his heels.

"What are you doing?"

"I'm getting rid of this trash," he announced.

Marin tried to take the packet from him, but Warner was too strong for her.

"Don't do that!" she screamed as he flushed it down the toilet.

Marin started hitting him with her fists as hard as she could. "I hate you! I hate you!" she screamed over and over again.

"You are an addict and you need help." Having said that, Warner picked her up carried her to the bed, and dropped her onto it.

He stormed out of the room, but not before Marin glimpsed him crying.

She knew Warner was right. She needed help to kick her drug habit. Deep down she wanted to rid her body of the cocaine, but she just wasn't strong enough.

I hate my life.

It was true. Marin hated what she had become and she would be all alone if she didn't go into rehab.

When Warner came back home, the boys weren't with him.

"Where are my babies?"

"They're with your parents," he announced. "I didn't want them to hear what we had to say. I need to know what you're going to do because we can't continue like this."

"I'm going to check myself into rehab. Warner, I don't want to be this way. I really want to get better. I just need your help."

Warner seemed relieved. "I'm glad to hear that."

"I'm so sorry for putting you through this."

He didn't respond.

"Please forgive me, Warner." Marin didn't know what else to say to him. She loved her husband dearly and didn't want to lose him.

"I do forgive you. I'm just at a loss for words. I never thought we'd have to worry about drugs. Not in our family."

His words only made Marin feel worse. "I can't tell you how sorry I am. Warner, I feel bad. I promise you, I'm going to kick this addiction and then I'm going to be the best wife and mother I can be. With God's help, I know I can do it."

After a tour of the facility, a fairly exhaustive admissions interview, and a family orientation, Marin was admitted into the Passages Malibu Treatment Center. From there Warner drove to pick up the boys and decided to stop by Chanelle's house.

They got the kids settled in Joshua's room with Mitch watching them, then went downstairs to talk.

"I just dropped Marin off at the treatment center. She checked herself into Passages Malibu. They told me she'll probably be in therapy until September."

"So what happens when she gets out in September?" Chanelle questioned. "What are you going to do then?"

"What do you mean? We're going to take it one day at a time. We're going to try and get our marriage back on track."

"Warner, have you lost your mind? Marin brought drugs into your house. I can't believe you're actually letting her back into the house, much less near the boys."

"She's their mother and my wife."

"Maybe you should remind her. Apparently, she's forgotten it."

"Chanelle, mind your own marriage and leave mine alone," Warner snapped.

She was clearly taken aback by his tone.

"I'm sorry for snapping at you, but, Chanelle, this is my problem. Marin is my problem. Stop acting like she's yours."

"She is a member of this family. That makes her *our* problem as well, whether you want to believe that or not."

"I love her, Chanelle."

"I know you do, which is why this angers me. Look at who you are, Warner. You have people all over the world watching you—looking to you for guidance. How can you lead your flock if you can't get your own house under control? You don't want to hear it right now, but you're going to have to divorce Marin!"

Warner didn't respond.

"I know how much this has to hurt you, but the truth is the truth."

"Is your marriage so perfect?"

"Excuse me?"

"Is your marriage a perfect one?"

"No," Chanelle admitted. "You know it's not. Mitch and I have been through a lot with his drinking and chasing women. You know all that changed when he gave his life to Christ."

"You stayed with him through it all."

This time it was Chanelle who remained quiet.

"When Mother suggested you divorce Mitch, you stood up and said that you wouldn't move until you heard from God. Remember that?"

"I remember."

"Well, I'm telling you the same thing. I'm not making a move toward divorce court until I know this is what God will have me do. I don't care what people think. I don't care what *you* think. I have to answer to God for everything I do in my life."

"You're right, Warner. But I still believe Marin is not the woman God has for you."

"It doesn't matter what you believe about my life and my choices. God spoke to *my* spirit, Chanelle. *He told me that Marin was to be my mate.* I don't want to be rude, but I need you to stay out of my business."

Chanelle looked hurt by his words. "I'm sorry if I happen to care about my brother."

"I'm glad you care about me. Chanelle, I care about you, too. But when it comes to marriage, we have to trust God and allow Him to guide us. Okay?"

Chanelle nodded. "Sure."

After a long pause, Warner said quietly, "I'm going to need your support. I don't know if I can deal with this alone. I never thought we'd have a drug problem in our marriage. I just never thought it would happen to us. Not us."

CHAPTER TWENTY-THREE

After Warner left Passages Malibu, the staff conducted a thorough search through Marin's luggage. Next, she was taken to her room and given time to unpack and settle in.

Laboratory tests were ordered and Marin underwent more interviews that would be evaluated before a plan of treatment could be outlined.

She was subjected to another orientation, this one covering the facility's schedule and rules.

"Meetings, lectures and counseling sessions are the heart of your treatment, Marin. You will probably be given a chance to talk one on one with your counselor, then in small groups."

Marin rubbed her arms as she listened to the administrator of the facility. Her skin was feeling warm and itchy, making her uncomfortable. She shifted in her seat.

"Do you have any questions for me?"

"Not at the moment," Marin responded.

She was sent back to her room.

The nights passed slowly for her, despite the twenty-four-hour nursing provided by the treatment center to make her detox period as comfortable as possible.

Her program began with a gradual reduction of medications over the course of a few days to regulate her moods and reduce the cravings.

The doctor had explained that round-the-clock support was important in the treatment of cocaine addiction.

Marin knew she would be here at least ten weeks and that it would take that long before she could once again enjoy life drug-free. She wanted that more than anything.

She was one week into her ten-week program and this was the first day she'd actually felt like her old self. She checked the clock. In ten minutes, she would be attending her first group therapy session.

She missed her husband and her children. Marin couldn't wait until the day she was free to walk out of the center.

Deep down, she knew she was free to leave anytime she wanted, but she truly wanted to fight her addiction. This was never supposed to be a part of her life. She'd tried coke in the first place to prepare for a role—how did it ever come to this?

"Can you believe that Marin Alexander is on drugs?" a woman said loudly enough for Warner to overhear during a recent visit to the supermarket.

"I was shocked. I mean, she's married to a minister and everything. She seemed like such a sweet girl," her friend responded. "I guess she got caught up in that Hollywood game."

"Her poor husband . . ."

Warner straightened his glasses and moved away from the aisle where the two women were standing. He didn't want to hear their comments on his wife or the state of his marriage.

What he and Marin were going through was painful enough, but to have to work on their problems in the public eye was worse.

A part of him was angry with Marin for putting them in this situation, but another part of him understood that her dependency was beyond her control. Together they would get through this.

Warner was prompt for their family appointment with Marin's counselor. He was curious to see if Marin was adapting well, but more importantly, if she was getting better.

He was seated in the reception area when Marin walked up. Her hair had grown out some and lay in soft, wispy curls. Her skin, free of makeup, had a healthy glow.

"I'm glad you could come," she said barely above a whisper.

Before Warner could respond, they were called by the counselor.

Inside the office, the counselor turned the meeting over to her. "Marin has some things she'd like to say to you."

Turning in his seat, Warner eyed his wife. "I'm listening."

She stared down at her hands for a moment. When she looked up, she had tears in her eyes. "You never once asked me why," she stated. "You never asked why I started taking drugs in the first place."

"I figured you'd tell me when you were ready."

Marin took a deep breath and exhaled slowly. "Warner, I thought my addiction started because I was researching a role. But since I've been here . . . I believe it was more than that." She paused for a heartbeat before saying, "When I was in high school, I tried out for cheerleading and I made it. I couldn't have been more excited and happy until my mother found out. In a matter of minutes the excitement passed right through me. It was gone, Warner. As quickly as it had come."

Marin twisted the folds of her skirt. "I felt so sad and I remember thinking, okay, what's next? What can I do to make my mother proud of me? I was so desperate for her approval. I guess I still am. But I can't blame all of this on her. I have always had these high periods that evaporate into lows. I'm happy one minute and then sad the next."

Warner glanced over at the counselor, then back at Marin. "It almost sounds like you go through a depression of some sort."

Wiping her eyes, she nodded. "It's like shooting up or something. I get a rush that's indescribable but then a few minutes later—nothing. I kept searching for whatever I needed to do next to reach my next high. When I tried cocaine for the first time, I felt like I'd found what I was looking for. It made me feel good, like I didn't have a care in the world."

"How do you feel now?" the counselor interjected.

"Like I have a better understanding of me," she responded. Looking at him, she said, "Warner, since I've been here—away from you and my babies—I've realized that all I want is to be your wife and their mother. We're a family and that's very important to me."

Warner wanted to believe her more than anything. "But what about those moments when you're feeling depressed? What then?" he wondered aloud. "Or when you're seeking approval?"

"I'm going to go to meetings. I'll have a sponsor . . . a support group and . . ." she paused a moment before adding, "I hope I'll have you, too."

Warner reached over, taking Marin's hand in his. "You will always have me. We are a team, sweetheart, and I love you."

He meant it. Warner loved his wife dearly and wanted their marriage to work. He'd never doubted that God had ordained their relationship and he was not about to just walk away at the first sign of trouble.

He sent up a prayer of thanksgiving. Warner had a lot to be grateful for—Marin was getting better. Since her admission six weeks ago, she now had a healthy glow. She looked beautiful and she was putting some weight back on. She didn't look anorexic any longer.

She was on the road to recovery.

Warner couldn't stop giving God the praise. He was so grateful and he prayed for Marin's continued strength to kick her addiction.

She would be coming home in a couple of weeks. Warner considered planning a special dinner for her, but decided he didn't really want to share her with anyone other than their sons.

He and Marin had a lot of time to make up for and Warner didn't want to waste a moment of it.

Thank You, Father God, for giving me my wife back. Satan tried to steal her from me, but I have the victory. Praise God, I have the victory.

The next day Irma Wooten and Mollie Ransom were in the church administration building when Warner arrived.

"Morning, Pastor." They greeted him in unison.

"Good morning, ladies."

Mollie followed him into his office. "Pastor, I want you to know that I'm praying for your wife. Marin is a nice young woman and I hate what's happened."

"Thank you, Sister Mollie. I appreciate that."

"When you talk to her, let her know that we're thinking of her. We gonna keep her lifted in prayer."

"I sure will."

Irma entered the office. "Pastor, you doing okay?"

Warner sat down at his desk. "I'm fine."

"My brother's boy—" Irma began. "He went to this party and somebody put something in his drink. That's how he got hooked on drugs. We been through a lot with him. One thing about Marin—she wants help."

"She does want to get better," Warner said. "Marin is taking responsibility and I'm very proud of her."

Mollie smiled. "We all are."

The two women didn't stay long. They soon left Warner to start his day. He heard a soft knock on his door and looked up. "Sister Hazel . . ."

"Pastor, how are you?" She walked into the office and took a seat without preamble.

"I'm fine. Doing just fine."

"How is your wife?"

"Marin is getting better each day."

"The devil sure is busy," Hazel stated. "Just busy."

Warner settled back in his chair, listening. He had no idea where Hazel was going with this conversation.

"You really have to stay prayed up."

He didn't respond.

"Elijah and I were talking and we think that it would be a good idea if you'd take some time off. You could tape your sermons ahead. You and your family could go away somewhere. Away from the media."

Warner knew that Hazel wanted her husband to have a larger role in Victory Baptist Church, so he silently questioned her true motives. "You think so?"

Hazel Pittman nodded. "Elijah's more than ready to take over in your absence."

After a moment, Warner responded, "I'll give it some thought and get back to Elijah. Thank you for your concern."

Satisfied, Hazel got up and left the office.

Shaking his head, Warner returned his attention to the computer monitor. He had several e-mails that needed a response.

He gave up after not being able to fully concentrate. He had heard from several of his deacons and some of the ministerial staff that members of his congregation were upset over Marin's actions.

What right did they have to judge her?

Marin made a mistake, but she was no different from anyone else in the world.

If God could forgive her, so could he.

Marin glanced around the room that had been her home since July. Ten weeks later, it was time to go home and for the first time in a long time, Marin felt like her old self. She was ready to be a wife and mother.

"Lord, please help me be a good wife to Warner and a good mother to my children. I want so badly to make my marriage work. Help me to do that. I don't want to mess this up, Lord. Please help me," she prayed.

She heard footsteps behind her and turned around to find Warner standing there. Marin smiled. "I'm so glad to see you."

He smiled back, giving her hope that everything would be okay between them. "Ready to go home?"

"Yes. I am."

Marin said her good-byes and followed Warner out to the waiting car. He pulled her into his arms.

"I love you," he whispered, bringing tears to her eyes. "I've never been so scared in my life."

"I don't want to ever put you through that again. You are my life and I love you. Just before you came to pick me up, I was praying for God to help me become a better person. A better wife and mother."

"I'm going to do what I can to be a good husband to you, Marin. I can't say that you are totally to blame for what happened—I have to accept some responsibility."

"We're going to get through this, aren't we?"

Warner nodded. "Now let's get you home."

"I can't wait to put some distance between me and this place," Marin said. She was finally going home, back to her life and to her family.

Marin vowed that this time she wouldn't screw up.

He wrapped his arms around her. "Honey, I love you and I married you for better or for worse. We just have to be honest with each other. If you're having a problem or feeling down, just come talk to me. I'm here for you."

Marin burst into tears. "I'm so sorry for being a screwup."

"You're not a screwup, Marin. Honey, stop saying that."

"The best thing I ever did was marry you, Warner." She wiped away her tears. "I missed you so much."

Marin begin unbuttoning Warner's shirt. "Let me show you how much."

The next morning, Warner served Marin breakfast in bed.

"This is a pleasant surprise. Thank you." She picked up a piece of toast and took a bite.

The telephone rang.

"It's Chanelle," Warner announced.

"Chanelle's going to bring the boys home in about an hour," Warner told her when he hung up the telephone.

Marin smiled. "I can't wait to see them. I really missed them." She sliced off a piece of her sausage. "I guess Chanelle probably hates me now."

"She doesn't hate you," Warner said reassuringly.

"She was never one of my fans and now—she probably thinks I'm really horrible for what I did to you and the boys."

"It doesn't matter what my sister thinks. You are my wife and we'll figure this out together."

Gabriel and Rylan ran up to Marin as soon as they spotted her, screaming "Mommy! Mommy!"

Grinning, she held her arms open. "Hello! I'm so happy to see you two!"

Chanelle intruded on her reunion with her sons. "Hello, Marin."

"Hi. Thanks so much for taking care of them for us. I'm sure they had a lot of fun playing with Joshua."

Gabriel began telling her about the trucks in Joshua's room. "He had a blue one and a red one. A yellow one and—"

CHAPTER TWENTY-FOUR

Warner unlocked the front door and held it open for Marin to enter the house. "Welcome home."

She waited in the family room while Warner took her suitcase upstairs to their bedroom.

"When are the boys coming home?" she asked when he came back down. "I really want to see them. I've missed them so much."

Warner took a seat in one of the wing chairs. "I asked my sister to keep them for the night. I thought we might need the time to talk."

She eyed him a moment before responding, "I've already told you how bad I feel for what happened. Warner, I'm sorry. I wish I could go back and change it, but I can't."

"I'm not asking you to, Marin. I just don't want this to happen again."

"It won't."

"How can you be so sure? This addiction will be with you for the rest of your life."

"I know that. Warner, I screwed up. I know it. But I promise you—it won't happen again. I'm going to do everything I can to keep that from happening. I love you and I love my babies. I don't want to lose my family."

"Neither do I," Warner admitted. "Marin, I've never been so scared."

Marin stood up and crossed the room to stand in front of him. "Please forgive me, Warner."

"Yeah," Rylan interrupted.

Chanelle gestured for Warner to join her in another room.

"If you're planning to discuss me, I think I should be present," Marin announced. She kissed Gabriel on the cheek and said, "Sweetie, you and your brother sit down here and watch television. Mommy and Daddy will be in the dining room talking to Auntie Chanelle. Okay?"

He nodded. "Okay, Mommy."

When they were alone, Marin inquired, "So what is it that you want to say to Warner? I'm sure it has something to do with me."

Chanelle glanced over at her brother.

"What did you want to talk to me about?"

"I was only going to ask how things were going so far."

"Warner and I talked for a long time last night and I think we're on our way to being back on track. Is that what you wanted to know?"

"I'm not sure I like your tone, Marin."

Marin met the challenge in Chanelle's eyes by saying, "I really don't care. I don't like that you're always in our marriage. Warner and I love each other and we're determined to make our marriage work. I'm sorry if this is not what you want to hear, but there's nothing you can do about it."

Chanelle sputtered in her indignation. "W-Warner! How can y-you let her t-talk to me like this?" She eyed Marin. "I'm not trying to be in your business, but I'm not going to lie. I was never convinced that you're the woman for my brother. After this—"

"It doesn't matter if you're convinced or not, Chanelle. I know what's in my heart and Warner knows what's in his. Like I said earlier, it has nothing to do with you."

Warner intervened. "Okay, I think this has gone far enough."

Chanelle agreed. "You know what? I'm not going to say another thing about your marriage, Warner. Whatever happens happens as far as I'm concerned. I apologize if I overstepped my bounds." She turned, walking through the living room, heading for the door. "I'll talk to you later, Warner."

"Good night to you, too," Marin said in a loud voice.

Warner looked down at her. "My sister doesn't mean any harm."

"I never said she did. I'm just tired of her trying to turn you against me. If I didn't know any better, I'd think she wanted you for herself."

"That's perverse, Marin."

Shrugging nonchalantly, she retorted, "Tell it to your sister."

Shirley Miller wasted no time in coming to see her daughter.

Marin greeted her when she blew into the master bedroom. "Hello, Mom."

She gave Marin a hostile glare in response. "How could you embarrass us like this?"

"I didn't do anything to you, or anybody else, for that matter," Marin replied sharply. "This is my life."

"Marin, what were you thinking? Do you have any idea what this could do to Warner?"

"I don't need this right now." Turning on her side, Marin said, "I'm going to take a nap."

"Your father and I came to visit with you."

"No, you didn't," Marin shot back. "You came to lecture me. And I really don't want to hear it right now. All you've ever done is tell me what a screwup I am. I don't need to listen to it again, Mom. *I got it.*"

"Well, you need to listen to somebody. Marin, I'm proud of you for accepting responsibility for your addiction. I'm just trying to make sense of it."

"I'm trying to make sense of this myself. Mom, I didn't do this to hurt you, Dad or Warner. It started out as research for a role and then I just wanted to feel better."

Shirley took Marin's hand, squeezing it. "Honey, what can I do to help you? Marin, let me help you through this."

She eyed her mother. "You really want to help me?"

"Of course, dear."

"Then please stop criticizing me."

"Honey, just listen to me, please. You have a good man and two beautiful little boys." Shirley gestured around the room. "This great big house. What more do you want?"

"Mom, I'm an actress—a pretty good one—and I love it. I want to go back to work. I want you to stop treating me like a child. I want Warner to take me out of that mold he's created for the perfect first lady.

When I needed you and Daddy to be parents you were too busy. Well, now I'm a grown woman. I don't want you making me feel bad. Just stop it, please."

"Your father and I did the best we could for you."

"I'm not saying you didn't. But Mom, you have to admit it—you and Daddy were on the fast track for success. It's okay. I survived."

"Why must you always try to blame me and your father for everything?"

Marin was quiet for a moment before saying, "I'm getting tired. I don't feel like talking anymore."

"That's what you do," Shirley stated. "You shut everybody out, but we're supposed to know what's going on with you? Marin, we can't read your mind."

She shifted in bed, turning her back to her mother. "Please leave, Mom. I'm really tired."

"You're never going to escape your demons this way, Marin. Cocaine isn't the answer either." Shirley placed a hand on her daughter's shoulder, patting her. "I love you, baby girl."

Marin refused to look at her mother. She didn't want to give her the satisfaction of seeing how her words had affected her.

Warner entered the bedroom a few minutes after Shirley left.

"I heard some of your conversation with your mother," he told her.

Marin stared down at her hands. "It's not something I wanted you to hear. I didn't mean it in a bad way. I want you to know that."

"I'm sorry if I made you feel that way."

Marin's eyes rose in surprise. "After everything I put you and the children through? *You're* apologizing to *me?*"

Sitting down on the bed beside her, Warner said, "I want you to know that your happiness is very important to me. I've never said that you should quit acting. I know how much you love it."

"But you have this way about you when it comes to certain roles. I'm not to the point where I can be a picky actress, Warner. I've sacrificed my career for you and for the boys and I don't regret it, but I'm ready to jump back in. I need this. Acting is the only part of my life where I feel totally free. It makes me happy. I don't want you making me feel bad about any roles that I decide to accept. I told you that I would never embarrass you."

"Are you saying that I don't make you happy?"

"Honey, no. Warner, you make me extremely happy. I'm talking about me. Remember what I told you? I'm happy for a while and then I have those moments of sadness. You would've had to live with my mother to understand. She just has this way of making me feel like such a failure. Like I can't do anything right. I live in constant fear of failing."

"I don't get that with her. I know sometimes she's very critical."

"I really don't expect you to understand, Warner. I just know it's not all in my head. *I'm not crazy.*"

"Nobody is saying that, Marin."

"But I feel like you and my mom just don't understand what I'm going through. It's such a terrible way to feel, like you're nothing more than a failure."

"You've got to fight this depression you've been experiencing."

"Don't you think I've tried? That I'm still trying? It's just not that easy. Warner, I don't like living this way. Feeling alone and scared all the time of messing up."

"Marin, listen to me. I trust you, sweetheart." Warner took her hand in his. "You are not alone. You have me, but more importantly, you have God. Honey, He will never leave you."

"God can't be too happy with me right now. I've let Him down so many times."

"The good news is that He still loves you, Marin. God loves you so much. When you feel down or lonely, call on the Lord, honey. Don't pick up a bottle of wine or buy cocaine. God is the answer, Marin. He is all you will ever need."

CHAPTER TWENTY-FIVE

A few days later, Marin slammed the telephone down in frustration. "What's going on?" Warner asked from his position at the table.

"That was my agent. I didn't get the part." Her eyes filled with tears. "I don't think anybody wants to work with me anymore. I'm not the first person who's had a problem. Why won't they give me a chance?"

Warner wrapped his arms around her. "I'm sorry, honey."

She wiped her eyes with the back of her hands. "I'm ready to get back to work, but nobody will give me a chance." Marin ran her fingers through her hair. "They think it's still too soon."

"Maybe they're right," Warner suggested.

"They're not. I know me better than anyone. I'm more than ready to go back to work." Marin didn't voice her feelings, but if she didn't find work soon, she didn't know what would happen.

She was bored sitting around the house. She leaned back against Warner. "I need to work. I really need to do something right now. Even if it's nothing but a commercial or a day actor. I just need something."

"Why don't you come with me tonight? You and the boys. Allow God to minister to you, sweetheart."

Marin felt like screaming. God wasn't the answer to her problem. She needed to work.

Warner tried to coax her to attend services with him, but she refused a second time.

After the boys fell asleep, Marin sent the nanny on an errand to pick up a bottle of wine for her. She needed something to drink.

She hadn't touched anything with alcohol since leaving rehab, but tonight she really needed an escape. Surely one little glass couldn't hurt.

After her third glass, Marin fell asleep on the sofa downstairs.

Warner woke her up when he returned home.

She sat up, momentarily confused. "Wha . . ."

He held up the half-full wine bottle. "You've been drinking."

"I just had some wine, Warner. What's the big deal?"

"Marin, what's going on with you?"

She looked up at him. "It was just a glass of wine. I'm not about to go off on a binge or something."

"From the looks of it, you've had more than one glass."

Marin rose sluggishly to her feet. "I'm going to bed. Good night, Warner."

The next morning, Marin woke up with a headache. She heard Warner moving about in the bathroom.

When he walked out, she sat up in bed. "I know how you feel about alcohol. I won't bring another bottle of wine into the house. In fact, I won't even touch it. You were really freaked out last night."

"Don't you feel I have every right to be? Not more than a couple of days ago, I told you that God is the answer to every problem—not wine, not drugs. Just God."

Marin rubbed her temple. "I get it, Warner."

They talked for a few minutes more before he had to leave for a meeting with his associate pastors.

Around noon, Marin decided to have lunch at Marino's. She'd hoped Warner could join her, but he had a meeting to attend at the last minute, so she was on her own.

She'd lost out on another part, this time to Carol. Depressed, she decided to bury her sorrows in seafood and pasta, followed by a slice of delectable chocolate mousse cake.

"Hello, beautiful."

Marin glanced up from her plate. "Danny, how are you?"

"I'm cool." He sat down in the empty chair facing her. "Haven't seen you around."

"I was in rehab," she responded. "Thanks to you."

"Hey, I was just trying to help you take the edge off . . . you know."

Marin stared at Danny. "I've been clean for six months now."

He smiled. "I've tried that a few times. It doesn't work for me. Maybe you'll have better luck. Well, I'm meeting an associate, so I'll see you around, Preacher's Wife." Danny moved on.

A part of Marin wanted to call Danny back. Her temptation to lose herself in a cocaine-induced high was great.

"I can't hurt Warner and the boys," she whispered. "I can't do that to them."

She signaled the waitress to bring her bill. After she paid for her meal, she jumped to her feet and rushed out of the restaurant.

She heard someone calling out her name and turned around.

"Marin! I thought that was you. How are you?"

"Hey, Tisha. I'm doing okay." Tisha was a makeup artist and had worked on Marin's face several times in the past.

"I was just asking Dru about you. I saw her yesterday on the set of *Missing*."

"I haven't talked to her in a couple of days."

"She told me."

"You doing okay? You're looking good."

"I wish I felt good. Tisha, I've been on I don't know how many auditions, but nobody's hiring me for movies. I did get the Breyer's ice cream commercial. Ice cream, Tisha. I've been reduced to doing ice cream commercials. I'm so depressed."

"When I'm depressed, I just lay back and get high." Tisha laughed. "I guess you know what I'm talking about. I was surprised when I heard you were in rehab. I had no idea you got down like that."

"I was going through a bad time in my life. I needed a pick-me-up."

"And what about now?"

"What are you talking about?"

Tisha grinned. *"You know?"*

Marin shook her head. "Oh, no. I don't do that anymore."

"Here's my card. Just in case you ever need me."

She accepted the card and rushed off.

Marin found another message from her agent waiting for her. She returned the call, asking, "What is so important?"

"I just spoke with the director for the Breyers Ice Cream commercial and they said you couldn't remember your lines. I've been thinking about this for a while and I wanted to inform you that I think it's best if we parted ways. I don't feel I can do any more for you."

"What do they mean I couldn't remember my lines? I messed up maybe twice. Is that why you're dropping me?"

"I just feel this is best. Perhaps another agent will be more suitable for you."

Tears in her eyes, Marin slammed down the phone. She dropped into a nearby chair sobbing.

My career is over. It's over now.

When she couldn't shed another tear, she pulled a tissue from her purse and wiped her face. Tisha's card fell out and floated to the floor.

Marin picked up the card.

She walked over to the phone and called Tisha.

"I need a pick-me-up."

"Marin, are you sure about this? When I spoke to you earlier, you said you were clean."

"Tisha, I really need something to make me feel better. How soon can you meet me?"

Marin's mood swings, her loss of appetite and inability to sleep reminded Warner of a time he'd thought was behind him. She'd been out of rehab five weeks and had been doing well until a few weeks ago.

He conducted a thorough search through the house while she was out at an audition.

When she came home, she looked around and said, "You've been going through my stuff, I see. You mind telling me why?"

"I hope I'm wrong, but I think that you're using again. Marin, we have two small boys living in this house. How can you do this? Haven't we been down this road before?"

"Did you find anything?" Marin asked calmly.

Warner shook his head no.

Before she realized what his intent was, he crossed the room and snatched her purse from her.

She tried to take it back from him. "Give it to me."

"Why?"

"Warner, have you no respect for my privacy?"

"Drug addicts have no rights in my house."

Marin was furious. "Warner, give me my purse!"

"I'll give it back to you after I make sure you have not brought any more illegal drugs into my house."

"Warner, why don't you trust me?"

"I want to trust you, but, Marin, it hasn't been that long. You got out of rehab in September, only a little over a month ago, and now you're using again."

Warner opened Marin's handbag and pulled out a small packet of white powder. Holding it up, he said, "You want me to trust you, huh?"

Her eyes flashed white-hot anger. "You had no right to invade my property. Now give me my purse, Warner."

"You can have your purse. I'm not giving this stuff back. If you want to live this kind of life, Marin, do it somewhere else. You can't live here."

Crying, Marin grabbed her purse from Warner and rushed out of the house.

Emotionally drained, Warner dropped down on a nearby sofa. *Lord, I can't go through this again. I just can't do it.*

Two hours passed and it was dark.

Warner called his in-laws' house when the clock struck ten thirty to see if Marin happened to be with them.

"What do you mean, Marin's gone?" Shirley questioned. "Where did she go?"

"I don't know. She just stormed out of here. We had a fight. She's using drugs again."

"Are you sure?"

"Yes. I found a packet of cocaine or something in her purse. I'm not sure I can go through this again. I told her if she wanted the drugs she would have to leave. Gabriel and Rylan don't need to see their mother high as a kite."

*   *   *

"Chanelle, I didn't expect to see you today," Warner said, greeting his sister. "What's going on?"

"I had lunch with a friend a couple of blocks away and thought I'd stop by for a minute." Chanelle glanced over her shoulder, gesturing. She turned back to face her brother.

"Warner, I have someone I'd like for you to meet, someone I went to college with. This is my friend Geneva Taylor. She's just moved to Los Angeles."

"It's nice to meet you. Thank you for coming to Victory Baptist this morning."

"Service was wonderful and I really enjoyed your sermon."

"Thank you. I hope you'll come back to visit with us again."

"I will. It was a pleasure meeting you." Turning to Chanelle, she said, "I need to get back to work. I'll give you a call later."

"She's the one I've been telling you about, Warner," Chanelle whispered as soon as Geneva left the office. "If you'd let me introduce you two back then, you might not have married Marin."

"You just don't get it, Chanelle. God ordained that Marin and I would become husband and wife. I didn't just pick her."

"I can't believe that God would bring someone like her into your life. I'm sorry, Warner, but I think you did that all on your own."

"I'm not going to debate this with you."

"So what did you think of Geneva?"

He shrugged nonchalantly. "She seems nice. Why?"

"You need a real wife. One who will put you and the children first."

"Chanelle, I know you mean well, but I need you to listen to me. Mind your own business, please."

"What does this woman have on you?"

"I need to get the boys," Warner told her as he rose to his full height. "I'll talk to you later."

"I'm not trying to upset you. I just think—"

Warner cut her off. "I don't want to continue this discussion, Chanelle. Just drop it."

"You deserve so much better, Warner. I'm sorry, but it's true. You know it."

He walked on ahead of his sister, ignoring her. Warner knew what God had called him to do and nobody—not even Chanelle—could tell him anything different.

Marin drove to Maxium Studios and parked her car on the street. She sat in her car for a moment, trying to gain her composure. Tisha was working on one of the sets and she needed to see her.

Warner had destroyed her stash and she needed more. She was still shaking all over from her confrontation with her husband.

How could she have been so stupid? How could she have risked doing drugs while the boys were there? Marin had had no idea that Warner had suspected she was using again.

She checked her watch, then pulled out her cell phone. "C'mon, Tisha. Answer the phone," she muttered. She hung up before leaving a voice mail.

Her skin felt itchy. Marin ran her hands up and down her arms.

She tried her call a second time.

"Hello."

"Hey, Tisha, it's me. Marin. I'm parked right outside the studio. When are you getting off?"

"I'll be off in about twenty minutes. I'll call you when I'm about to walk out."

"Okay."

Marin's cell phone rang as soon as she hung up with Tisha. It was Warner.

She didn't answer. She couldn't talk to him right now. She was too ashamed.

Her cell phone rang again. This time it was her mother. She definitely wasn't in the mood to talk to Shirley.

Marin spotted Tisha and stepped out of the car.

When she saw Marin, Tisha came over, saying, "Hey, girl, what are you doing out here?"

"I need some snow. Warner threw away my other stash."

"Follow me back to my place."

She made her purchase and forty-five minutes later she was driving to Santa Monica, where she checked into the Marriott. She just needed some time alone.

Using her credit card, she chopped the cocaine into a fine powder. She formed several lines then used a tiny straw to inhale the drug up her nostril.

A few minutes later, she was floating. It was almost one in the morning and she was tired. She closed her eyes.

When Marin opened her eyes, the clock on the bedside table read nine forty-five. She sat up in bed, pushing away the covers.

Swinging her legs to the side, Marin climbed out of bed and rushed over to the window.

I've been gone overnight. Warner is going to be furious.

She sat down on the bed and reached for her cell phone. *What do I say to him? He's going to think . . .*

Her head throbbed.

She stayed in the room another night because it was much easier than going home and facing Warner. By now her parents were probably camped out at the house.

She was too ashamed to face any of them.

CHAPTER TWENTY-SIX

"Marin, what are you going to do about your marriage? You can't hide out forever. And with you being famous—girl, you can't hide."

"I don't know. I don't think there's much I can do right now. I guess they're out looking for me."

"Maybe you should call them," Tisha suggested. "You don't want them thinking something bad happened to you."

"You're right. I'll call Warner later."

When Tisha left, Marin reached for the phone.

She called the house.

Warner answered on the first ring. "Where are you?"

Clearing her throat, Marin replied, "I'm staying in a hotel. I just need a few days to get myself together."

"You can't come home?"

"Not right now. Warner, I need some space. Please just give me a few days."

"Are you doing drugs?"

Marin didn't respond.

"I mean it. You can't come home until you've decided once and for all you want to be delivered from this addiction. Marin, you have to decide what you want most. Your family or the drugs."

"You know I want you and the boys. Warner, I love you dearly. You're my life."

"If that were true, you'd still be here in the house with us. We'd be working together to kick this addiction."

"I don't want to go back to rehab. Warner, I feel like I'm drowning and I need to save myself. Can you understand that?"

"Honey, you can't do this alone. Trust me on this. We can get through this together, but you've got to trust me, sweetheart. Marin, I love you. Just come home."

"I'm not ready," she confessed. "I just can't face you right now."

Two weeks passed and still no sign of Marin. Warner and Marin's parents checked every hotel, looking for her.

"She must be using an assumed name. That's the only explanation." Shirley wrung her hands in frustration. "I can't believe Marin would just run off like that."

Robert declared, "I think it's time for more radical measures. You need to secure a power of attorney and have her bank accounts closed."

"Cancel her credit cards, too," Shirley said. "That way she'll have to come home. Have the car declared stolen. You might want to have your locks changed here at the house."

"Why would I want to do that?"

"She's a drug addict. You don't want her coming into the house stealing or scaring the children. Worse, she might bring other addicts with her." Shirley clutched a fist to her chest. "I can't believe I'm talking about my own child."

"I know what you mean," Warner said. "I never thought we'd be in this situation. Never. . . ."

Warner spent the early afternoon canceling his wife's credit cards and closing her bank accounts. He also called a locksmith to change the locks. If Marin was still using, he didn't want her home around the children. She would have to go back to rehab.

"What am I supposed to tell my family?" he wondered. Warner hadn't informed them of Marin's absence. He already knew what Chanelle would say. She would push him toward a divorce, but he would continue to hold his ground.

Warner intended to pray for God's wisdom concerning his marriage.

A couple of hours later, Chanelle stopped by the church to drop off the new hymnals.

She cornered Warner in his office. "Why are the boys here with you? Where's Marin?"

"She's away."

"Warner, I know you're not telling me something. What's going on?"

"Marin's gone. She left two weeks ago. I've been trying to find her. She—"

"You don't need to go searching after that woman. Just let her go. But if I were you, I'd cancel her credit cards and restrict her bank access."

"I've already done that," Warner confirmed. "Her parents suggested it."

"They knew that Marin was missing?"

"Yeah. They're her parents. They needed to be told something."

"And we didn't? We're your family. Don't you think we had a right to know?"

"At the time, I didn't," Warner responded. "Chanelle, I'm worried about my wife. I have to make sure my children are alright. I have enough on my plate right now."

Hitting the side of the ATM machine, Marin muttered a string of curses.

She desperately needed money. She'd already given away her car and her wedding rings to feed her habit, but now she needed more. She had even tried to sneak back into the house, but the locks had been changed. Proof that Warner wanted nothing to do with her.

He'd even prevented her access to her own personal accounts. Her credit cards had been canceled. Warner was ruining her life.

Marin placed a call to Dru.

"Where are you?" her friend demanded. "We've been looking all over for you, Marin."

"Dru, I need a big favor. Can you loan me two hundred dollars? I need it to fix the car."

"Marin, your car was found stripped in El Segundo. I know what's really going on."

"I don't know what you've heard . . ." Marin cleared her throat. "I just need a little money to tide me over. I need some food, Dru."

"Why don't you let me come pick you up and take you home? Warner is so worried about you."

"He changed the locks on me. Warner doesn't love me anymore."

"Where are you, Marin?"

"I just need money. Just twenty dollars, Dru. Please."

"I'll give you the money if you let me come get you and take you home. You can even stay with me for a couple of days until we can get you into rehab. Marin, you need help. You can't do this alone."

"There's nothing wrong with me," she snapped.

Next, Marin called her mother and father.

"Mom, I need a favor. I need some money."

"I'm sorry, but we can't help you, Marin. You need to check yourself into rehab."

"Why can't you ever be there for me, Mom? Just once."

Warner hung up after his conversation with Dru. Marin had called her, asking for money.

His mother walked into the room. "Was that about Marin?"

He turned around, facing her. "It was Dru. She said that Marin called begging for money. She tried to get Marin to tell her where she was, but she wouldn't. She just wanted money."

"Do you think she'll go to her parents?"

"She tried, but they couldn't get her to come home either. They refused to give her any money."

"Maybe they shouldn't have refused. Marin would've had to show up to get the money. We could've had her picked up and taken to a hospital."

"I didn't think about that." Warner picked up the telephone. "Maybe I should give them a call. In case she calls back."

After his conversation with Shirley ended, Warner sat down with his mother.

"This is such a shame," Millicent murmured. "What in the world must your congregation think?"

"A lot of them have relatives on drugs," Warner stated.

"But they're not the first lady. What are you going to say to your congregation? They are going to want some type of explanation."

"I don't know. It'll come to me when the time is right."

Millicent rose to her feet. "Why don't you let me take the boys home with me? Your father and I would love to spend a couple of days with our grandchildren."

"You're sure?"

She nodded. "Right now, you have enough to deal with."

He went upstairs, quickly packed a bag for Gabriel and Rylan and took the boys downstairs. "I want you two to behave for Nana and Poppy. Okay?"

"Okay!" they yelled in unison.

He hugged his mother before seeing them off. "Thanks so much for this."

"I hope you find Marin," Millicent whispered.

"Me, too."

Warner went back into the house.

Alone, he didn't know what else to do other than pray. Falling down to his knees, Warner closed his eyes, saying, "Heavenly Father, I know that You know my pain, the suffering, the grief and the fears I have right now. Lord, I feel so broken because my wife is out there somewhere in a sea drifting away by the currents of drug use, abuse, and addiction. Please give me the strength to do battle in this chemical warfare for Marin's life. In Jesus' name I pray. Amen."

Marin threw a mug against the wall of the room she was staying in. She had no money and she needed something—she needed it badly.

She had left home three weeks ago and she knew that there was no way Warner would let her come back. Not after this. So she had nowhere to go and she had no money.

There was a knock at the door.

Marin rushed to answer it. "Danny, what took you so long?"

He walked into the room. "I'm here." Holding out his hand, he asked, "Where's the money?"

"I don't have any. Warner's closed out my credit cards and I can't get any money out of the bank. I can't even get to my own money."

"So how do you plan on paying for this?"

Marin started removing her clothes.

After paying for the cocaine with her body, Marin turned her back to Danny.

"You know, with this body, a pretty girl like you could make a lot of money."

Sitting up, Marin demanded, "What are you talking about?"

"You need money, don't you?"

Marin couldn't believe what she was hearing. "You want me to be a prostitute?"

"We can work something out. You need me and I need you."

Marin shook her head. Disgusted, she said, "I don't need you."

"Oh, you don't think so?" He reached for the packet of snow white powder, but Marin backed away, sparking his laughter.

"You don't have any money. This snow ain't for free. I run a business."

"I can't sell my body. My husband—"

"Doesn't want you anymore because you're an addict. Look at you— you're nothing now."

Marin winced at his words. Tears formed in her eyes. "You shut up. Just shut up."

"And you better start earning you some money to pay for your habit. I don't want no more jewelry. You don't have a car no more. Unless you have cash or you willing to work it off, lose my number."

"What about you? Don't you want me? How about you and me? We just work something out between you and me. Huh? What about that?"

Danny looked disgusted. "I told you. This is a business. Like I said, unless you got cash or you willing to work it off—don't call me." His tone had a ring of finality to it.

He tossed a shopping bag on the bed. "Oh, you're going to need these." Without another word, he left the room.

Marin picked up the bag and looked inside. She pulled out a long-haired wig, a halter top and a pair of shorts she'd never be caught dead in.

"I'm not doing this," Marin vowed, throwing the bag and its contents across the room.

Two days later, Marin walked out of the room and down the steps of the motel where she was staying. She ventured slowly to the street, standing on the sidewalk.

I can't do this. I'm an actor. No, I was an actor. Nobody wants me anymore. People are calling me a has-been, a drug addict.

A car coming down the street slowed to a stop. The man rolled down the window on the passenger side and leered at her a moment before saying, "How much?"

"Fifty dollars," she stated flatly.

"What's your name?"

"Mary," she responded.

She was no longer Marin Alexander or Warner's wife. From this moment forward, she was just another addict hooking on the streets for enough money to support her habit.

CHAPTER TWENTY-SEVEN

The next time was easier.

Marin could barely remember what happened, she was so high. All she cared about was her drugs.

She was in a cloudy haze, her eyes bouncing around the room. Tisha was stretched out on the sofa, sleeping soundly.

Marin struggled to sit up. "Hey, Tisha. I th-thought you had to go to work this morning."

Tisha stirred, but didn't wake up.

Marin called out to her again. "Tisha, wake up."

"Wha—what?" she mumbled, rubbing her eyes.

"I thought you had to work today."

Tisha sat up, running her fingers through her elbow-length weave. "What time is it?"

Marin glanced over at the bedside clock on the nightstand. "Eleven . . . eleven thirty."

Tisha released a string of profanity. "I'ma lose my job for sure." She rose quickly, then fell back against the couch. "I can't do nothing, I'm so messed up."

Marin burst into laughter.

Tisha cut her eyes at her. "What you laughing at?" After a moment she started laughing too. "I guess I'ma need to find me another job. I guess I can always start hooking like you."

Marin turned up the television to drown out Tisha's words. She didn't need to be reminded of how low she'd sunk.

Switching channels, Marin stopped when she glimpsed Warner on television. His sermons were telecast daily, several times a day on the Christian channel. He looked so handsome, standing there in the navy suit she'd given him for his birthday last year.

"What are you watching that for?" Tisha asked. "You can go home to hear a sermon." She broke into another round of laughter.

Marin didn't think it was funny. She wished it were that simple, because that's all she wanted—to be able to go back home.

"Have you heard from your wife?" Millicent asked Warner when she stopped by the house to pick up the boys Friday afternoon. They were spending the weekend with their grandparents.

"Not yet," Warner responded. He was tired of everyone asking him that one question. He'd done everything he could. Cut off her credit cards, froze her bank accounts—still no Marin. Warner had no idea how she was surviving. He called her cell phone daily, but no answer.

It was clear that she'd chosen the drugs over her family.

"Well, have Shirley and Robert spoken to her?"

"Nobody's talked to her, Mom. She obviously doesn't want anything to do with us."

"I just can't believe this. We did everything we could to make Marin feel like family. What is her problem?"

"She's on drugs, Mom," Warner explained. "Marin can't help it. She's sick."

"But what I don't understand is how did this happen?"

"I don't think we'll ever really know. Marin has a relationship with the drugs. It's almost like a marriage, Mom. You know how you feel you can't function without Dad? Well, Marin feels she can't function without the drugs. In a way, it makes her feel secure, so she's seeking that oneness with the drug. She's sick without it. She feels she can't function without it. Everything else becomes secondary, including her family." Warner's voice broke and it took him a moment to compose himself before he continued.

"She betrayed the relationship by going into rehab before, but this time she will try harder to make it work because once she can no longer contribute to the relationship, she's going to fall. What most addicts fail to see is that a relationship of this kind is one-sided. It's an abusive relationship and definitely not a healthy one."

Millicent shook her head sadly. "I've always heard how it could rip a family apart. I just never thought it would happen to us."

"I didn't either. I love Marin and I want her to come home so that she can get the help she needs. She can kick this addiction—but she has to want to do it."

"Are you and the boys reason enough to fight back?"

"Mom, I hope so. Lord knows, I hope Marin feels that way, because if she doesn't, we're going to lose her forever."

Marin tried to move her arms with the handcuffs, but she couldn't. If she hadn't propositioned an undercover cop, she wouldn't be in this mess. On top of that, the guy recognized her and was telling anyone who'd listen.

Once they booked her down at the jail, Marin knew it was only a matter of time before the media heard about it—they lived for this kind of scandal.

Not only was Warner going to be humiliated—he was going to be furious as well.

Tears filled her eyes as she was shoved roughly into a police car.

"I wondered what happened to you," the policeman fingerprinting her was saying. "How could you let yourself get this way?"

Marin stared out the window. "I'm a screwup," she whispered.

"What do you think your husband will say when he finds out about this? Pastor Brice is a good man."

"I know," she murmured.

Marin was allowed one phone call before a policewoman took her down to a holding cell.

Three hours later she was released.

"Thanks for bailing me out," Marin said. "I didn't know who else to call. I couldn't call Warner or my parents. Dru and I aren't exactly friends anymore."

"Why don't you let me call Pastor Brice?" Carol inquired. "I'm sure he must be worried sick about you."

Shaking her head, Marin said, "I can't go home like this." She fingered the wig on her head. "Carol, look at me. I don't want my babies to see me like I am. I have to get myself together first." She removed the wig from her head and tossed it in the backseat.

"Pastor Brice loves you, Marin. You guys made it through the last time. You can do it again."

She shook her head. "I can't face him, Carol. Just look at me. I'm an addict and a prostitute. Warner's never going to want me again. He won't be able to put all this behind him. I know it."

Carol embraced her. "I can take you somewhere. You can get help. You beat your addiction before, Marin. I know you can do it again."

"I really appreciate you bailing me out of jail. I need to get out of here."

"Marin, please don't leave. Let me help you."

"You can't help me. Carol, no one can help me. Just let me go and please don't tell Warner that you saw me. He's been humiliated enough."

"He loves you."

"I love him, too. I'm just tired of hurting him and my boys."

"Marin, please let me help you. I'll go with you to a treatment center. Warner can meet us there. He really loves you. I know he does, Marin. He's so worried about you. If you don't want him to come, how about your parents?"

"I don't want my mom anywhere near me. All she's going to do is talk about how much I've embarrassed her. I already know how I humiliated them. I don't need to hear it from her."

"What about your father? You told me once that you and he were close. Can I at least call your dad?"

"Carol, you don't have to worry about me. I'm going to get my life straight. I promise. I just have to do it on my own. I've let too many people down in the past."

"I have some clothes upstairs you can put on. Why don't you take a nice hot shower? It'll make you feel so much better."

"Thanks so much, Carol. I really appreciate all you've done for me."

"Marin, promise me that you're going to get some help. I'm sorry, but I only have a hundred dollars on me. I'm going to give this to you, but I want you to understand something. If you don't get any help, please don't call me for any more money. I'm not going to aid in your addiction." Carol wiped away her tears. "I love you, Marin, like a sister. I don't want anything to happen to you."

Carol went upstairs to get a change of clothes for Marin.

Marin glanced down at the money in her hands. "I'm sorry, Carol," she mumbled and ran out of the house.

"What did I tell you?" Chanelle exclaimed as she tossed a newspaper in Warner's direction. "Marin was arrested for prostitution. She's selling her body . . . for drugs."

"You can't possibly believe this. The *National Star* is a gossip magazine."

"It's in *all* the newspapers, Warner. Check your *L.A. Times*. And her face is splashed all over the television."

Warner shook his head in disbelief. Surely this was some sort of mistake. His wife arrested for prostitution? No way.

He couldn't accept the idea. "She's my wife. She wouldn't do something so disgusting."

"Warner, I know you don't want to believe it, but—"

"It's a mistake, Chanelle. I'm telling you, this is a big misunderstanding."

The telephone rang.

Warner answered it. "Hello."

"Pastor Brice, this is Carol. I just wanted you to know that I bailed Marin out of jail this morning. I tried to talk her into going home, but she refused. She's worried that you won't forgive her. I offered to take her to a treatment facility and I thought I'd gotten through to her, but she just took off when I went upstairs to get something for her to wear. I brought her here so that she could shower and put on clean clothes."

Warner's eyes watered. Blinking rapidly, he responded, "Carol, thanks so much for trying to help Marin. We can't really help a person if they don't want to be helped. That's just the way it is, no matter how painful."

Warner hung up the telephone.

"Did Carol see Marin?" Chanelle inquired.

He nodded. "She bailed her out of jail. Carol tried to get Marin to check herself in to rehab, but she disappeared when Carol went to get her some clothes."

"She doesn't want to be helped."

Warner had to agree.

"I feel bad for Marin. This life she's leading is only going to end one way and that's tragic."

He shrugged. "I'm not giving up on her. I'm going to continue to pray for her. I know God can get through to Marin when nobody else is able to. I have to believe that."

"Your church members are very concerned for you, Warner."

"I have a ministry meeting tonight. I'm going to address some of their concerns. Chanelle, I need you to understand that I have to let God lead me. It's the only way I can get through this painful period in my life. If I don't give this to Him, I'll go insane."

CHAPTER TWENTY-EIGHT

Marin called Tisha from a pay phone. "I need you to come pick me up, please. I'm on the corner of LaBrea and Exposition." "Give me a few minutes to get there," she responded sleepily. "I'm not dressed."

Marin heard rustling on the other end, then Tisha saying, "I saw you on the news."

"I don't want to talk about that right now. Just come get me." Marin kept her head down when a couple of people passed the pay phone she was using.

Tisha kept Marin waiting for nearly two hours, giving her time to think over her conversation with Carol. Why didn't people understand that she wanted to go home? She wanted to be with her family. But it just wasn't possible. Too much had happened. Warner would never welcome her back into the house.

The drugs, and now prostitution . . .

"I can't go back," Marin whispered. "No matter how much I want to."

Tisha drove her back to the motel in Santa Monica, where Marin paid for a weeklong stay, thanks in part to Carol's contribution. She was afraid to start hooking again, but she didn't know what else she could do to make enough money for cocaine.

"God, please help me. I can't do this alone," Marin prayed.

*   *   *

Warner stopped by the supermarket to pick up something for dinner. He was planning on making spaghetti for the boys. Chanelle had invited them over for dinner, but he didn't think he'd be good company. He felt it was time for them to move on—without Marin. The thought made him sad.

The longer she was gone, the more apparent it was becoming that Marin would no longer be a part of his life. She had chosen to follow her addiction.

It pained him that he couldn't save his own wife. *God, I don't understand,* he said in his heart. *I just don't understand.*

He heard someone walk up behind him and turned, hoping he would find Marin standing there. But he was disappointed.

"Are you following me?" Geneva teased. "I'm beginning to see you everywhere."

"I guess we like the same places." Warner gave her a tiny smile.

"You look tired. Are you okay?"

Warner nodded, not really wanting to go into his personal life in the middle of a busy supermarket.

"I'm thinking about going to the movies tomorrow afternoon. If you don't mind, I could take the boys with me. I love Disney movies and if I take them, my secret will remain safe."

"That's real nice of you, Geneva, but I don't want to impose on you like that."

"It's no imposition at all. I'd be more than happy to do it. You look like you could use a few hours to yourself."

"You sure you won't mind?"

"It'll be fun," she assured him. "Your boys already know me from church and from seeing me at your sister's house."

"You're sure this isn't an imposition?"

"Not at all. I'd like to do what I can to help you. I'm sure this is a very difficult time for you."

"This is the biggest storm of my life," Warner acknowledged. "It's only the grace of God that keeps me going. That and the love of my children. They need me and I'm not going to abandon them, too."

*   *   *

Bored, Marin switched her purse from one side to the other. She needed to make some money, but not one car had stopped so far. Since being arrested, Marin had decided to frequent another area. The problem was that there were several other girls working the same corner.

A small sigh of relief escaped when a guy driving a black Cadillac pulled to a stop.

"Get in," he practically growled.

For a split second, Marin felt something akin to fear. A small voice inside screamed for her to run, but she chose to ignore it.

Her need for cocaine was greater.

Three hours later, Marin eyed her reflection in a mirror at the hospital.

Once considered one of the ten most beautiful and sexy women in the world, here she stood, pale, pained, bruised and beaten. Her left eye was blackened and her arms swollen and bearing an assortment of cuts and bruises.

She gingerly touched her split top lip, wincing from the pain. She adjusted the fit of the hospital gown she was wearing and glanced around, looking for her clothes. She needed to get out of here. She didn't want her picture splashed all over the tabloids or the fact that she'd been raped and beaten getting back to Warner. He'd been through enough because of her.

Marin crept down the hall to a nearby supply closet. Inside, she slipped on a pair of scrubs. As soon as she was dressed, she walked with her head down right out of the nearest hospital exit.

Warner drove the short distance to Geneva's house. She met him in the driveway.

"I really appreciate your doing this for me," he told her after the boys climbed out of the car. "They're basically good boys."

"I don't expect them to be any trouble. We're going to have a good time at the movies," she said. "Aren't we, Gabriel?"

"Yeah," he responded. "We going to have lots of fun."

Warner didn't hang around long. He left Geneva's house and drove back home.

He truly appreciated her offer to help him with the boys. Geneva was beautiful and she seemed to laugh a lot. Since meeting her, Warner couldn't remember a day she wasn't smiling.

It was Chanelle's wish to see him and Geneva together, but even though Marin was nowhere to be found, Warner was still married and he intended to honor his vows.

Not having to worry about the children gave Warner some time to think about his life without interruption. He sat down, going through his wedding album and family pictures, reliving happy memories.

Warner missed Marin. His eyes filled with tears until they ran down his face. "Lord, I don't understand," he whispered.

Warner sobbed until no more tears would come. He didn't feel any better afterward; instead he was left with a profound sadness.

He drove to Geneva's house to pick up the boys shortly after three.

Geneva opened the door, saying, "Gabriel and Rylan are sleeping. I think they had a wonderful time today."

Warner grinned. "I think so, too. They're both knocked out. What did you do to get them to fall asleep like that? They give me a hard time when it's nap time."

"I lay down with them. We all had quiet time. When they fell asleep, I got up. Rylan was the first to go and Gabriel went to sleep a short time later. He was trying to fight it though."

"I can't thank you enough. I was able to get a lot of stuff taken care of while the boys were with you."

"Anytime you need a break, I'd be more than happy to have the boys come over here. I don't know if Chanelle told you, but I love children. I can't wait to have some of my own."

"They are a blessing," Warner murmured. He checked his watch. "I'd better get them home."

"Have you eaten?" Geneva asked.

"No, I haven't. I was planning on hot dogs for dinner tonight. That's about the only thing the boys will eat when I cook."

"Why don't you and the boys eat with me? I made a lot of food."

Warner hesitated a moment before saying, "We'd be more than happy to share a meal with you. Thank you for your kindness."

Geneva laughed. "You don't have to be so formal."

Warner relaxed some.

She gestured for him to take a seat. "You're not gonna get any taller."

Chuckling, Warner sat down on a nearby chair. Geneva was a delight and he enjoyed her company. But it made him feel a little guilty, too. She was a single woman and he was married. Warner didn't want to give Geneva false hope.

With his emotions in turmoil, he had to tread carefully.

CHAPTER TWENTY-NINE

Warner ran into Hazel and Elijah in the church parking lot. He gave a slight wave.

"Pastor," Hazel called out, "how is your wife doing? Have you heard anything from her?"

He stopped walking. "No, I haven't, Sister Hazel."

She patted his arm. "I'm so sorry. I've been praying for the Lord to bring her home. He can do it, you know."

Warner nodded in agreement. "It's my prayer."

Elijah cleared his throat. "Pastor, I think it's time you address what's been going on . . . to the congregation. Your members care about you and they—well, they hear things on the news."

"You're right, Elijah. I'll do just that on Sunday."

"Pastor, you're going through a lot right now. The members would understand if you wanted to take a little sabbatical. Elijah can take over for you," Hazel suggested. "Just for a little while."

"I'll give it some thought." Warner checked his watch. "I need to make some phone calls."

"Pastor, we're praying for you and your family."

He gave a tight smile. "Thank you, Sister Hazel."

Inside his office, Warner groaned in frustration. He was sick and tired of people asking him about Marin. He didn't have any answers.

He didn't know why Marin refused to come home, why she wasn't strong enough to break the hold this addiction had over her.

"I'm not understanding this, God. I know in my heart that you told me to make Marin my wife. Why is this happening to us? What are you trying to show me?"

Sunday morning, Warner stood in the pulpit, staring out at the thousands of people in the congregation.

"I'm sure most of you know that my wife . . . my wife has a problem with drugs. She has an addiction. She's somewhere out there. Nobody knows where."

Tears filled his eyes.

"C'mon, Pastor. We here for you," someone yelled out.

"Drug addiction has affected all of us in some way. From the standpoint of a husband, I know the realities of addiction. And as your pastor, I am well acquainted with a variety of shameful emotions and filled with humiliation. I hope that by my opening up with you, you or people you know will come to realize that you're not alone. Drug dependency can attack anyone at any time."

"Tell it," someone called out.

Warner prayed that by sharing his personal pain, he would be able to encourage others and that they could find a degree of solace in knowing that God could turn even this situation around.

When he finished speaking, Warner was stunned when the congregation rose to their feet, showing support in thunderous applause.

He was touched by the standing ovation.

After the service, Chanelle found Warner in his office. "I wanted to check on you."

"I'm okay."

"What you said this morning was really nice. And heartfelt."

"I meant it."

"I know you did."

Warner met her gaze. "I know what you're thinking and, Chanelle, I really don't want to hear it. Just drop it."

"I was simply going to invite you over for dinner. Geneva will be there and—"

"I'm a married man."

"I thought you and Geneva were friends. I know she's been helping you out with the boys and here at church."

Geneva had become a great help to Warner. In her spare time, she'd taken over the administrative tasks at church for him until he could find a replacement for his former clerical assistant. She taught Sunday school and his sons loved her.

On those days when the nanny couldn't stay, Geneva would keep them at her house until Warner returned to town.

She had also become a good friend to him. She listened without judgment and often gave solid advice.

Warner was careful not to send the wrong signals. Despite the fact that Marin had disappeared from their lives, she was still very much his wife. He was a married man and he resolved to carry himself in that manner.

It was the middle of January. Marin had been gone for almost three and a half months and Warner wasn't sure if he would ever see her again.

Back in December, Marin's parents had gone to court during her appearance to try and talk some sense into her, but she had refused to hang around long enough to have a conversation. She'd gotten off with a slap on the wrist thanks to her parents' connections, but she didn't seem to care. She'd strolled out of the courthouse and disappeared after taking off for the bathroom.

Her parents had hired a detective to find her, but he had yet to locate her. Warner suspected that she'd left California. She could be anywhere by now.

He prayed God would guide her back to him.

New York

There were flashing lights, squad cars and police everywhere.

Marin stayed back, hiding among the growing crowd, watching as members of DEA escorted her friend Tisha and her boyfriend to a van.

They were being arrested. The drugs, no doubt. Marin was grateful she'd left early that morning to try to buy groceries. There was no food in the house.

But now with Tisha and Moe gone, where would she live? She had nowhere to go. After nearly being killed with that last john, Marin had refused to sell her body again.

She'd hooked up with Tisha and left Los Angeles a couple of weeks after her court appearance and a week before Christmas. She was still angry with Carol for telling her parents about it, but then again, her mom and dad could've easily found out for themselves. They had many friends in the court network.

Shortly after moving to New York, Tisha met Moe and they moved in with him. He was into all kinds of drugs—people on the streets called him the Pharmacist.

He looked out for them. Marin didn't have to hook for money to pay for her cocaine; instead Moe had her selling to some of his VIP clients, as he called them.

It was freezing outside and snow was on the ground, but Marin was afraid to go near the apartment now because she suspected it would be watched for the next few days. If they knew about Tisha and Moe, then there was a possibility that they knew about her.

This was definitely not the life she wanted for herself.

She eyed a pay phone nearby.

Warner crossed her mind. Her heart urged her to call him, but she shook her head. She couldn't call him now. Not after all she'd done.

She was too ashamed.

Her eyes watered. She couldn't even call her own parents. There was no way they'd help her now. Her mother was right all along—she was nothing but a screwup.

After the way she ran out on Carol, Marin figured she probably wouldn't talk to her now. Dru had given up on her a long time ago.

She recalled passing by some type of drug rehabilitation facility a few blocks away.

Rubbing her arms, she turned around, having made the decision to leave that part of her life behind. It was time to save whatever was left of her future.

Marin stood outside the treatment center, summoning up the strength she needed to enter the building. All she had to do was reach out and open the door.

"I can do this," she whispered. "I want help. I want help," she repeated over and over again.

Marin opened the door and stepped inside.

"Can I help you?" the receptionist asked from behind a huge table.

"I hope so," Marin responded. "My life depends on it."

"I was about to grab some lunch," Geneva announced from her position at the door. "Would you like something to eat?"

"If you don't mind picking up a sandwich for me, I'd appreciate it." Warner straightened his glasses. "I didn't eat anything for breakfast this morning. I was too busy trying to make sure the boys had what they needed."

She returned ten minutes later.

He accepted the sandwich she held out to him. "That was quick."

"I called the order in ahead of time. I figured you'd need something to eat."

Warner laughed. "You know me so well." He gestured to one of the visitor chairs. "Join me?"

She smiled and sat down.

He took a bite of his sandwich.

Watching him, Geneva said, "I can only imagine how hard this must be for you. I pray for your strength and courage every day."

"There are days, I'm not sure I know what I'm doing. I love Marin. If she would just come home, we could get her into a treatment facility. She needs help."

Geneva agreed. "You haven't heard anything from your wife?"

Warner shook his head. "Not a word."

"I pray for her, too. She's not in her right mind, but God can still reach her. I believe that."

"So do I. He's the only one who can help her now."

CHAPTER THIRTY

Four months had passed, and still there was no word from Marin. Warner had half expected to hear from her, mostly because yesterday was their seventh wedding anniversary.

From inside his office, Warner could hear Gabriel and Rylan, laughing and playing with Geneva.

She's good with them, he silently acknowledged, a smile forming on his lips. Warner wasn't blind. He was very aware of Geneva's feelings for him, but he couldn't act on them. He still loved Marin and was still holding on to his faith that she would one day come home.

Deep down, Warner didn't really blame Marin for her actions. He blamed Hollywood. The very same Hollywood he had once defended.

The hardest part of this for Warner was that he didn't know where Marin was. He and her parents had searched everywhere, including walking up and down streets that drug addicts were known to frequent. She was nowhere to be found.

Marin hadn't called Dru or Carol either.

Warner swallowed his anger. How could she treat them like this? *We're the people who truly care about you. Why, Marin? Why would you give up on us? On yourself?*

He didn't want to be angry. He wanted to forgive her, but he couldn't. Not yet.

"God, I need You to help me with this. I can't do it alone. I still love Marin, but there's a part of me that hates her. I'm so angry and disappointed in her. I know this is the addiction, but why can't she love us enough to fight it? Why did You bring her into my life?"

Tears ran down his face. "My heart is broken, Lord. The boys don't understand why their mother is gone. My family is in disarray. I know this is not Your will for my life. How can I lead my flock if I can't find my own way? Please help me, God. I need You."

Warner heard his children's voices and wiped away his tears. He didn't want them to see him so upset.

Gabriel ran into his bedroom, Rylan hot on his heels. "Daddy, will you tell Rylan that Mommy isn't dead. He keeps saying that Mommy's in heaven."

"Where did you hear that, Rylan?"

"When people go away, they go to heaven. Auntie says that."

Warner made a mental note to call Chanelle. He picked up Rylan, sitting him on his lap. "Mommy isn't dead. She didn't go away to heaven."

"Then where is she? Why did Mommy leave?"

"Did we do something bad?" Gabriel asked.

"No," Warner assured them. "We didn't do anything bad. Mommy is sick. She's real sick and just can't be home with us right now."

"Daddy, pray for her. Ask God to make Mommy better so that she can come home. I miss her."

"I miss Mommy, too." Warner embraced Gabriel. "I have an idea. Why don't we pray for Mommy right now?"

The boys agreed.

Heads bowed and holding hands, Warner led them in a prayer for Marin.

After Warner had the boys settled in bed, he called his sister.

"Chanelle, I need to talk to you about something you told Rylan," Warner said. "You have a minute?"

"Sure."

"Rylan mentioned earlier that his mommy was in heaven. He said that you told him when people leave they go to heaven."

"Mrs. Summers, our next-door neighbor, died a couple of months ago. She used to make the boys cookies whenever they were here with us. Rylan asked about her and I told him that she'd gone to heaven. I never said anything about Marin."

"I guess he just came to that conclusion on his own." Warner straightened his glasses. "Have they asked you about her lately?"

"Not really. They just talk about missing her." There was a brief pause. "I'm sorry if I said something I shouldn't have. I didn't even consider that Rylan would make a connection like that to Marin."

"It's not your fault," Warner assured her. "It's mine. The boys need some type of closure with this. So do I."

Warner ended his conversation a few minutes later and spent the rest of the evening in deep thought.

Sitting on a narrow bed in a small room, Marin shivered, feeling a chill from deep within. She was hungry but it wasn't the type of hunger that could be alleviated by food.

She eyed the television, listening to a voice that she'd been running from for most of her adult life. It was the same voice that had haunted her day and night, the voice that penetrated her brain no matter how high she was.

It was Warner's face on TV, but it was the voice of God that she heard.

Marin glanced down at the ragged and worn clothes draping her body. Hers was a body that men had once loved and openly admired, a body that was now nothing but skin and bones, except for the small mound in the middle.

Marin could still remember what her life was like before the drugs. She could remember her babies—her little boys—images of them in her mind, making her eyes grow wet. In her heart, she cried out to God.

I want to go home, but how can I? How can I ever face Warner, my parents . . . his family? I'm too ashamed.

Marin began to cry. This was not the way she'd ever seen her life turning out. What had happened to her?

Drugs.

She hadn't touched any since finding out about the baby she carried, and she'd even tried to pick up the pieces of her life, but she couldn't keep a job because she was sick a lot.

She was grateful to be living in transitional housing because otherwise she'd be homeless.

She'd called home a few times but hung up whenever someone answered. She had even called her parents' house but couldn't summon the courage to say anything.

She cried harder.

All she wanted was to be able to go home. But it was something that could never happen. Even if Warner forgave her for the drugs, he could never forgive her for selling her body and for being pregnant with another man's child. He was a good man. A man of God, but even men who loved God had their limits.

Marin got out of bed. She needed to go to the bathroom. As soon as she took a step, Marin doubled over in pain. She called out for help.

One of the other residents rushed into her room and was instantly by her side. "Mary, are you okay?"

"I don't know," Marin managed between groans. "I think I might be losing the baby." She hadn't been able to see a doctor this time around, so she didn't know what was going on. She'd had preeclampsia before and knew there was a chance that she would develop it again with subsequent pregnancies.

Her neighbor said, "Here, lay back down for a moment. Maybe this will pass."

Marin did as she was told.

When the pains persisted, an ambulance was called and Marin was on her way to Brooklyn Hospital Center.

Once at the hospital, Marin was seen almost immediately. When she was asked to describe her symptoms, she said, "I have some pain on my right side. And I feel dizzy at times. I've experienced bad headaches in the past during my pregnancies. I know something's not right."

She and Warner had tried for years to have another child, but she never could conceive. Now she was pregnant again. Out of such a terrible ordeal, God had given her a little girl.

After the rape, Marin couldn't summon enough courage to sell her body again, but it wasn't enough to keep her off the drugs. She didn't find the strength to fight her dependency until Tisha and Moe were arrested. While she was undergoing treatment, Marin discovered she was pregnant. Her daughter had given her a reason to keep fighting.

Marin endured a round of blood, kidney and liver tests. During the ultrasound scan, she watched her baby's heart beat and silently urged the little girl to keep fighting to survive.

They monitored the baby's heart while they waited for the results of the tests to come back.

She was scared. Not for herself but for her child. Marin didn't want to lose this little girl. "Please don't punish my baby, Lord. Please don't let her die. She deserves a real chance to make it in this world. Father God, I know what You can do. I know You are a miracle worker and I'm counting on my miracle."

Marin raised her eyes and her hands toward the ceiling. "Father, I'm counting on You to be here with me and my baby. You didn't give up on me and I'm not about to give up on this child. She's here for a reason—I believe that. Only You, God, can make something so beautiful come out of something that was so ugly. Father, I've never trusted You before . . . I trust You now. I have mustard-seed faith and I thank You for what You're about to do. I thank You. In Your holy name I fall before You. Amen."

Marin's body went as limp as a washrag. She fell back against the pillows, feeling exhausted mentally and physically. A feeling of warmth enveloped her body and she knew without a doubt that God had heard her plea. He had heard her prayer.

Placing a hand on her belly, Marin whispered, "It's going to be alright, my little sweetheart. God is not going to leave us."

CHAPTER THIRTY-ONE

"I've made a decision about my marriage," Warner announced when he sat down in the booth with Adrian. "I'm getting a divorce."

Adrian nodded in understanding. "I hate to say it but I think you're doing the right thing, Warner. Marin's too strung out on that stuff. Truth is, you don't even know if she's still alive."

Wincing at his friend's words, Warner responded, "I wish I knew for sure. That's the part that's really getting to me. And that's why this just doesn't feel right to me. Adrian, I'm not an advocate for divorce, but I don't know what else to do." Warner sighed in resignation. "I surely never thought I'd be getting one."

"Man, nobody's going to blame you for getting a divorce," Adrian responded. "You did everything you could for Marin. You tried to help her."

"I'm not worried about what people will say or think. I'm more worried about what the Word says in regards to marriage."

"Warner, your marriage isn't ending because of you. Do you really think God would want you to stay with a woman who you haven't heard from or seen in months? I don't think so."

"I know what God told me to do. He told me that Marin was the woman I should marry. *I know it.*"

"I can't argue with you about that, but did you ever consider that maybe your season with Marin is over?"

"I don't think she's dead," Warner said. "At least I hope she isn't. I think I'd feel it in here," he said, pointing to his heart.

"Maybe she was just to be with you long enough to give you Gabriel and Rylan."

"I've thought about that myself. I just know that I can't continue to live with the way things are right now. My children are hurting and I don't know how to help them because I can't help myself."

"You need some closure, Warner."

"The detectives have turned up no leads. It's like she just vanished into thin air."

Adrian gave him a sympathetic look.

"I have to have closure."

"I agree. You and your sons need to move forward with your lives. You can't just keep waiting on her to suddenly come back home."

"I know, but my heart tells me to just hold on—not to give up on her."

"So what are you going to do?"

"I have to do what's right for me and my sons." Warner picked up a menu. "I have to file for divorce. I don't really see where I have any choice."

His heart was breaking, but Warner refused to let it show. He'd prayed for so long and he'd worried for even longer. It was time to let Marin go. If God ordained it, they would find their way back to each other.

Geneva closed the door to her prayer room and fell down to her knees. Her heart was in turmoil.

"Heavenly Father, I'm in trouble. I'm in love with Warner and I know he is married to another woman, but she's not here. No one knows where she is. I love Gabriel and Rylan as if they were my own children. I need Your guidance. Father God, please show me what Your will is for my life. I don't want to go against Your will. Please show me and give me the strength to accept Your answer. In Jesus' name I pray. Amen."

Geneva sat there for a moment, quiet and listening. She needed to hear a word from God. She felt so guilty for loving Warner, but she couldn't control her feelings. They had so much in common and he was a good man who truly loved the Lord—everything she'd ever wanted in a man.

Life wasn't always fair. She knew that, but she desired God's best for her and she believed that His will was better than anything she could ever imagine.

Geneva emerged from her prayer room an hour later, still feeling a little unsettled.

She made a dinner salad and dined alone in front of her television.

"A love story . . ." the voice on the TV intoned. Geneva turned the channel to an action adventure movie. Right now that was all her heart could handle.

She answered her telephone on the first ring. "I knew it was you," Geneva said with a smile. "Hey, girl."

"What are you doing?"

"Eating a boring salad."

"I thought you might be with my brother. I called Warner a few minutes ago and he wasn't home. The nanny said he'd gone out to dinner."

"Chanelle, your brother is still very much a married man."

"Warner is getting tired of waiting on Marin to come home. Personally, I don't think she's ever going to do that, but nobody wants to hear what I have to say."

"Chanelle, Marin is an addict. She needs help."

"I agree. I just don't think she's the person to be married to Warner. She's put him through so much that he's barely holding it together."

"He loves Marin, whether or not you approve, Chanelle. I know how much you love your brother, but you've got to let him live his own life."

"I hate to see him hurting. It nearly breaks my heart."

"Chanelle, I understand. My sister and I are very close and I can't stand the guy she's married to. He's nothing but a cheating dog. The thing is, she loves him and it's her life. No matter what I say, Jenn wants to try and make her marriage work."

"I know what you're saying, Geneva. Really, I do."

"I think we should just continue to pray for Marin and Warner."

"You really are such a sweet person. That's why I love you, Geneva. And why I think you're so perfect for Warner."

"It's out of our hands. I've given this over to God and regardless, I want God's best for my life."

Marin hated hospitals.

She was lying in bed with an IV stuck in her arm and monitors attached to her belly. She ran her hand across her belly. "I've put you through so much, little one. I'm so sorry. I messed up with everyone. But I promise you—when we get out of here, I'll make it up to you. I'll find a way."

The doctor entered the room.

"Is my baby okay?" Marin questioned.

"You have preeclampsia. It's—"

Marin cut him off, saying, "I know what it is, doctor. I've had it before—with my first child. What I need to know is if you're planning to take this baby. It's too soon. She won't survive."

"We're going to take hourly blood pressure checks and several urine collections to see if the condition is getting worse. Rest assured, we're going to do everything we can to keep both you and your baby healthy."

Sunday morning, Warner walked up to the pulpit to give his first sermon in almost a month. He gave a short prayer.

Afterward he began by saying, "This morning we are going to talk about God's love for us." He opened his Bible. "For those of you who have your Bibles, please turn to the book of Hosea. I'm going to talk about what I consider to be the greatest love story ever told."

Warner straightened his glasses, then said, "The very first thing God tells us in Hosea is about what others may consider a very strange or unlikely marriage. *When the LORD began to speak through Hosea, the LORD said to him, 'Go, take to yourself an adulterous wife and children of unfaithfulness, because the land is guilty of the vilest adultery in departing from the LORD.'* When you read this chapter, what goes through your mind?

"God *directed* Hosea to take Gomer as his wife. I imagine that during their newlywed years their marriage was wonderful. When God blessed their marriage with a child, Hosea was probably floating on the clouds. I'm sure he was convinced nothing could destroy their marriage."

Warner spoke from his heart, instead of giving the sermon he'd struggled to prepare all week long. God planted the seeds of this one and Warner allowed God to move upon him.

"After the birth of Jezreel, Hosea noticed a change in his wife. She became restless and was very unhappy, but he kept on preaching. Gomer was not interested in his ministry. I believe she resented it. She probably thought he loved his ministry more than he loved her."

Warner removed his glasses and set them on the podium. "Church, the scripture doesn't outline the details of what exactly happened between Hosea and Gomer, but we have some idea. Hosea began to suspect that she was being unfaithful. When she became pregnant, he didn't believe the baby was his. It was a girl this time, and at God's direction he called her Loruhamah, meaning 'unpitied' or 'unloved.' Gomer had another child and God directed Hosea to call him Lo-ammi, which means 'not my people' or 'no kin of mine.' "

Warner walked down the steps and stood yards away from the congregation.

"It was all out in the open now. Everybody knew about Gomer's affairs. But Hosea, being a true man of God, would take her back in loving forgiveness and they would try again. It worked for a short time, then Gomer ran off with another man. I know it must have wounded Hosea to no end. He loved his wife and he was heartbroken that Gomer would choose a way of life that would no doubt end tragically. I'm sure his friends and family were telling him to move on. He was now free of the tramp, but Hosea didn't feel that way. He wanted his wife to come home. He just wanted her to come home."

Warner observed the expressions on the faces of the congregation. Shock, bewilderment, confusion. They couldn't believe that a man like Hosea would want someone like Gomer back.

It just didn't make sense. Who in his right mind would willingly welcome that kind of drama back into his life?

CHAPTER THIRTY-TWO

Her heart breaking, Geneva listened as Warner preached.

"Hosea wanted to see Gomer restored as his faithful wife and he had faith that God was great enough to do it. He soon heard that Gomer's lover had dumped her and so she'd hit rock bottom. God spoke to him, saying, *Go again, love a woman who is loved by her husband, yet an adulteress, even as the Lord loves the sons of Israel, though they turn to other gods.* God directed him."

Warner repeated his words. "God *directed* him; church . . . God wanted Hosea to go out there and find his wife, therefore proving his love to her."

The story of Hosea and the prostitute Gomer resonated with Geneva, confirming what God had placed in her spirit. Brokenhearted, she silently thanked God for His answer, although it was not the one she wanted.

Warner would never be hers.

She wiped away a lone tear sliding down her cheek. Geneva felt like she could hardly bear the pain of her heartache. Deep down, she felt like she was dying.

After church Chanelle walked over to her. "Hey, you."

Geneva pasted on a smile. "Joshua looked so cute up there singing. I don't know why Rylan won't sing in the choir. He has such a nice voice."

"He's so shy."

Geneva agreed. "He and Gabriel are so sweet. I never have any trouble with them when they come over. We just hang out, having fun."

"It sounds like you've fallen in love," Chanelle responded with a smile.

Fighting back her tears, Geneva nodded. "I have. I love those boys like they were my own."

"And Warner?"

"I need to get going. I didn't take anything out for dinner, I was in such a rush this morning."

"I have an idea. Why don't you have dinner with us? You know your godson's a little jealous that you've been spending so much time with Gabriel and Rylan."

"Thanks for the invitation, Chanelle," Geneva replied. "But I think I'll just go home and take a nap. I'm not feeling my best today."

"You can lie down in one of the guest rooms." Chanelle looped her arm through Geneva's. "C'mon."

"Okay, I think I will. I really don't want to be alone right now."

"What's going on?"

"I just have a lot on my mind."

"Does it have anything to do with Warner?"

"I'd rather not get into it right now, Chanelle. To be honest, I don't want to talk about it at all. Let's just move on."

"Sure. Whatever you want."

What I want doesn't matter, Geneva thought to herself.

Warner was just about to walk out of his office when Chanelle caught up with him.

"I've been looking for you," she said. "I wanted to see if you and the boys wanted to eat with us."

"I'm sure Mitch is tired of us coming over so much. He would probably appreciate just having you and Joshua to himself."

"Mitch doesn't have a problem with you and the boys coming over for dinner. He adores Gabriel and Rylan."

"Are you sure Mitch is okay with this?"

"Okay with what?" a voice from the hallway asked. Mitch strolled into the office.

"I invited Warner and the boys over for dinner. Tell Warner that it's okay with you."

"It's okay with me," Mitch repeated with a chuckle. "Man, you're family. You're welcome in our home anytime."

They walked out to the parking lot together.

Joshua, Gabriel and Rylan were playing under the watchful eye of Millicent. Warner greeted his mother with a kiss.

"When will Dad be back?" he questioned.

"His plane comes in around six this evening," she answered.

They arranged the time for dinner, then Warner and the boys went home to change clothes. He put the boys down for a nap before lying down himself.

An hour later Warner was up and about. He woke up Gabriel and Rylan and gave them a snack.

Shortly after four they left for Chanelle's house. Warner was surprised to see Geneva there when he arrived. His sister hadn't mentioned that she would be joining them.

"I see your sister is still up to her matchmaking," she murmured.

Warner smiled. "Maybe it's not such a bad thing," he replied. "I didn't get a chance to talk to you before you left church this morning. You looked very nice today."

"Thank you." Geneva glanced over her shoulder. "I'm helping Chanelle with dinner. We can talk later."

He was puzzled by her demeanor. Geneva always had a smile for him, but today she was acting strangely, almost as if she was upset about something.

Warner noted Geneva was quiet throughout most of dinner. She didn't smile—something she'd done frequently in the past. Warner could tell something was really bothering her.

Instinctively, he knew whatever was making her so sad had to do with him.

When Geneva got up to leave shortly after she helped Chanelle clean up the kitchen, Warner decided to walk her out.

"I haven't said anything to my family yet, but I'm filing for divorce," he told her. "Marin's not coming back and I can't go on living like this. It's not fair to me or the children."

"Are you sure about this?" Geneva questioned.

Warner nodded. "I think it's the right thing to do."

She met his gaze. "But do you know in your heart that your divorce is the answer?"

Warner met her gaze. "No," he responded truthfully. "I just can't go on like this, Geneva. It takes two people to have a marriage. Mine is short one person."

"I listened to your sermon this morning. I think the message was not only for the congregation—it was also for you. Actually, it was probably more for you than anyone else."

"What do you mean by that?"

"I didn't realize it until this morning when you gave your sermon. Warner, you're like Hosea. I think—no, I know in my heart—that God wants to restore your marriage. He wants you to go out there and find your wife. Bring her home." A lone tear rolled down her cheek. "Warner, you don't know how much this hurts me to tell you this, but I have to be obedient to the will of God."

Silence enveloped them.

"You are a very special woman, Geneva. I want you to know that I care deeply for you."

She nodded. "I know. I also know that you love Marin. She is the woman of your heart and you have to find her. I will do all I can to help you find Marin. I want you to know that."

"Geneva, I can see how much this hurts you and I'm so sorry."

She gave a slight shrug. "I'll be fine. Don't worry about me." She wiped her eyes. "I'm alright."

"I'm sorry," Warner said a second time.

"I'm going to be just fine. With God's help, I'll get through this."

"You're going to make some man a wonderful wife." Warner embraced her. "Thank you, Geneva."

She stepped away from him. "You know what they say. If you love someone, let them go. If it's meant to be, they'll come back to you." Her voice broke. "I have to let you go."

"You will always hold a place in my heart."

"I know it's supposed to make me feel better when you say that but, Warner, it doesn't. It only adds to my heartbreak." She wiped away her tears. "Go find your wife. Marin needs you." Geneva paused a moment before saying, "I forgot my purse. I need to go back inside."

Warner watched Geneva as she brushed her hair back, away from her face before going back into the house. She was a beautiful and intelligent woman, and he prayed God would bless her with a good man. He'd meant what he told her. She would make some man a wonderful wife.

Chanelle scanned Geneva's face when she walked through the front door. She looked like she'd been crying. "Honey, what's wrong?"

"It's nothing, Chanelle. I had a brief emotional moment back there, but now I'm fine."

Chanelle pulled her friend into the first-floor bedroom. "Did Warner say something to upset you? He looked so intense when you two walked outside."

"He told me that he was thinking about filing for divorce."

"Thank you, Lord," Chanelle muttered. "My brother has finally come to his senses. It's been long enough. The woman's not coming back."

Geneva held up her hand to interrupt. "Whoa. Chanelle, don't go getting too excited. I think I talked him out of it."

Chanelle gasped. "But why would you do that? I know you have feelings for my brother."

"I love him," Geneva confessed. "But Warner is a married man and he has to honor those vows."

"He's married to a prostitute. You can't be serious. Warner needs to get a divorce and marry you. You two are so good together. Everybody can see it."

"I know how you feel about Marin, but Chanelle, I prayed about this and Warner needs to find his wife. That's the right thing to do. It doesn't matter what you or I may think."

Chanelle gasped. "Geneva, what's going on with you?"

"Did you listen to Warner's sermon this morning?"

"Of course," Chanelle huffed.

"Well, remember how he compared the relationship between Hosea and Gomer to God's love and what He did when He allowed His Son, Jesus, to go to the cross?" When Chanelle nodded, she continued. "No matter how much we have sinned and gone against God's word, He's never forsaken us. He loves us no matter what. Christian husbands are commanded to love their wives as Christ loved the church, Chanelle."

"I know what you're trying to say, but you don't know Marin. She—"

"You're right, I don't know her. But I feel in my spirit that she's just someone running away from God by drowning her miseries in empty pleasures such as drugs. In the end she will be redeemed. In the end Marin will come home, Chanelle. I'm not just talking about home to Warner and the children, but home to the Lord."

"You've certainly got more faith in her than I have."

"How would you feel if God felt about you the way you feel about Marin?"

"I've never been on drugs or sold my body."

"But you have sinned. *Sin is sin.* We are all sinners, Chanelle. What if God just wanted to write us off because of what we've done?"

Geneva reached over and took Chanelle by the hand. "No matter what Marin has done, God still loves her and He wants her to come home. We should have that same attitude of forgiveness. Warner realized it and so do you. We can't sit in judgment of others when we are just as sinful. Our heavenly Father is the only judge and if He doesn't hold our sins against us, how can we hold the sins of others against them?"

Marin sat on the edge of the hospital bed, struggling to find the courage she desperately needed. If she wanted to have a safe and healthy baby, she was going to have to make some changes. And for that she needed help.

God, I need You to give me strength and courage to do this. I'm scared to death, but I don't know where else to turn. I need help and I'm not ready to deal with my mother. As hard as it is to face Warner, I know that he'll try not to judge me. I know he's not going to be happy with me, but I believe he'll do what he can for me. Please don't let him turn his back on me.

Marin picked up the telephone, then put it back down. She couldn't do it just yet. She wasn't ready to make that phone call.

God, please help me. Give me courage. This isn't about me anymore. This is for my little girl.

She picked up the phone again, vowing that this time she wasn't going to chicken out.

Marin dialed the number etched in her memory.

"Hello."

Just hearing Warner's voice sent a myriad of emotions coursing through her. Marin took a deep breath and exhaled slowly.

"Hello. Is anybody there?" After a moment he asked, "Marin, is that you?"

It was now or never.

CHAPTER THIRTY-THREE

"Marin . . ." Warner said a second time. "Is that you?"

He was about to put the phone down when he heard a voice barely above a whisper say, "Warner, I need to see you." His knees buckled, forcing him down into a nearby chair. "Where are you?"

"I'm in New York. In Brooklyn Hospital Center."

"Why are you in a hospital? Are you okay?"

"I'm as well as I can be." Marin paused for a heartbeat before saying, "I know I have no right to ask, but I really need to see you, Warner. I'm hoping that you'll say yes."

"Of course I'll come. Marin, I have been so worried about you. Everyone has. Nobody knew if you were dead or alive. To tell you the truth, we didn't know what to think."

"I'm sorry. I wasn't myself, Warner. My addiction—"

"I know."

"I've been off the drugs for almost five months now," Marin blurted out.

Warner sent up a silent prayer of thanks. "I'm so glad to hear that, Marin. But I don't understand why you never called before now."

"I've called—just didn't wait around for anyone to answer. I was too ashamed."

"I need to make arrangements for the boys and for my flight. I'll get there as soon as I can."

"Thank you, Warner. I know I don't deserve it."

They hung up.

Warner called Chanelle next.

"I just received a call from Marin," Warner told her happily. "She's in a hospital in New York. I need to leave as soon as possible. Can you watch Gabriel and Rylan for me?"

"Sure," Chanelle answered. "Just bring them over. What's going on with her? Did she overdose?"

"Marin said she's been off the drugs for months now. I don't know what's wrong with her, but it sounds like she's really sick. She sounded pretty weak on the phone."

"Don't worry about the boys. They'll be fine. Did you get a chance to speak to Pastor Elijah?"

"He's my next phone call. I'm sure, though, that he'll have no problem covering for me until I can get back."

"Warner, all I'm going to say is just guard your heart when it comes to Marin. Be careful around her."

"I'll call you once I find out what's going on. Thanks for helping me out with the boys."

After making arrangements with Elijah, Warner packed a bag for himself and one for the boys. After dropping them off at Chanelle's, he headed straight to the airport. Luckily, he'd been able to book a flight that would be leaving in two hours.

"I'll be there as soon as I can, Marin," he vowed. "Thank You, Father God. Thank You."

Marin would be coming home.

Warner was ecstatic. At least now their marriage had a fighting chance.

Warner was coming to New York.

Marin sent up a short prayer of thanksgiving. She knew that it was only because of God that Warner was making this trip.

She hoped and prayed that Warner wouldn't bring her parents with him. She wasn't ready for that. She wasn't in any shape to have a confrontation with her mother.

She glanced down at her swollen belly. "It's going to be okay, little one," she whispered. "I just want him to help us get a place of our own and to release my money so that I can take care of you. We need to be around family. I want you to know your brothers and your grandparents. We both need that."

Marin looked upward. "God, please give me the right words to say when Warner gets here. He's going to have to deal with a lot when he sees me."

Doubts crept into her head. *What if this isn't the right thing to do? What if Warner freaks out?*

"God, please don't let that happen," she whispered. "I just need a chance to apologize to him. Warner deserves that much."

In her mind, Marin went through a series of scenarios involving her and Warner, all of them ending up with him slamming the door in her face or divorcing her and taking custody of their children.

There was no way of avoiding it. Warner was going to be hurt and he would be angry. Marin just prayed that he wouldn't be vindictive.

He wasn't that kind of man, she told herself. Warner was a good man. He wouldn't be cruel. It just wasn't in his makeup.

Warner would forgive her. He might divorce her, but he would forgive her.

Marin was sleeping when Warner arrived at Brooklyn Hospital Center.

She barely resembled the woman he'd fallen in love with. Marin had been through a lot. The evidence showed clearly on her face. Her hair was much longer, almost to her shoulders. She had dark circles under her eyes and her face was pale.

Noting the sprinkling of freckles across her nose brought a smile to Warner's lips. Even now he still found her beautiful.

She stirred in her sleep but didn't wake up. Warner stepped outside of the hospital room, walking down to the nurses' station.

"Marin is my wife and I'd like to speak to her doctor."

"He'll be with you shortly."

"I hope it's not necessary to say that I'd like my wife's privacy respected. Please do not distribute any information about her to the media."

"Pastor Brice, you don't have to worry about that. We have strict rules about stuff like that. Your wife is entitled to her privacy."

Warner gave her a smile. "Thank you."

"Here's the doctor now."

The two men shook hands.

"I'm Dr. Ross. I'm sure you have lots of questions, but Mrs. Brice asked that I wait until the two of you were together before we discuss anything."

Confused by Marin's request, Warner replied, "Then I guess we should go in to see her."

Warner followed Dr. Ross back into the hospital room.

Marin was awake and sitting up when they walked in. She gave Warner a tiny smile. "You're here," she murmured.

Warner turned to the doctor and asked, "Okay, we're in here. What is going on with Marin?"

"Your wife is suffering from preeclampsia. She mentioned that she had it during a previous pregnancy. If her condition continues to improve, we might not have to worry about delivering the baby early . . ."

Warner's eyes nearly popped out of his head. Surely his ears had deceived him.

Marin was pregnant? She was carrying another man's child?

His heart broke into a million little pieces.

When Dr. Ross mentioned the word "baby," Marin noted the change in Warner's expression. Saying he was completely shocked to discover she was pregnant didn't come close.

Warner didn't say a word. He just listened.

When they were alone, Marin was the first to speak. "I'm sorry you had to find out like this. I wanted to be the one to tell you. He just didn't give me a chance."

Stunned, Warner sat down in the visitor's chair, holding his head.

"Who is the father?" he asked after a moment.

"I was raped and beaten a few months back. It was the wake-up call I needed. I went into rehab after that. After a couple of months there, the doctor told me I was pregnant." Marin looked down at her hands. "Please say something, Warner. Talk to me. Yell—just say anything."

He met her gaze. "Marin, what do you want me to say? I don't know what to say to you right now. I didn't expect to come here and find you like this."

"I'm so sorry for what I did to you. I hope that in time you'll be able to forgive me."

"This is a lot to deal with right now." Warner straightened his glasses. "We didn't know where you were for months. Marin, we didn't know if you were dead or alive."

"You have every right to be angry. I treated you horribly and, Warner, I'm truly sorry."

He held up his hand to silence her. "Marin, why did you want me to come here?"

"I need your help, Warner. As you already know, I'm about to have a baby. I need to be able to access my bank accounts so that I can find a place to live. I'm going to find work after the baby's born."

"Where are you planning on living?"

"I don't know. I was hoping to go back to Los Angeles though. I think I'm ready to be around family again. I need that right now."

Warner was quiet.

"I've been going to my meetings. Warner, I'm doing everything I'm supposed to be doing. I've been clean for months. I know I've hurt you and my parents. My children. All I'm asking is that you please help me move back to L.A. Once the baby's born—I'll find work and . . ."

Warner held up his hand to silence her. "I'm in shock right now, Marin. I need some time to . . . to think." He headed toward the door. "I'll see you in the morning. It's late and you need your rest."

She could see how much he was hurting and it pained her. Warner probably hated her now. "Are you coming back here? Or do you plan on catching the first flight to Los Angeles?"

"I'll be here in the morning. I wouldn't dream of running out on you. Good night, Marin."

Tears fell from her eyes. It broke her heart knowing that she was the source of Warner's pain.

CHAPTER THIRTY-FOUR

Warner had a long talk with God as soon as he entered his hotel suite.

"Lord, I need You to help me on this. I need to make sure I heard You right. Now, did I, or did I not, hear You say that You wanted me to marry Marin? I mean, did I jump the gun on this? I need to get this straight. I dealt with her drug use the first time and I was ready to deal with it again. But now she's pregnant with a child that isn't mine. Lord, what are You asking me to do?"

His question was met with a deafening silence.

Tears streamed down Warner's face. How could Marin do this to him?

She claimed to have been raped, so Warner was supposed to assume the baby was conceived during that violent act. Warner didn't know what he believed—after all, Marin had been arrested for prostitution.

He spent the night tossing and turning. When he still couldn't sleep, he got out of bed around four and fell to his knees praying, hoping God would give him some direction.

Later that morning Warner returned to the hospital.

He found Marin standing by the window, looking out. She turned around when he entered the room.

"Good morning," she said.

Warner returned her greeting. "Looks like you're feeling better."

"This is the first time they've let me get out of bed." Marin scanned his face. "How did you sleep?"

"I didn't," he responded. "Not much anyway. I had too much on my mind."

Her eyes became bright with unshed tears. "Warner, I'm so sorry."

He nodded. "Marin, I did a lot of praying about this. We married for better or for worse. We took vows and I take those vows seriously. I have to obey God."

"Warner, wait," Marin quickly interjected. "I know how much I hurt you. I don't expect you to take me back. I know that God would understand if you wanted a divorce. I messed up—not you."

"I thought about divorce," Warner admitted. "I can't deny that I'm still considering it—strongly. But the truth is that I don't believe that's what God wants. Until I know for sure, we need to figure out some things and we can't do it apart. I don't think so anyway."

"So what exactly are you saying?"

Warner met her questioning gaze. "I want you to come home with me."

Marin was stunned. "You *want* me to come home with you?"

"Let's be clear on this. I'm only doing it because I think it's the right thing to do. We've got to figure out where we go from there."

"Warner, I want more than anything to be with you and the boys," Marin blurted out. "I love you. That's never changed. I just want you to know that."

The room was suddenly filled with tension.

Warner cleared his throat noisily. "When you're released, I'm taking you home. I hope you don't mind, but I called your parents last night to let them know that you've been found."

Marin pulled the folds of her robe together. "What did they say?"

"They want you to know that they love you very much, Marin. Your parents want to see you."

"I want to see them, too."

"Marin, I don't know what's going to happen between us."

"I understand." She slowly made her way back to her hospital bed.

Warner was instantly by her side. "Let me help you get in," he murmured.

"Thank you."

While Marin lay in bed, Warner stood by the window looking out.

"We had so many plans," he uttered.

Marin wiped away her tears.

He turned around, facing her. "I'm not sure we can survive all this."

"We can, Warner," she responded softly. "If you give me a chance, I can make this up to you. Going through all this—it changed me. Made me grow up. I'm a different person now."

Warner turned back to stare out the window, wondering if his marriage was doomed.

Two days later Warner, Marin and her doctor flew to Los Angeles via a private plane.

During the flight, Warner was deep in thought. Marin was carrying another man's baby and it not only hurt him. It angered him as well.

God, why would You want me to stay with a woman like this? Warner thought back to the last sermon he'd preached. The one on Hosea. He recalled his words. *It is a love that bears all things, believes all things, hopes all things, endures all things, a love that never ends.*

Warner shook his head, trying to shut out the words. *How many times should I forgive Marin? If I keep forgiving her, she'll think she can do whatever she wants and I'm going to forgive her. Lord, I can't take another hurt.*

He was aware that these were his human responses. If he allowed bitterness and resentment to eat at him, he would never be able to forgive. It was going to take some time to recover from everything that had happened.

Every time Warner looked at Marin, he would be reminded of her unfaithfulness. He would be reminded of the way she'd walked out on him and their children. It would constantly prey on his consciousness. There was no way to avoid it.

But, like God's love for His people, marriage was a covenant and it couldn't be irrevocably broken by one person. Even if that one person failed to live by the terms of the covenant. He couldn't just give up on Marin because of her actions.

Warner spent the next hour silently meditating on how much God had forgiven him. He prayed in earnest, asking God to take away his destructive, unforgiving thoughts.

However, forgiveness did not necessarily mean that he had to suffer in silence.

"When are they getting here?" Marin asked for the third time since they'd arrived home. "Did Chanelle say they were on their way?"

"The boys should be home soon," Warner replied.

"I'm sorry if I'm getting on your nerves. I just really want to see my babies."

Warner didn't respond.

"I know that you're thinking I waited all this time to see them, I can wait a few minutes longer."

"Something like that," he admitted.

Marin watched him for a moment before saying, "I know you might not believe me, but I really missed my boys, Warner. I missed them every day."

"Even when you were stoned out of your mind? Did you even think about them then?"

This time it was Marin who remained silent. She had no defense— Warner was right. Nothing mattered to her when she was high. "What do you want me to say?"

"I don't expect anything from you, Marin." Warner stalked out of the room, leaving her alone with her thoughts.

He was angry and his words hurt her, cutting her deeply. *I deserve this,* she thought silently.

Chanelle and the boys arrived a few minutes later.

Gabriel and Rylan openly stared at their mother but wouldn't go to her, no matter how much she tried to coax them. "You remember me, don't you? This is Mommy . . ."

"You shouldn't try to force them, Marin. Don't forget that you've been gone a long time."

Marin sent Chanelle a sharp look. "Thank you for watching *my* sons. But now that they're home, Warner and I will see to them."

Chanelle's eyes traveled down to Marin's stomach, then back up to her face. "I think you have enough to worry about right now."

Warner grabbed his sister by the arm. "Not in front of my sons.

Thank you so much for taking care of Gabriel and Rylan. I'll give you a call in the morning. Okay?"

"You just remember what I told you." Chanelle turned and walked out of the house.

Marin smiled at Gabriel. "Come here, sweetie. Mommy just wants to give you a hug."

Gabriel looked up at Warner, who gave a slight nod. He walked over to Marin. She pulled him into her arms. "I missed you so much, baby."

Seeing his big brother with Marin, Rylan slowly ventured closer. Smiling, she held out her arms to him. "C'mere, sweetie. I want to give you a hug, too."

Tears ran down Marin's face as she reveled in the nearness of her boys. Her babies. She was home—finally.

Marin offered to give the boys their bath, but Warner insisted on handling the task himself.

"I'm their mother. I know how to bathe them."

"You've been gone a long time, Marin. Give them some time to adjust."

She backed down. "You know, when your sister was here, I really thought that you would come to my defense since I'm still your wife and the mother of your children."

"Defend you," Warner repeated. "How can I defend you when I feel the exact same way?"

Stunned by the look of disgust on his face and the tone of his voice, Marin didn't respond.

Warner took the boys upstairs for their bath.

She picked up their wedding album, thumbing through and remembering happier times.

Marin heard Warner coming down the stairs and put the album back on the coffee table.

"I put your things in the guest room across from the boys' room," Warner announced when he walked back into the family room.

Surprised, Marin could only nod. She hadn't really considered where she would be sleeping or whether she would sharing a bed with him, but his announcement still stunned her. "I'm staying in one of the guest rooms?"

"We have a lot to deal with right now. It's going to take some time to sort everything out. Sleeping together is just not something I think we should do."

"I understand, Warner."

"I thought you might want to be near the boys."

"That was very thoughtful of you," Marin said with an ease she didn't feel. She had no right to feel hurt, but she did. Warner's actions wounded her deeply.

"I think I'll go upstairs and lie down for a little while," Marin announced. "I'm feeling tired."

"I'm going to fix Gabriel and Rylan something to eat. Would you like something?"

Marin shook her head no. She didn't know how much she could bear Warner being overly polite to her. She knew he was trying so hard, but that only added to her guilt.

"Where is she? Where is Marin?" Shirley questioned as soon as she entered the house. She and Robert arrived twenty minutes after Warner called to let them know Marin was home.

"She's upstairs resting," Warner responded. "In the first guest room on the right."

"The first guest room . . ." Shirley's eyes widened in her surprise. Looking at him, she demanded, "Why is she in a guest room?"

"We have a lot to work out," Warner explained. "A lot has happened over the past few months to change both of us."

Robert nodded in understanding. "We appreciate you bringing Marin home. Especially after all she's put you through."

"Warner, tell me something . . ." Shirley began. "Why did you bring her here? You could've brought her home to us while you two sort everything out. Her father and I would love to have her stay with us. We could keep an eye on her."

"She's my wife and the mother of my children. She should be home with us."

"Are you sure that you're up to this?" Robert queried. "Is Marin?"

"We're going to take it one day at a time. That's all we can do. If it doesn't work out . . . we'll have to see what needs to be done at that time."

Shirley pointed toward the staircase. "I'm going up to see my daughter. Did you tell her that we were coming by?"

"You asked me not to."

Robert gave his wife a puzzled look. "Why would you do that?"

Shirley shrugged nonchalantly. "I didn't want to give her a chance to say she didn't want to see us."

Warner watched his mother-in-law take the stairs up to the second level. He hoped Shirley's visit didn't upset Marin. She was still in a very fragile state.

"Marin . . ."

She glanced up from her reading. "Mom, what are you doing here?"

"I wanted to see you. Your father will come by later." Shirley surveyed her. "Honey, you look . . . Where have you been?"

"On the streets. I stayed in shelters whenever I could until I was able to get into transitional housing."

"Marin, why didn't you come to us?"

"I did, remember? You turned me away."

"You were on drugs. Warner told us that you've been off drugs for months. You could have come to us. For goodness' sakes, we're your parents. What can we do to help you now?"

"I just need to know that you and Daddy still love me. I know I'm a big screwup and I know that I've embarrassed you both, but I hope that somewhere deep inside you . . . you still love me." Marin wiped her eyes. She didn't want to fall apart like this in front of her mother.

Shirley embraced her. "We will always love you."

"I really messed up."

"We'll get you all the help you need, darling. Don't you worry."

Marin removed her blanket. "Mom, I'm afraid you and Daddy can't help me with this."

Shirley gasped. "Y-You're pregnant?"

"Yes."

Shirley was thoroughly disgusted. "No wonder Warner has you in here. It's a blessing he even let you back into the house. Most men wouldn't."

Marin's tears wouldn't stop flowing. "I know that. Warner is a wonderful man, but he's also human. I can tell he's hurt by all this. He'll hardly look at me and he won't even stay in the same room with me too long."

"Well, you can't possibly blame him."

"I don't."

"Has he spoken of divorce?"

"Just briefly, but he said he needs to make sure it's what God wants." Marin combed her fingers through her hair. "I'm sure it's coming though. Maybe it's because I'm not feeling well right now, but I don't expect him to stay married to me. I've put him through too much for that."

"I believe Warner still loves you, but I agree. You have put him through entirely too much. I think maybe you should just come home with us."

Shaking her head, Marin responded, "Not just yet. I want to try and make up for what I've done. I don't want to just give up yet. I have to try and fight."

"Fight for what?"

"My marriage."

"Marin, dear, you need to be realistic. Your marriage ended the day you walked out of this house chasing after the drugs you were taking. Warner will never accept that child you're carrying. *You know that.*"

Marin folded her arms across her chest. "I'm not going to give up hope until I have no other choice."

"I worry about you, Marin. You're not a very strong person. I'm afraid Warner's rejection will kill you. Please come home with me and your father."

Marin shook her head no. "Not yet. I have to try and see if there's a chance to save my marriage. Mom, I can see it in his eyes. Warner still loves me."

"I know he cares for you, Marin. You are the mother of his children. He will probably always care for you—he just won't be married to you."

Marin refused to give up hope. "It's more than that, Mom. Deep down, Warner still loves me. I know he does."

"I don't want to see you get hurt, dear."

"All I can do is try to make things work. If I'm wrong, then I'll pick up my pride and move on with my life. Even if Warner is never able to forgive me, I will still be a mother to my boys. I'm not going to lose them again."

CHAPTER THIRTY-FIVE

Shortly after Marin's parents left, Warner went upstairs to check on her mental state. He wanted to make sure Shirley hadn't upset her. He paused for a minute outside the room. He wasn't sure what he'd say to Marin. He was trying to deal with his own bitterness.

He breathed in deeply and exhaled slowly. He knocked before walking into the bedroom. Marin was sitting in a chair by the double window.

She glanced over at him. "Mom asked me if you'd brought up the subject of divorce."

"What did you tell her?"

"I told her the truth—that you hadn't completely put it out of your mind. That you wanted to be sure divorce was the right thing to do." Marin paused a moment before adding, "She asked me to come home with her and my father. She thinks that would be best for me."

"How do you feel about it?"

Marin shrugged. "I really don't know. I want to stay here with you and the boys, but I have to be honest—I feel like I'm walking around waiting for the other shoe to drop. Warner, are you going to divorce me? Because this is what I believe. I believe that you're just waiting to make sure I'm okay health-wise. I just need you to confirm it for me so that I can move on with what's left of my life."

"Right now, I don't want to speak of divorce. Let's just get you better."

"So I'm right. You are waiting on me to get well." Marin chewed on her bottom lip a moment before continuing. "You don't have to do that, Warner. I don't deserve your kindness. It's not a problem for me to just move in with my parents until I figure out what I'm going to do. I don't want you to have to see me like this. I know how much it must hurt you."

Warner couldn't deny that it hurt to see her pregnant with another man's child, so he didn't respond.

"I told you the truth. I was raped and beaten. The guy left me on the street to die. I considered having an abortion, but when I thought of how long you and I tried to have another baby—I just couldn't discard this child's life that easily. This baby is a miracle—my miracle. Regardless of how she was conceived."

"It's a girl?"

She nodded. "Warner, I love you and I want to give our marriage a fighting chance, but if you don't want me here . . . I understand."

"Right now, I think it would be best for you to stay here in the house with the boys. You need to rebuild a relationship with them and you can't really do that if you're at your parents' house."

"Warner, are you sure about this? Do you really want me here?"

"I think it's for the best," he responded. "At least for the time being."

"I'm sure your family—especially your sister—most likely disagree."

"It doesn't matter." Warner picked up his Bible, saying, "I'll be in my office for the next hour or so. Call me if you need anything."

He left the room without waiting for a response.

Lord, he's so hurt. Please show me how to help Warner through this storm. Heavenly Father, it was You who helped me kick the drugs. I don't think I knew it then, but I do now. You have been with me every step of the way—even when I didn't acknowledge You or give You the glory. Father, this prayer is not for me. It's for Warner. I am so sorry for everything I've done and I want to be a better person. I love my husband and I know he loves me, too. We made vows and we both want to honor them. I have to believe that, Father. Only You can bring restoration to our marriage, if it is Your will.

When she finished praying, Marin felt better, although her heart still ached for Warner.

*   *   *

Warner stepped inside his office, shutting the door, and immediately began praying.

Lord, what do you want me to do in this situation? I know what my flesh is telling me, but I strive to do what thus says the Lord. I'm angry. I'm so angry. My family is angry. On top of that, what am I supposed to say to my congregation?

Surely you haven't called me to stand for You and be ashamed and publicly humiliated.

Warner paced back and forth in his office for a moment before picking up his Bible and turning to Hosea. Sitting down on the leather sofa, he began rereading the first chapter.

Meditating on the scriptures, Warner allowed God to speak on his heart.

God tells us how much our sin grieves Him. If I want my marriage to be restored, then I have to be honest with Marin. I have to share with her what is on my heart. I can't give in to my wanting to retaliate. I have to absolve Marin of all guilt. That's what it means to have a forgiving love. God uses that kind of love to melt the hardest of hearts. This is the lesson of Hosea and Gomer—a story of love and redemption.

"I'm going into the office today," Warner announced when Marin came down to breakfast the next morning. "I won't be late. Mrs. Kelly will be here to prepare some meals for us. She'll be coming around noon. Just let her know what you'd like from the store and she'll be more than happy to pick it up."

"You hired a cook?"

"It was necessary. Don't you agree?"

Nodding, Marin sat down at the table with her sons. "Good morning," she said to them.

"Morning, Mommy," Rylan responded.

"I can't believe how big you boys have grown. I've missed you both so much."

"Are you still sick?" Gabriel blurted out.

Marin glanced over at Warner before responding, "I'm feeling much better this morning."

He broke into a big grin. "I'm glad. I don't want you to be sick no more."

"If you come give me a hug, I think that'll make me feel so much better."

Gabriel hugged her.

"I wanna give you a hug, too."

Laughing, Marin embraced Rylan. "I love you both so much."

Warner stood by, watching his sons with their mother. He hadn't seen them this happy in months. Bringing her home had been the right thing to do.

Two day later, Chanelle was in his office when Warner arrived at the church.

"Warner, what on earth are you thinking about?" She demanded, closing the door so they wouldn't be overheard. "I know it's not your children because I know you wouldn't dare let that woman back into the house."

"Marin is my wife."

She sighed in frustration. "You sound like a broken record. She walked out on you and on the children. The woman was a prostitute. How can you let her back into your bed?"

"She didn't move back into our bedroom, Chanelle. Just back into the house. Not that it's any business of yours."

She released a sigh of relief. "Thank You, Jesus. At least you had enough sense to keep her out of your bedroom. Marin broke your heart."

"Give her a break. Marin was on drugs, Chanelle. She wasn't in her right mind."

"And she is now?"

"She's clean. She's been clean for months."

"By whose account? And I noticed that she's pregnant again. I know that can't be your baby. Probably some trick's baby." Chanelle wore a look of disgust on her face. "I just don't understand how you can let her come back here carrying another man's child."

"It's the right thing to do."

"God won't hold you accountable for divorcing Marin. She committed adultery. You have the Godly right to divorce her."

"Sis, we're talking in circles."

"Fine . . . Warner, I'm going to stay out of this thing between you and Marin."

"I've been asking you to do that for months, Chanelle. You never liked her. You can't see things objectively."

"Geneva is a wonderful woman and she cares a great deal for you. You missed out on a very special lady. One day you're going to realize it."

"I know how wonderful she is, Chanelle. *I know.* And if I weren't married to Marin—who knows what would've happened? But the fact of the matter is that I am a married man. Until God tells me otherwise, Marin and I are not getting a divorce. I'm not having this discussion with you ever again, Chanelle."

Warner turned on his computer. "If you don't mind, I have a lot of work to do."

Marin was getting frustrated with the way Warner hovered around her and the boys. It was as if he didn't trust her to be alone with them. She would never hurt Rylan and Gabriel.

She fought back tears as she watched them playing with trucks in their room.

Gabriel looked up and saw her standing in the doorway. His smile disappeared. "You okay?" he asked.

She nodded.

"Then why do you look like you're gonna cry? Are you sad?"

"No. I'm happy, sweetie. Very happy." Marin strode into the room. "Can I play with you?" she asked.

Rylan broke into a grin. "Yeah."

Gabriel suddenly pushed away his truck, saying, "I don't want to play anymore."

Marin sat down on Rylan's bed. "I'd like to talk to you two about why I was gone."

"You were sick," Rylan supplied.

"I was." Marin confirmed his statement. "Because I was sick, I wasn't able to be a mother to you and I'm so sorry about that. I love you both so much. I want you to know that. I really do."

"What if you get sick again?" Gabriel asked. "Will you leave us again?"

"I'm going to do everything I can to keep from getting sick like that again. But I want you to know something. No matter what happens, I will always love you." Marin put her hand on Gabriel's chest. "I want you to keep me in here. If you do that, you'll always feel my love."

"I love you, Mommy, and I missed you so much."

Rylan snuggled up to her, saying, "Me, too. I love you."

Marin wrapped her arms around both of her sons. "My babies . . . I love you and I don't want to ever let you go."

She was thrilled to be back at home. This was where she belonged—if only she could've seen it before.

Shirley accompanied Marin to her doctor's appointment the following day.

They sat down in the reception area, waiting for the nurse to call Marin.

"Mom, thanks so much for coming with me today. I thought it would be too much for Warner."

"I think you're right. Have you thought about what you're going to do?"

Marin glanced over at her mother. "About what?"

"About the baby," Shirley responded in a whisper. "If you want any chance with Warner, you're going to have to put that baby up for adoption."

"I've thought about it," Marin confessed. "But, Mom, I don't think I can do that. This may not be Warner's child, but she's mine. This is my little girl."

"Warner will not ever accept that child. You're asking too much of him if you expect him to."

"Mom, you don't know that. Stop being so negative. I can't handle that right now. I've given this to God and I have to leave it there."

Marin released a short sigh of relief when the nurse called her name. She was trying so hard to maintain her optimism, but her mother's negativity wasn't helping.

Inside the examination room, the doctor checked her out and ordered blood tests.

She scheduled her next appointment and they left.

On the way home Shirley said, "I have an idea. Why don't you make a special dinner for you and Warner tonight? The boys can stay with me and your father."

"I think that's a wonderful idea, but I would rather the boys stay home with us. Maybe a family dinner will help bridge the gap some, though."

Marin pulled out her cell phone. "I'll call Sylvia and have her pick up some stuff for me from the supermarket."

"What are you going to have her cook?" Shirley inquired.

"I'm going to do the cooking. This dinner has to be prepared by my hands. It's special."

"Honey, are you up to taking on a task like that? Why don't you let me prepare the meal for you?"

Marin shook her head. "Mom, I want to do this. I need to do this for myself and for Warner. We need to find a way to put all that's happened behind us. I want it to start with a dinner that I cooked with my own hands."

"Then just let me help you. It would be a shame for you to end up getting sick."

Marin laughed. "You are just so positive today."

"Sweetie, I'm just trying to help you."

"I know and I thank you for it. I really do appreciate you, Mom. I don't know what I'd do if I didn't have you right now. Warner's so distant, but I can't really blame him." Marin played with the ribbon on her shirt. "I've got to find a way to reconnect with him. If I don't—I'm going to lose him."

Shirley reached over, taking Marin's hand. "Now who's being negative?"

CHAPTER THIRTY-SIX

Warner wiped his mouth with the corner of his napkin. "Dinner was delicious. You did an outstanding job."

Warner's compliment made her smile. Marin had wanted tonight to be perfect. "I'm glad you enjoyed it. I can't believe I actually remembered how to cook beef Stroganoff. I only cooked it that one time and I found a recipe in one of the cookbooks on the shelf."

After dinner he helped her clean up the kitchen while the boys watched cartoons on the television in the family room.

"They're getting so big," Marin murmured. "Gabriel's looking more like you every day."

Warner chuckled. "He's something else. Just yesterday, he came and told me that God spoke to him and said that he's to be a good boy every day."

"He told you that?"

"Yeah. I asked him if he was going to do what God told him and he said, "I have to, Daddy, because God told me to do it."

"You've done a wonderful job with them," Marin acknowledged. "I'm so proud of them."

"They are very smart. And Gabriel has a nice singing voice. That boy can sing."

"I can't wait to hear him. Do you mind if I help you get them ready for bed tonight?"

"I think the boys will like that."

After getting the boys settled in bed, Warner walked Marin over to the guest bedroom. "I think I'm going to turn in early. I'll see you in the morning."

"Tonight was good, don't you think?" she asked.

Warner agreed.

"Warner, I miss you so much. I—"

"Marin, don't . . ."

"Warner, I thought—" Marin stopped short, then began again. "I thought you said you still loved me."

"I do. I will always love you, but this . . . I can't go back there with you."

"Because of the baby?"

"Yes," Warner admitted. "That and everything you've put me through."

"You speak of forgiveness in church on Sundays, but you haven't forgiven me."

"Marin, I have forgiven you. If I hadn't, you wouldn't be in this house. I am human. I can't just dismiss the past—everything you've done. I'm sorry."

"I thought you wanted us. I thought you wanted the marriage."

"I am just as committed to our marriage as I was on our wedding day. But you can't expect me to just act like nothing's changed. Marin, you're carrying the child of another man."

Tears slipped from her eyes. "A man that raped me. He raped me, Warner."

"But that wasn't the only time you—" He removed his glasses. "I don't want to talk about this. We were having a pleasant evening and I don't want to ruin it."

"You can't ruin it," Marin muttered. "I did that a long time ago."

Warner didn't respond.

"I just want a chance to make it up to you. Please let me try, Warner. Please." She was crying harder now.

"I don't want you to get upset, Marin. It's not good for your child."

"I can't take this distance between us."

Warner wiped his eyes. Making sure to keep his voice low, he said,

"Marin, how do you think I feel? Do you realize that I'm dying inside having to see your body growing with another man's child? What do you think people are saying? Read the tabloids. You've made me look like a fool."

Marin could feel the heat of his anger. She could feel his heartache. She opened her mouth to speak, but he wouldn't let her get a word out.

"I am the laughingstock of Los Angeles. The whole world knows that you—my wife—were a hooker and now you're carrying the baby of one of your tricks. What did I do to deserve this?"

"You didn't do a thing, Warner." Tears ran down her face. "I'm the one at fault and I take full responsibility. All of this is my fault."

"Marin, this is getting us nowhere. I'm tired and I'm sure you must be exhausted. Thank you for dinner, but I need some time alone. I'm not ready for such an emotionally draining discussion. I'm just not ready."

"Warner, we have to find a way to get past the pain. If we can't, then I don't need to be living here." Marin wiped her face with the back of her hands. "Maybe I should move in with my parents for a while."

After a moment, Warner muttered, "Maybe you should." Without another word he walked away from her.

The next morning Shirley arrived shortly after Warner left to go to his office. "Good morning, dear. How did your dinner go last night?"

Marin released a long sigh. "Mom, I made a complete fool of myself. Warner is so angry with me—I don't think we'll ever get past this." She burst into tears.

Embracing Marin, Shirley responded, "Honey, give him more time. Warner's been through a lot."

"I know that." Wiping her face, she replied tearfully, "Mom, I love him. I really love Warner. Being in this house has reminded me of how much I had with him. I don't want to leave. I want my family back."

"Has he asked you to leave?"

"Not really. I mentioned that maybe I should move in with you and Dad. Warner agreed."

"Oh, honey, I'm so sorry."

"I will do anything to save my marriage. Mom, I don't want to lose him."

Shirley poured herself a cup of coffee. "What if he wants you to give up that baby you're carrying?"

"This baby is part of my family. Besides, Warner and I always wanted a little girl."

"She's not his daughter," Shirley gently reminded her.

"I can do without your negativity. If Warner loves me enough—we can get through this. I have to hold on to that belief . . ." Marin's voice died.

"What is it, dear?"

She shook her head. "Just forget about it, Mom. Let's change the subject."

Shirley shrugged. "Sure. No problem. I was thinking that if you're feeling up to it, we should do a little shopping. You're going to need some decent maternity clothes."

Marin pulled a newspaper out of the wastebasket. "I can't believe Warner actually brought this into the house." She laid the tattered *National Star* on the counter. "This isn't helping things between us. Why won't they leave us alone?"

On the front page, the headline read, AN ACT OF FORGIVENESS: FALLEN ACTRESS MARIN ALEXANDER IS CARRYING LOVER'S CHILD & HUSBAND ALLOWS HER TO COME HOME.

"This sounds so ugly. No wonder Warner's so upset." Marin turned to her mother. "Mom, I need you to help me pack what little stuff I have. I can't do this to him. I can't keep torturing Warner. He deserves better."

"Are you sure this is what you want to do?"

"What I want is to stay here in my home with my family, but I don't want to humiliate them."

That evening when Warner walked into her parents' house, a strange expression on his face, Marin tried to mentally prepare herself for what she thought was about to happen. He was going to ask for a divorce.

"Warner, what's wrong?" she asked, although she already knew the answer.

"I was surprised to find that you'd moved out of the house."

Marin laid down the book she was reading. "You shouldn't have been. When we talked the other night, I was left with the impression that this is what you wanted."

He sat down in one of the chairs facing her. Warner looked as if he was struggling to find the right words.

She decided to make it easy on him. "I think I know what you're about to say," Marin stated quietly. "You want a divorce, don't you? I saw the *National Star* and I can imagine how humiliated you must feel."

"I don't think you can ever imagine what I'm feeling." Warner eyed her for a moment, straightening his glasses. "I came here to apologize for coming down so hard on you. I was wrong."

"I deserved it."

"The reason I came here is because I . . . Marin, I'd like for you to come back home. The boys are confused and they're asking for you."

"Is that the only reason you're asking me to come home?"

"I think we should take it one day at a time. I can't promise any more than that."

"I'm not asking for any more than that, Warner."

Marin jumped.

"What's wrong?" he asked out of concern.

Placing her hand on her stomach, she said, "The baby—she just moved. She's so active."

"The doctors . . . are they saying that she's okay?"

Marin's eyes traveled to Warner's face. "Do you really want to hear about the baby?"

"Yeah."

"Do you mind if I ask why?"

"She's your child and you're my wife. If we are going to have even the smallest chance to work this out, we have to address this issue."

"My baby is not an *issue*, Warner. She is an innocent little baby who was conceived out of a horrible situation. She saved me, you know. I was about to leave rehab, but I passed out before I could walk out the doors.

That's when I found out I was pregnant. She's the reason I stayed clean. I didn't want to bring a drug baby into the world. I couldn't do that to a child."

Warner nodded in understanding.

Smiling, Marin said, "She's moving again. This girl has a strong kick. I'm thinking she's my football player. The boys never kicked me so hard."

"Marin, I don't know if I've told you this, but I'm very proud of you. It takes a lot of courage to kick an addiction—any addiction."

"It's going to be a battle for me for the rest of my life, but as long as God gives me the strength to resist temptation, I intend to fight with everything I have in me."

Marin rose slowly. "I'm going to bed. I'm kind of tired." She leaned against the chair, a tiny moan escaping her lips.

Warner stood up and wrapped an arm around her. He pressed his other hand to her stomach. "Give your mother a break, little one."

He felt the baby move—maybe she was stretching. It didn't feel like a foot. Warner imagined it was a little hand, pressing against his large one. Warmth radiated within him. He snatched his hand away.

"She's an innocent baby, Warner," Marin whispered. "She can't hurt you."

Two days later Warner announced that his parents had invited them to dinner.

"Maybe you and the boys should go to your parents' house without me. You know how they feel about me."

"Marin, you're my wife and we have to find a way to be a family once again. Hiding here won't do that."

"I'm just not ready. Especially if Chanelle is going to be there. I don't want to deal with her attitude."

"My sister won't bother you, Marin. I'll see to that."

"I really think you'd have a better time if you and the boys go alone, Warner. I don't mind staying home by myself."

"We have to start the healing process somewhere. Marin, I want you to come with us."

She gazed at her husband. "You're sure about this?"

Warner nodded.

"Okay . . . I guess I'll get dressed, then." Marin went upstairs to her room and searched through the closet, looking for something to wear. She decided on black pants with a black and white top.

Warner and the boys were in the foyer waiting when she came downstairs.

"You look nice," he complimented.

"Thanks," Marin muttered.

Reaching for the doorknob, Warner said, "We'd better get going. We don't want to be late."

They drove to Beverly Hills in silence except for the music drifting from the radio and random questions from the boys.

When they pulled into the circular driveway, Marin could feel her heart racing. She prayed the evening would pass with little or no drama.

Warner came around the car, opening the door for her. Marin took a deep breath, then exhaled slowly before getting out. "Here we are," she whispered.

"It's going to be okay, Marin."

She looked up at him. "Warner, I really hope you're right."

"Hello, Marin," Millicent greeted her.

"Thank you for including me."

She nodded stiffly, then stepped out of the way.

Chanelle and Mitch were in the family room with Garfield. She waved at Warner, but she totally ignored Marin.

The boys spotted Joshua on the floor watching a Disney video and joined him.

Garfield got up and gave Marin a hug. "I'm glad you're well. We were very worried about you."

"Thank you for saying that." Marin glanced over her shoulder at Chanelle, then back at him. "It's nice to see a friendly face."

"I realize you were sick. I just wish you'd turned to us."

"I'm sorry. I wish I could go back and do this all over again, but I can't."

"No point in looking in the past, Marin. You have to learn from your mistakes and move forward."

Dinner conversation was forced and Marin noted that Chanelle refused to even look in her direction.

No one made reference to the baby she was carrying, although that didn't really surprise Marin. She fully expected them to act just the way they were because they didn't care for her and made no bones about it.

It didn't matter to her. Marin cared only about what Warner and her children thought of her.

CHAPTER THIRTY-SEVEN

Marin couldn't seem to get rid of her headache. She stayed in bed most of the day. The cook Warner had hired kept coming upstairs to check on her.

Her father stopped by the house shortly after two.

Smiling, she sat up in bed when he walked into the bedroom. "Hey, Daddy."

He sat down beside her. "You look tired."

Lifting a hand to her head, Marin responded, "I have a headache. I've had it for a couple of days now. It's probably stress-related."

"How is Warner treating you?"

"Good," Marin murmured. "Daddy, he's a good man."

"Your mama tells me that he's not taking you to church with him. Why is that? Is he ashamed of you?"

"No, that's not it at all. Warner just doesn't want me to overdo it. My blood pressure's been a little elevated lately."

She watched his eyes widen with concern. "I'm worried about you, Marin. If that headache doesn't go away, you need to call the doctor."

She embraced him. "Daddy, I love you, but you worry way too much. I'm going to be fine. I just need to take it easy. I've been stressing a lot about my marriage. I don't want to lose Warner."

Robert kept Marin company until she fell asleep. When she woke up two hours later, he was gone.

Her headache, on the other hand, was still there.

Everyone at church continued to ask about Marin. Warner assured them that she was fine and on the road to recovery. He considered the matter settled until he heard Hazel and Elijah talking.

"I think he either needs to get a divorce or step down as pastor of this church, Elijah. How can he lead us if he can't manage his own household?"

"Hazel, stop talking like that. Warner built Victory Baptist. This is his church."

"It could be our church if you weren't so meek. I like Pastor Warner, but that's got nothing to do with the truth. He married an actress. There are plenty of God-fearing folk right here in church but he didn't pick not one. You know he's been running around with that lady Geneva. It's a mess, I'm telling you."

Warner stepped into the office, interrupting them. "I couldn't help but overhear your conversation."

Hazel's mouth dropped open. "P-Pastor . . ."

"I know that you probably don't understand this, but then again, it's not about you. Obeying God means to go against all human wisdom and judgment, against all of your own desires, against your religious convictions and your moral standards. It means that you have this willingness to trust God for the outcome. Even if it means being ridiculed by everyone. It's what we all must do in our marriages, Hazel. We have to place our relationship in God's hands and trust Him."

Elijah nodded in agreement. "We have to love people in spite of their faults."

"Yes," Warner stated. "That's what every marriage is about—loving someone in spite of their faults."

"Pastor, I'm sorry," Hazel murmured. "I had no right discussing your personal business."

Elijah walked over to Warner and said, "You preached on Hosea and Gomer a while back and God just placed this in my spirit. All Hosea wanted was for Gomer to be a good wife and to love him. He just wanted her to do right. Gomer became an inspiration to Hosea's life. He was reminded of God's love every time he looked at her. Through his experience, Hosea came to understand why it was so important to God that Israel do right and that they love Him. It's what we all want. I'd like to think that Gomer did come to love Hosea."

Warner smiled his gratitude. "Thank you, Elijah. I really needed a word today. Thank you."

Warner left the church and stopped by the grocery store to pick up a few items.

"I see you're following me again."

Standing in the cereal aisle, Warner turned around, looking surprised. "Geneva, how are you?"

"I'm okay. And you? Things going well at the house?"

"Marin and I are talking," Warner told her. "Right now, that's all I have to offer."

"You've been through a lot. I'm sure she has too. Just take it one day at a time."

"We are," he confirmed. "Geneva, I'm so sorry. I—"

Cutting him off, she said, "Warner, you did the right thing. I'll be fine. Don't worry about me."

"I never meant to hurt you."

"Warner, it's okay," she assured him. "You did the right thing. Just be happy."

"Thank you, Geneva."

"Good seeing you again, Warner. You take care."

He gave a slight nod, then watched Geneva leave. Warner thought about Marin and how much he loved her. For so many months he'd prayed for her to come home. That prayer had been answered, but not in the way he'd imagined it.

To say he was hurt just didn't aptly describe his emotions. He was angry and he resented Marin, although he was diligently trying to work through his feelings.

Forgiveness wasn't out of the question, but deep down Warner didn't know if he and Marin could ever recapture the love they'd once shared. He still loved her, but maybe it was already too late for them.

❉   ❉   ❉

"Lord, I know what I need to do," Marin murmured. "I've given my life back to You, but I can't just let it go at that. I need to tell others how You brought me out of the darkness. I need to testify how You redeemed me. I can't hide out in this house any longer. I'm going to church with Warner on Sunday."

Marin wasn't so sure she was ready to stand up in front of Warner's congregation, but she felt she had no other choice. She loved her husband and she wanted him to see how far she'd come in her walk with God.

"You look like you're feeling better," Warner told her when she came downstairs.

"Actually, I am," Marin confirmed. She pointed to his face. "You have new glasses. I like them."

He smiled. "Thanks."

Marin sat down at the breakfast bar beside Warner. "How are things going at the church?"

"In what way do you mean?"

"I'm sure people have had something to say about me. Are they giving you a hard time?"

Warner shook his head no. "Everything is fine, Marin. You don't have to worry about me. I can handle whatever is thrown my way."

"You shouldn't have to go through this alone. I'm the one who messed up."

Warner's eyes traveled to her swollen belly. "There's nothing we can do about it now."

Marin was up and dressed by the time Warner and the boys came downstairs the following Sunday.

He looked her up and down before asking, "Where are you going?"

"To church with you and the boys," she announced with a smile. "We're still a family and my place is with you at Victory Baptist."

"I think it would be better if you just stayed home."

"Why? Are you ashamed of me?"

He didn't respond.

"Are you?" Marin prompted. *"Tell me."*

A flash of anger showed in Warner's eyes. "I will not have you make a mockery of me in my own church. We've been the subject of gossip for long enough. I would rather the members focus on my sermon and not on you." Turning to the boys, he said, "C'mon, let's head out to the car."

Marin was not going to be deterred.

She grabbed him by the arm. "Warner, I'm going to church with you and my sons. I need to go. Please. How can you deny me a chance to get my life right with God?"

Her question was met with silence.

Shoulders slumped, Warner sighed in resignation, then said, "Let's go."

Marin released a short sigh of relief. She'd crossed one hurdle. The next would come once they were at the church.

Warner didn't know why Marin had suddenly decided to come to church, but he didn't want to deny her a chance to worship the Lord.

He'd never pressed her about attending before because she'd not been feeling well; then he'd just assumed she was too embarrassed to show her face, but the truth was that he would be the one humiliated.

There were days when he felt he could deal with his situation head-on, but then there were the times when he just wanted to bury his head in the sand.

Marin's appearance in church this morning certainly caused heads to turn. He admired her courage as she strolled down the aisle, her head up, as if she didn't have a care in the world.

Warner got up and preached a sermon he'd been working on for a couple of weeks. A couple of times, his eyes teared up and his voice broke, but he continued on.

"So how much do you trust Him?" he asked. "Do you trust Him enough to let go and let God?"

Marin noticed there was a new tone in Warner's preaching. His sermons were no longer spoken with thunder, but with tears.

Warner closed out his sermon and did the altar call. Chewing on her bottom lip, Marin rose slowly.

She walked up to the front, clearly surprising Warner.

He'd had no idea what she was about to do. She hadn't told him.

Warner met her at the bottom step. "Are you sure you want to do this?"

"No," she confessed truthfully. "But I have to do it now. It's what God laid on my heart."

"What are you going to do?"

"Just listen."

Warner handed her the microphone.

"Good morning, church. I'm sure you're all probably wondering why I'm standing up here."

Marin could hear the low murmurings and whispers floating throughout the sanctuary, but she ignored them. "I'm up here because . . . because I need your prayers and your forgiveness." Her eyes teared up.

"I'm sure all of you know that I had a problem. A drug problem. It was a problem so addictive that I would do anything to score some coke."

A tear rolled down her cheek. "I lied to my husband . . . to my family and my friends. Getting high was all I wanted to do. I'm standing here right now because I want you to know that God delivered me of my dependency. God saved me."

The applause was deafening.

Warner embraced her, giving her the support she needed while facing the huge congregation. A few of the church members eyed her with open disdain, but Marin didn't falter.

"We search and we search for something to make us happy—to make us feel satisfied with our lives. I thought I knew what was best for me, what I needed. I don't know if you realize it, but you can get in a lot of trouble when you're out there just trying to survive on your own. I had to hit rock bottom before I realized that God is all I ever needed. He will allow us to go our own way and make mistakes. And when we realize how much we need Him, God will rescue us from the pit that in our sin we dug for ourselves. The good thing is that God doesn't rub our faces in our shame. He forgives us and restores us."

Marin looked over at Warner. "That is unconditional love."

Several *amens* were heard around the sanctuary.

"I came across this verse in the Bible. *I have chosen you and have not rejected you. So do not fear, for I am with you; do not be dismayed, for I am your God. I will strengthen you and help you; I will uphold you with my righteous right hand.* This verse made me realize that God had not forgotten about me—instead, I'd forgotten about Him. That's why I'm standing up here now. I want to renew my relationship with God. I'm grateful to have the opportunity to stand here asking for His forgiveness—for your forgiveness—and for a personal relationship with God through His Son, Jesus Christ. I could've died so many times, but God wouldn't let me. I ask that you please keep me lifted up in prayer. I need your prayers and your strength to help me fight drug addiction. I've been clean for seven months now."

Another round of applause rang out.

Marin's emotions overtook her and she began to sob.

Warner held her close, comforting her.

They stood before the congregation and the entire television community, holding each other. Warner reassured Marin over and over of God's love for her.

To the congregation, he said, "God loves us—even though we're sinners. He hates sin; it grieves Him. But because He is a loving God, He offers us His divine forgiveness. The people of Israel kept going back to their sins and because God never stopped loving them, He never stopped pleading with them to return to Him."

Warner paused for a heartbeat before continuing. "God will redeem humanity as many times as it takes. This is why Jesus died for our sins. Church, we need to love like that. We need to forgive like that. We need to drag the festering hurts we have been harboring in our hearts to the cross of Christ and we need to leave them there. Once we fully forgive, our minds are released from the bondage of anger, bitterness and resentment. Once we fully forgive, we are free to grow in our relationship with each other."

Elijah and the associate pastors came down out of the pulpit, surrounding them.

One of the pastors led them in prayer.

At the end of the service, several members of the congregation came up to encourage Marin or give her a hug.

"I thank God for giving you the strength to stand up here and give that testimony. I will keep you lifted up in prayer."

"Thank you," she murmured.

Marin's eyes traveled to where Chanelle stood with her parents. It was clear her sister-in-law hadn't been moved by her words. She was not convinced of Marin's sincerity.

It didn't matter to her what Chanelle or anybody else thought. God knew her heart.

Marin slowly made her way to Warner's office, where he was changing out of his robe. She knocked on the door and announced, "It's just me."

"Come in," Warner called out.

Marin stepped inside, closing the door behind her. "Thank you," she said.

"For what?"

"For standing beside me—supporting me. I really appreciate it."

"You're my wife, Marin."

"There aren't many men like you, Warner. Most wouldn't have had anything to do with me after seeing me like this." Her eyes watered. "There's something I want you to know. God allowed me to hit rock bottom. I was ashamed and disgraced, but Warner, it's the unconditional love that I see in your eyes that breaks my heart. Because of your love and your steadfast prayers, I want to be a better person. I want to be the wife you deserve."

CHAPTER THIRTY-EIGHT

Warner was moved by Marin's words and ashamed of the way he'd treated her this morning. In his heart, he repented and prayed for forgiveness.

"I'm so proud of you," he told Marin, embracing her. "What you did this morning took courage."

"I had to say what was on my heart. And it wasn't for show. I meant it, Warner. I really did."

"I believe you."

"I don't think your sister does. It doesn't matter though."

"How are you feeling?"

Marin pasted on a smile. "I'm okay. Just a little tired."

"I'll be ready to go in about fifteen minutes," Warner announced. "I need to speak to Elijah."

"I'm fine, Warner. Take all the time you need. I'm going to check on the boys. They're still in children's church."

"Marin, I do love you."

She nodded. "I know you do, Warner."

"I forgive you."

"It's been a lot for you to deal with. I know that."

"I was angry. I'm not anymore. I'm not saying that—"

Marin cut him off. "I know. Our problems won't disappear overnight."

"I am trying."

"That's all I can ask. It's all anyone can ask of you."

Warner watched her walk out of his office, her head held high. She was determined to put on a brave front for everyone.

He couldn't deny she was fighting hard for their marriage. He wanted to just forget the past and go back to before, when they were so happy. But one question stayed on his heart.

If they were so happy, how did it come to this?

While waiting on Warner to finish his meeting, Marin watched a slender woman sitting in the banquet room talking and laughing with her boys.

She seemed very familiar with them. Marin couldn't help but notice that this woman appeared to be everything she wasn't. She was the type of woman who would be perfect for Warner—at least by Chanelle's standards.

She heard Rylan address the woman as Miss Geneva. "Chanelle's friend," she whispered. Apparently she was also Warner's friend, too. A thread of jealousy wove its way through her body.

Marin walked over to where they were standing. "You're very good with them," she said.

Geneva glanced over her shoulder. Her eyes rose in surprise. Recovering quickly, she turned around and offered her hand. "Mrs. Brice . . . it's nice to finally meet you. Your testimony was very moving."

Marin shook her hand. "Thank you, but just call me Marin."

"I'm Geneva Winston. I'm friends with your sister-in-law," she explained. "Chanelle and I went to college together."

"And a friend of Warner's, I suppose."

"Warner and I are friends," Geneva admitted. Her eyes never left Marin's face.

"I'm sure he needed a good friend during all those months I was gone."

Geneva didn't respond.

Marin wasn't in the mood to play games. "Miss Winston, you're very transparent. I know that you have feelings for my husband. I also know that you know all about my sordid past—the whole world knows. Warner has allowed me back into his life and into our home. I want a chance to make things right again."

Meeting her gaze, Geneva stated, "I have no plans to interfere in your marriage."

"Thank you for being a friend to Warner and for caring for my children, but I hope you won't be offended when I tell you that you're no longer needed. I'm back home and I intend to stay."

"Have you ever read the story of Hosea and Gomer, Mrs. Brice?"

"Excuse me?"

"The story of Hosea and Gomer? I think it's one of the greatest love stories in the Bible."

Marin had no idea where Geneva was going with this. Hosea? She'd heard of him, but she couldn't remember anything about him. "I think he's a minor prophet or something," she answered.

"He was," Geneva confirmed. "Pastor Warner preached on Hosea and Gomer some weeks ago. When you get a chance, I think you should read the book of Hosea."

"Why?" Marin wanted to know.

"Because I believe God has a word for you."

"Why don't you tell me what that is?" Marin searched her memory. "Wait . . . Hosea . . . he married the prostitute." Angry, she laid her purse on a nearby table. "Okay, I see where this is going."

"Do you know what the name Gomer means?"

Folding her arms across her chest, Marin said, "Why don't you just tell me?"

"Gomer means 'complete.' The root word is *gamar* which means to perfect or finish. Psalm one thirty eight, verse eight says that the Lord will not leave us in the lurch. He has a plan for our lives and *He will finish what He has started*. You and Warner are not finished. I believe that God will restore your marriage, Mrs. Brice. I pray that He will walk with you every step of the way throughout your recovery." Geneva blinked rapidly, fighting to hold back her tears. "I want you to know that I will be praying for you and Warner."

Marin observed her for a moment before responding, "I believe you mean it. Thank you."

"God bless you."

"And you, Miss Winston." Marin watched Geneva leave before saying, "C'mon, boys. Your father's waiting on us."

After dinner, the boys went upstairs to play while Warner and Marin decided to relax in the family room.

Marin picked up the Bible, located the book of Hosea and began to read.

When she finished, her eyes were filled with tears. Gomer was a prostitute and God told Hosea to marry her. She understood that God wanted to use their marriage of Hosea as a symbol of His love for the people of Israel.

What tore up her emotions was just how closely her life resembled Gomer's. Like her, Gomer left Hosea after giving birth to her children. She figured that her former life was better than her present life as a wife and mother.

Marin had never really felt that way—she just made the wrong choice to try cocaine and then couldn't fight her addiction. But like Gomer, Marin hadn't really realized how wonderful her life with Warner was.

This story reminded her of the Prodigal Son and what he went through before returning home to his father.

The amazing part of Hosea and Gomer's story was when God asked Hosea if he still loved Gomer and he answered that he really did. Then God told Hosea to go find his wife and bring her back home. God told Hosea to forgive her, clean her up, and make her as his own again.

Marin's eyes traveled over to where Warner was sitting. He was a modern-day Hosea.

He had to endure public ridicule and humiliation because he'd chosen to stand by her through her pregnancy and recovery—just as Hosea had to buy his own wife from the slave trader and God had to buy His own children back with the blood of His Son.

Her heart was so convicted on many levels. For what she'd put Warner through and for forgetting that God paid so much for us. He stood by and watched His only Son die a horrible death, when He could have stopped it.

Marin couldn't imagine just standing by and letting someone kill her sweet boys or the child she carried. Her emotions threatened to overcome her, so she rose to her feet and rushed off to the bathroom.

She fell to her knees, sobbing. "Oh, Father God, I am so sorry for everything. I know that You have already forgiven me, but Lord I just want to say I'm sorry for taking the life You've given me for granted. The wonderful man You blessed me with—I never should've taken him for granted. Father, I repent of my sins and I just want to be washed in the blood of Your Son, whom You stood by and allowed to die to save us. We are so unworthy, yet You love us. Thank You for that love, Father God. Thank You so much. In Jesus' name I pray. Amen."

"Do you love her?" Marin asked when she returned to the family room.

Warner looked up from his book. "Excuse me?"

"Are you in love with Geneva Winston?" Marin gave a slight shrug. "Warner, you can be honest with me. There's absolutely nothing I can say to you after everything I put you through."

He removed his glasses. "Marin, let's not do this."

"Do what? Have a conversation? Be honest with each other? Isn't this what you always wanted?"

Warner took a deep breath and said, "I care for Geneva. She has been a good friend to me."

"But do you love her?"

After what seemed like an eternity, Warner answered. "No. Marin, I love only one woman. You are that woman—even though you have done all you could to destroy that love."

"She's in love with you. Did you know that?"

"What made you ask me about Geneva? Did you overhear something at church?"

Shaking her head, Marin responded, "I talked to her this morning after church services ended."

"Why?"

"I saw her in the banquet room with the boys. I stood back and watched them for a while. They were laughing and playing around like we used to do. It was like she had taken my place as their mother. Gabriel and Rylan really like her."

"She's been very good for them."

Marin couldn't hide her true feelings. She was jealous. "I realize that, but the fact is that I'm their mother—not her."

"Geneva's never tried to replace you, Marin. She couldn't even if she tried."

"She wants to be your wife, Warner. The woman is in love with you and I know you can see it. It's written all over her face."

"It doesn't really matter, Marin. You are my wife. End of story."

"But only in name," she retorted. "We sleep in separate rooms, Warner. Can you truly call this a marriage? You spoke about forgiveness this morning. You talked about laying the anger, resentment and bitterness down at the cross of Christ. Is this what you're doing?"

"Yes. But Marin, it doesn't mean we're going to jump back in bed together. Some wounds take longer to heal. I love you, but I just can't—"

"Even after everything I put you through, you still love me and I love you, too. Warner, I love you more than my own life. I want you to be happy. I really do. You've been so good to me."

"We have to take this one day at a time, Marin. Right now, I just want to take it slow."

Marin nodded.

"When is your next doctor's appointment?"

"Tuesday at nine," she responded. "Why?"

"I'd like to go with you."

A tear escaped her eye. "Warner, I'd like that. I'd like that very much."

Another hurdle had been crossed.

CHAPTER THIRTY-NINE

"Is my brother home?"

"No, he's not, but he should be here shortly." Marin held the door open wide enough for her to enter. "Chanelle, why don't you just wait in here for him?"

Without responding, her sister-in-law brushed past her and sat down in the living room.

Marin followed her. "I can tell you have something on your mind. Why don't you just say it, Chanelle?"

"I have to be honest with you, Marin. I wish you'd never come back. How can you do this to Warner? He deserves so much more."

Marin agreed. "You're right, Chanelle. Warner deserves so much better than me. So do my children." Tears filled her eyes. "When I met Geneva, I knew immediately that she was the type of woman Warner probably should've married. She seems like a really nice person."

"She is," Chanelle confirmed.

"But the fact of it is that he married me. He chose me, Chanelle. So no matter what you think or what I think—Warner thought I was his soul mate."

"Marin, I want you to know that I truly wanted you and my brother to be happy."

"Oh, is that why you introduced Geneva to him the first chance you got? Let's be honest, Chanelle. You never wanted me with Warner. You never once thought I was good enough for him."

"Do you disagree?" Chanelle queried. "You're standing here pregnant with another man's baby."

"I was raped."

"Are you really going to lie and say you've never slept with other men? For goodness' sake, you were arrested for prostitution."

"I'm not saying that, but I do know that this baby was conceived the night I was raped."

"And that makes it okay?"

Marin shook her head no.

"Why don't you just let Warner go? He deserves to be with a woman who loves him."

"I love him, Chanelle," Marin announced. "I love Warner with my whole being. I made mistakes. I got hooked on drugs and . . ." She couldn't finish her sentence because of her sobs.

"Marin, calm down." Chanelle walked over and embraced her. "You shouldn't get upset like this."

"I'm so sorry. Oh, dear God . . . I'm so sorry. Please forgive me . . . please forgive me . . ."

"It'll be alright," Chanelle said, soothing her. "We'll get through this."

Marin sobbed harder. "Please don't hate me."

"I don't hate you. I don't like what you did to Warner and the children, but I don't hate you." She handed Marin a tissue.

Wiping her tears away, Marin responded, "I'm sorry. All I want is a chance to prove that I'm not a bad person."

"Are you expecting . . . Marin, are you planning to keep the baby you're carrying?"

"Yes. This is my child, Chanelle."

"How does Warner feel about the baby?"

"We haven't really talked about her."

"It's a girl."

Smiling, Marin nodded. "I've always wanted a little girl. Regardless of how she was conceived, she's worthy of being loved."

"I agree. But I'm sure this has to break Warner's heart. I know Mitch would've kicked me out of the house a long time ago. He couldn't handle something like this. Most men couldn't."

"It's hard for Warner—I can't deny that—but we're trying. He's trying to put all this behind him. Warner's even going with me to my next doctor's appointment."

Chanelle tried to hide her surprise. "Really?"

"He's really trying to get past all the . . . all my mistakes."

Shaking her head in confusion, Chanelle said, "I don't know what Warner sees in you."

"It's not for you to see, Chanelle. There are only three people in this marriage—Warner, God and me."

Marin ran into Geneva again at Bible study on Wednesday night.

"Mrs. Brice. It's good to see you again."

"It's Marin," she responded. "How are you, Geneva?"

"I'm doing just fine." She gave Marin a handout and quickly moved on.

Feeling like she was being watched, Marin glanced up and found Hazel's eyes trained on her. She smiled and waved.

Hazel waved back.

Marin was sure to avoid looking at Geneva during the Bible study because she was under intense scrutiny by several of the women. They apparently knew of Warner's relationship with Geneva.

Her pangs of jealousy threatened to overtake her by the end of the meeting, but Marin had to remind herself that she was in no position to be upset with Geneva and Warner. Besides, it wasn't as if he'd actually committed adultery.

She was the adulteress.

Marin found herself comparing her strengths and weaknesses to what she considered to be Geneva's. The woman was striking and she seemed intelligent. She possessed a thorough knowledge of the Bible. As far as Marin was concerned, Geneva was everything she was not.

The next day, Marin was completely surprised to find Dru and Carol standing at her door. She hugged them both before inviting them inside.

"Oh my goodness! I can't believe you guys are here!"

Dru laughed. "Honey, I would've been here sooner but with Larry playing in Atlanta now, I spend a lot of time there. Marin, you look great. I like the hair."

She touched her ponytail. "I'm letting it grow out."

Carol agreed. "You really do look wonderful. Pregnancy agrees with you. You—"

Holding up her hand, Dru cut Carol off. "Why don't we discuss something else?" she suggested.

Marin's gaze met Dru's. "It's okay. We can talk about it."

They settled down in the family room.

"How is Warner taking it?" Dru asked as soon as they were all seated.

"It's hard on him, but he's trying. He's just started going to my doctor appointments with me."

"I've been praying for you both," Dru responded. "I know God can restore your marriage. You just have to give it to Him. Give God your marriage."

"Dru's right," Carol said. "I'm a living witness to how God can restore a marriage. I know y'all know that Cameron cheated on me a year after we got married. Well, what I didn't tell you is that he had a child with that woman. Cameron has a daughter. She's eight years old."

Marin's mouth dropped open in her surprise. "Nooo."

"Wow!" Dru uttered.

"It was so hard for me to forgive him in the beginning. Girl, it was even harder to accept Mya, but I had to do it. She's innocent in all this. I finally allowed her to come to the house to spend time with us, but it's only been about five years. She's a sweetie."

"How do you feel about her?" Marin asked. "Really? Like, deep down."

"I resented her at first, but now I love that little girl like my own. She's a part of my family. She and Cameron Junior get along so well. He loves his big sister to death."

"Thank you for sharing this with me," Marin stated. "It encourages me."

"It's not easy, but it can happen, Marin. You and Warner can be as close as you used to be. Your marriage can be restored, but you have to give it to the Lord."

"Sometimes I think it might be too late."

"Why do you say that?" Dru questioned.

"I don't know if you know it, but he was spending a lot of time with a woman from church. One of Chanelle's friends."

Carol was shocked. "Pastor Brice?"

"It was mentioned a couple of times in the *National Star*," Marin told them. "Her name is Geneva."

"How do you feel about it?"

Marin looked at Dru. "How do you think I feel? It hurts so bad. I hate it. But what right do I have to feel anything?"

"I don't think Warner and Geneva . . ." Dru's voice died. "I think they were just good friends."

"I think she would be a better wife to Warner."

Carol and Dru exchanged looks. "Why would you say that?" they asked in unison.

"She seems more the first-lady type, I guess."

Dru laid her purse on the coffee table. "So you think that first ladies have a certain look?"

Marin considered her friend's question. "No, not really. Just certain qualities. In the beginning I didn't have them, but I've changed and now—now I'm ready to stand with my husband and serve the Lord."

"Praise God!" Carol shouted. "Girl, I have prayed and prayed for God to just speak to you, Marin. Oh, praise God."

"I'm so glad to have you both back in my life. I owe you an apology. I'm so sorry for the things I did and said when I was on cocaine. Please forgive me."

The three women embraced, then spent the rest of the afternoon catching up on their friendship.

Marin hated to see them leave. "Thanks so much for coming by. I had a good time."

"Give me another hug," Dru said. "I've missed you so much and I'm so glad to have you back. I love you, girl."

"I love you, too." Marin hugged Carol. "And I love you, sweetie. Thank you for your prayers while I was out there."

"We are supposed to pray for one another. Anytime, Marin. If you need a friend, just call me."

"Me, too," Dru chimed in. "Honey, don't forget—be still and know that He is God. Trust Him."

Nodding, Marin responded, "I'm standing still. I'm letting God be God."

She was in the bathroom throwing up when Warner came home that evening.

"Marin? You awake?" He called out.

"I'm up," she managed to respond. When she heard him walk into the bedroom, she said, "I think my nausea's back."

Warner entered the bathroom. "When did it start up again?" Marin didn't look well at all. He was immediately concerned about her and the baby.

"Yesterday. I was sick last night, but I thought maybe I'd eaten something that didn't sit right with me." Marin put a hand to her head. "I have a terrible headache, too."

"C'mon, let me help you back to bed," he suggested.

Marin accepted his assistance without comment.

While Marin rested, Warner first went to check on the boys and then he went downstairs to fix some tea for her.

He sent up a short prayer for her and her unborn child.

After bringing her the lukewarm tea, Warner stayed with her until after midnight. He watched her sleep for a moment, his heart filled with love.

Just as he stood up, he glimpsed movement under her shirt. The baby was moving.

Warner's lips curved into an unconscious smile. A little girl. An innocent little baby. How could he turn his back on a child that was blameless?

Her doubts were getting the best of her.

Marin couldn't help but wonder if she was doing the right thing by Warner, wanting him to remain by her side. She couldn't help but wonder if she was being selfish. He was such a good man and he deserved a good woman.

Marin wasn't sure she was that person. She desperately wanted to be, but she couldn't deny the mess she'd made of her life. Warner deserved so much more.

God, please show me what to do.

It didn't help that she seemed to be running into Geneva everywhere lately.

Just this morning, on the way to the doctor's office, Marin and Warner saw her leaving the medical building.

Geneva quickly explained that she'd had a dentist appointment.

Marin observed both Warner and Geneva. She was pretty sure that her husband had not broken his marital vows and that pleased her.

While they were waiting on the nurse to call them, Warner reached over, taking Marin by the hand. "Geneva has been nothing but a good friend to me when I really needed one. That's all."

"I believe you." Marin wasn't blind. Warner had feelings for Geneva. He wouldn't act on them, but they were there.

There's nothing I can do, Lord. This is all in Your hands.

CHAPTER FORTY

Marin stared at the date on the calendar. It was Warner's birthday.

Warner and I can't go on this way. It's not fair to him. I've got to do something. She'd listened to Dru when she told her to give God her marriage and she had tried to do just that.

But her insecurities and her guilt were getting the better of her. Tears in her eyes, Marin pulled a notepad and pen out of the bedside table.

The pain in her head was killing her, but Marin didn't falter. She began to write. It was something that should've been done a long time ago, but this was her present to Warner. She would give it to him tonight during the birthday dinner that was being hosted by his parents.

Warner knocked on her door. "Marin, can I come in?"

She quickly stuck her letter into their wedding album before answering, "Sure."

"How are you feeling?"

"I still have a headache, but other than that, I'm okay. At least for the moment." Smiling, she said, "Happy birthday, Warner."

He embraced her. "Thanks."

She gently stroked his face. "I wish I could just take away all the pain I caused you."

Warner was still very noncommittal. "It's going to take some time, Marin."

"It may never happen, Warner. We have to face the truth. I put you through a lot."

"Nothing is impossible with God."

Marin committed his words to memory. She had to hold on to that promise of hope.

For now, it was all she had to hold on to—besides her faith.

God, I'm going back and forth with this, I know it. I really am trying to sit back and wait on You, but my flesh just takes over. I'm still a work in progress, Lord. Please don't give up on me.

While Warner worked in his office downstairs, Marin decided to lie down to rest before the dinner party. She wanted to look her best.

An hour later, she dragged her body out of bed and padded barefoot into the bathroom to shower. Even after the short nap she'd taken she still felt like ugh. If they hadn't been celebrating Warner's birthday, she would've chosen to just stay home.

"Lord, please help me make it through this evening," she prayed.

The air in the room was suddenly filled with tension when Warner and Marin arrived, and small talk was kept to a minimum.

Garfield did what he could to make Marin feel welcome, touching her beyond words. Warner had the same warm, soothing nature as his father.

Mitch talked to her, too, despite the sharp glares being sent his way by Chanelle. Marin couldn't believe the woman was being so childish.

Dinner was served.

They gathered around the dining room table. Garfield offered the blessing of the food.

"Marin, aren't you going to eat something?" Millicent inquired. "You really must keep up your strength."

"I don't feel well," Marin confessed, placing a hand on her stomach. "I don't know what's wrong with me."

Chanelle picked up her water glass and took a sip. "Have you talked to your doctor?"

"Not yet. I have an appointment tomorrow morning."

"Mommie, come watch TV with me, peeze," Rylan requested from the family room.

"Okay, sweetie," Marin responded. Pushing away from the dining table, she rose to her feet. "I'll be right there."

Pain ripped through her body and she felt dizzy. "Warner . . ."

He reached out for her. "Marin, you okay?"

She looked at him. "Something's wrong. Help me . . ."

Darkness descended upon Marin with a vengeance.

Warner stayed by her side during the ambulance ride to the hospital and even now he was right beside her in the hospital emergency room.

After a battery of tests, the doctor finally was able to make a diagnosis.

"Your wife has a condition called acute fatty liver of pregnancy, commonly known as AFLP," Dr. Appling explained.

"What exactly is that?" Warner asked.

"It's a rare disorder that occurs toward the end of pregnancy, when there is an excessive accumulation of fat in the liver."

"So, what can be done to treat this condition?"

"We're going to have to deliver the baby now. Mrs. Brice is being prepped for surgery as we speak."

Warner glanced over at Marin. Two nurses were busy checking her vital signs and getting her ready to be taken down to the operating room.

"I'm scared, Warner."

He walked over and sat down in the chair beside the bed. "It's going to be alright, sweetheart," he assured her. "They're prepping you right now for a C-section."

"Please don't leave me."

"I'll be right by your side," Warner promised. He reached over, taking her hand in his.

"I need to tell you something."

"What is it?"

"I love you and I want to say thank you for loving me in return. You gave me . . ." Her voice weakened.

"Honey, don't talk. Just rest. Before long the baby will be here and you'll be on the road to recovery. We can talk then."

"Warner, I want my children raised together. I don't want them to be separated. Promise me that you'll keep my babies together."

"Relax, sweetheart. You don't need to get all excited."

"Promise me," Marin insisted. "I need you to do this for me. And make sure they know how much I love them—all of them."

"Honey, you're going to come through this fine. You and the baby."

"Warner, I don't know. I'm not trying to be negative, but this just doesn't feel right."

Warner prayed that what he was saying would turn out to be true. *Lord, I can't lose her now. Please keep her and the baby—our little girl—safe. Please do it for me.*

CHAPTER FORTY-ONE

At precisely 9:32 p.m., Marin's daughter made her entrance into the world, protesting loudly. She didn't stop crying until she was placed in Warner's arms.

He checked out her fingers and her toes. When she pressed her tiny hand flat against his, Warner's mind traveled back to the first time he'd felt her kick in Marin's stomach.

Warner planted a kiss on her forehead. "You are loved, little one." He glanced over his shoulder to where his wife lay on the operating table. "I can't wait until your mom sees you."

But Marin's eyes never opened again.

She hemorrhaged during the night and in her weakened state it was too big a battle for her to fight.

Warner was still sitting beside her bed, holding her hand when Marin's parents arrived.

"We got here as soon as we could," Shirley said. "I knew I shouldn't have gone to Florida."

"I'm so s-sorry," Warner began, his voice breaking. "Marin . . . They c-couldn't s-stop the bleeding." Tears ran down his face. "She's gone."

Shirley stared at Warner as if he was crazy. "Gone? What do you mean, she's gone?"

"She passed away," he responded slowly.

His mother-in-law collapsed, falling against her husband, crying.

"Dear Lord," Robert whispered, "why did You take my baby?"

Shirley sobbed loudly.

They were soon joined by Warner's parents.

Geneva walked up to Warner. "I don't mean to intrude, but Chanelle called and told me about Marin. I came to offer my sincere condolences and see if I could take the boys for you."

"The boys should stay with family," Shirley said. "How dare you come around here? My daughter's barely gone a few hours."

"Mrs. Alexander, I assure you, I didn't come here with ulterior motives." Geneva glanced over at Warner. "I'm sorry. I should leave."

"Yes, you should," Shirley agreed.

"Geneva didn't mean any harm," Chanelle stated.

"You just need to shut up," Shirley said nastily. "Don't think I don't know what's really going on. You never liked my daughter. Didn't think she was good enough for Warner. None of you did."

Robert embraced his wife. "Shirley, now is not the time for this."

"It's their fault that my daughter's dead. My baby . . . all she wanted to do was try to make everybody happy. She tried to fit into the Brice family mold, but she couldn't. That's why she started using drugs."

Shirley let out a scream. "My baby's dead. Oooh, Robert . . . she's gone."

Chanelle wiped away a tear.

"Don't you cry for her," Shirley sniped. "I will slap your lying face. You never once cared for her. Marin wasn't perfect, but she loved Warner and she loved her boys."

Chanelle nodded. "I know."

"Nobody really gave her a chance except for you, Warner. But the rest of you—you didn't give her a chance. Nobody . . . not even me . . ."

"We need to discuss the baby," Warner stated after everyone had had a chance to settle down. "She'll be in the hospital for a few more days, but she'll have to go somewhere."

Everybody looked over at Robert and Shirley, who sighed softly. "I don't know what we'll do with a baby, but we'll have to manage, I suppose."

"Actually, I'd like to raise the baby," Warner told them. "She should be raised with her brothers."

"Warner, are you sure about this?" Garfield questioned.

"I love Marin with my entire heart and now she's gone. The least I can do for her is to keep her three children together. Besides, I have a nanny."

"Can you love her, Warner?" Shirley inquired. "Can you love that little girl as much as you love your sons?"

"Marin and I always wanted a daughter. When this baby was born and they placed her in my arms, it was love at first sight."

"I don't know about this, Warner. I just don't know."

"Marin is my wife and this little girl will bear my name. She is my child. Nothing will ever change that."

On a balmy afternoon in August, Marin Alexander Brice reigned from her gleaming walnut-finished throne amid rows of rainbow-colored flowers and elaborately designed wreaths.

This day belonged to her, although she was totally unaware of it.

Or was she? Warner wondered.

Wrapped in white satin, his wife and the mother of his children lay resting in a dark coffin, with her eyes closed and the barest hint of a smile on her face. She looked more peaceful than he'd ever seen her during their short time together.

She was not the first love that he'd had to bury, but this time Warner could barely hide the pain of his heartbreak. He'd loved Marin with his entire being. If only things had turned out differently.

Marin was gone and there was no point in looking back now.

Among the mourners sat a mixture of Hollywood royalty and Marin's fans. There were people standing outside the church waiting to glimpse the coffin when it was carried out to continue the journey to her final resting place.

Warner could barely make it through the burial at the cemetery. He was relieved when the sleek black limo pulled into his driveway.

He couldn't stand to hear another well-meaning person approach him offering condolences. He'd heard enough. What he needed now was some time alone.

He slipped upstairs to his bedroom, hoping no one would notice his absence. When he sat down in the sitting room, he noticed that the wedding album had been moved from downstairs to up here.

Marin or one of the children must have brought it up here, he decided.

In his grief, Warner couldn't bear to look at the photos of him and Marin commemorating the beginning of their life as husband and wife. He picked it up, intending to hide it in one of the cabinets below the built-in bookshelves.

An envelope fell out, floating to the floor.

Warner bent to pick it up. He recognized Marin's handwriting.

Inside a beautifully designed birthday card, there was a letter addressed to him. He opened it and began to read.

Dearest Warner:

Today is your birthday and there is so much I want to say to you, but the words just won't come out right. There are no words to fully express my sorrow over the way I ruined our marriage. You honored me by allowing me to become your wife and all I gave you in return was shame and disgrace. I am so sorry for the pain I caused you and the boys.

I love you so much and I am extremely grateful that you have allowed me back into our home. But I'm not blind. I can also see how hard this is on you. Especially when everyone thinks you should have left me on the streets somewhere. Anyone who really knows you knows that's not the type of man that you are. You are a true man of God— you shouldn't be criticized, or considered weak and stupid. If anything, you should be admired and respected.

Thank you so much for praying for me even when I couldn't pray for myself, Warner. Thank you for caring when others advised you to forget about me.

I never deserved your forgiveness, but I am so grateful for it. Thank you for helping me find my way back to the Lord. It is in Him that I place my all. I surrender to Him and I am at peace knowing that I have been redeemed spiritually.

I haven't had the privilege of spending a lot of time with Geneva, but she seems to be a wonderful woman and I've heard nothing but good things about her. The boys certainly love her—they talk about her all the time. I believe that she will make you very happy. I know how you feel about divorce, but I believe that God would not hold you in error if you decided to end our marriage.

It is because I love you so very much that I feel I must let you go. I brought you nothing but disgrace and scandal. My only request is that I be allowed to visit with my children from time to time, as I know you're not comfortable enough to give me shared custody.

Warner, I can't stress enough how much I love you and while I can't change all that's happened, I want you to know that I will do everything I can to earn your respect once more. I promise I will not take this second chance at life for granted.

Even though I pushed God out of my life, He never forgot me. Being a godly man, you didn't abandon me either. Please make sure my boys know how much I love them and that I'm not running out on them again. They are truly my best work ever.

God bless you, Warner, and I wish you and Geneva nothing but the best. If she's who you truly want in your life. Chanelle was right about one thing. Geneva is the perfect woman for you and she'll be an asset to your church. You can't imagine how much it hurts me to admit that.

As painful as this is for me, the best birthday gift I can give you is your freedom. I love you enough to let you go and find your happiness.

I've made arrangements to stay with my parents until the baby is born, and I've already signed the required legal documents for our divorce. They are in the bottom drawer on the nightstand in the guest room.

With all my love,
Marin

The love emanating from Marin's letter moved him to tears. She loved him so much that she was willing to sacrifice her happiness.

"Warner . . ."

He wiped his eyes, the glanced over his shoulder.

Chanelle came closer. "What's wrong?"

"Marin wrote me a letter and stuck it in our wedding album," Warner announced. "She wrote it the day she got sick." He handed the letter to Chanelle.

As she read, her eyes became wet with unshed tears.

"She really did love you."

He nodded.

Chanelle sat down in the chair facing her brother. "I was wrong about her in some things. She really wasn't a bad person."

"No, she wasn't. She wasn't a bad person at all."

"How did she know about Geneva?"

"She wasn't stupid, Chanelle. Marin said she could see the way Geneva felt about me in her eyes."

"Warner, I need you to forgive me."

His gaze met Chanelle's. "For what?"

"I pushed Geneva toward you. I thought she was the better woman for you. I never really accepted Marin. I feel so bad because my friend was the one who got hurt as a result of my actions. I never should have done that to her. Or to you and Marin."

"Geneva is a wonderful woman. If I'd met her before Marin, who knows what could've happened? She is a dear friend to me and I care a great deal for her."

"She loves you so much, Warner."

"I know. I admire her because when I was ready to give up and file for divorce, Geneva wouldn't let me. She reminded me of my marriage vows and encouraged me to find Marin."

He sighed softly. "If the day comes for me to take another wife . . ." His eyes filled with tears. "I just don't know if I can do it. Marin will always be the love of my life."

Warner asked Shirley and her husband to stay behind after everyone had gone home.

"I found a letter from Marin," he announced. "She had planned to free me. She planned to divorce me."

"Marin loved you, Warner. I don't think she was able to forgive herself for what she'd done to you. She just wanted you to be happy."

"I know. The thing is that Marin was the love of my life. She *is* the love of my life. She really wanted this baby."

Shirley nodded in agreement. "Yes, she did. She really wanted this little girl."

"Marin and I always wanted a little girl and this baby . . . I've felt her kick, watch her move when she was in her mom's belly. I didn't realize just how much I loved her until we rushed Marin to the hospital. I love that little girl. I want you both to know that I truly love her like my own."

Taking Shirley's hand in his, Robert's eyes traveled to Warner's. "So have you decided on a name for your daughter? She needs a name."

Nodding, Warner said, "I think we should name her after her mother. Marin Danielle Brice."

"It's perfect. I think my daughter would be so pleased." Shirley wiped her eyes. "Little Marin's a real beauty, isn't she?"

"Just like her mother."

Robert said, "You're certainly going to have your hands full, Warner."

"I'm glad that I'll have the two of you to help me. The children—all three of them—are going to need us."

Before leaving, Shirley turned to him, saying, "Warner, this feels right. I'm at peace with this decision."

EPILOGUE

Geneva plucked up a weed, then another and another. "I hate these things," she muttered to no one in particular. "Don't worry, Marin. I'll never let you go out like that—weeds everywhere."

She tossed away the old flowers, replacing them with a bouquet selected from her own rose garden.

"You should see little Marin. She's growing like these weeds out here. She's so beautiful and such a joy. And she's so smart for just three years old. She has Warner wrapped around her little finger. He loves her like his own. We both do, so you don't have to worry about her."

Warner walked up to the grave and sat down beside her. "You come out here and fuss with those flowers—I appreciate it, Geneva, but you don't have to do this."

"Warner, I want to," she insisted. "I know how much Marin meant to you. How much she means to the children. I intend to honor her."

"You're an incredible woman."

She smiled at her husband, resting her hands on the rounded mound of her stomach. "This one is so busy."

"Soon we're going to have four children in the house. You ready for that?"

"We can handle it, Warner," she assured him. "We're a family. With God's help, we can do anything."

AUTHOR'S NOTE

I hope you enjoyed reading *Redemption*. The idea for this novel came to me after reading the biblical story of Hosea and his wayward wife, Gomer (Hosea 1–3) in the Old Testament. For those of you who haven't read it, this is one of the most powerful stories of love and redemption.

It is a love story with a good beginning, then a time of pain and heartache, and a touching reconciliation at the end.

God calls Hosea to marry a harlot. Although Gomer has a wonderful husband, her philandering ways take her away from home and into a world of sin. Her spiritual life fades from her as she drifts into a world of hopelessness and falls onto hard times.

But this is not the end of the story. Hosea eventually finds his wife being offered up for sale as a slave. The redemptive elements are woven into the story when he purchases his wife and brings her home.

While it sounds like a great story for talk shows, Hosea and Gomer's relationship clearly demonstrates God's unfailing love for us. The story shows that He loves us no matter how often we break His heart. I want *Redemption* to be a reminder that He is a God who longs to forgive us, to redeem us, if we just turn to Him.

REDEMPTION

JACQUELIN THOMAS

A CONVERSATION WITH
JACQUELIN THOMAS

1. When did you start writing? Did you choose it, or did the profession choose you?

I was painfully shy as a child, and writing was my outlet. I also loved reading, and when I couldn't find a book to read, I would make up my own stories. I found that I loved the craft of writing, and by the time I was sixteen, I knew that I wanted to be a writer. My mother writes in her spare time and is a wonderful storyteller, and my father writes screenplays—I guess it's in my blood.

2. What inspires you?

Life. I'm inspired by newspaper articles, news interviews, people—I find stories in just about everything I come in contact with or that I experience.

3. How much of yourself and the people you know manifests into your characters?

I think there's a little bit of me in all of my characters, but they are not me. In *Redemption*, my characters were inspired by Hosea and Gomer in the Bible. I have a strong reluctance to base my characters on "real" people.

4. In your current novel, Warner and Marin's marriage is tested with drug abuse, prostitution and an unplanned pregnancy. What inspired you to write a controversial story like Redemption*?*

I believe the Biblical story of Hosea and Gomer's marriage is one of the greatest love stories. Because of obedience to God, Hosea went against what I can only assume would be normal human reactions and continued to honor his marriage vows, despite the fact that his wife was unfaithful and bore children who were not his. Even after she left him, Hosea eventually found her and brought her back home. It's a wonderful example of God's love for us—no matter how many times we sin and/or turn our backs on Him.

5. When someone reads one of your books for the first time, what do you hope he or she gains, feels or experiences?

Joy . . . joy in the knowledge that God will never leave you. Joy in that no matter how big the problem or how small, God is the answer. I want to leave readers with a moving but satisfying and entertaining experience. And if they shed a tear or two, I really like that.

Discussion Questions

1. Hosea's relationship with his adulterous wife, Gomer, was given as a picture of God's relationship with His people. The same can be said about Warner and Marin's relationship. What message do you believe God is trying to send?

2. Warner said in the beginning of the story that God told him Marin was to be his wife. Do you believe that God would send someone like her to a man of God? Why or why not?

3. Do you think that Marin was just another golddigger as Chanelle accused her of being, or do you believe that she truly loved Warner but just got caught up in the wrong crowd?

4. Warner was considering divorce. Why do you think he changed his mind? Was it out of love or was it because he knew this was what God desired?

5. In the Bible, Gomer was eventually restored to God. Do you feel that Marin was redeemed and restored before her death? Why or why not?

6. Geneva was in love with Warner, a married man. Although she never crossed that marital line, do you feel that she was wrong for feeling this way? She loved him enough to free him by advising him to give his marriage a second chance. What would you have done if in her shoes?

7. Chanelle pushed Geneva toward Warner. Do you agree with her actions? Despite the fact that Marin abused drugs, committed adultery and became pregnant with another man's child, should Chanelle have acted in this manner?

8. Some thought Warner was a fool to bring Marin back home. But in reality, Warner chose to follow God's example. To have a love that always protects, always trusts, always hopes and always perseveres. The kind of love that never fails. Can you say that you have the same forgiving spirit that Warner had?